CRITICS RAVE ABOUT NINA BANGS!

THE PLEASURE MASTER

"An irreverent, sexy and hilarious romp . . .
Nina Bangs has done a fabulous job of creating
a funny, sexy off-beat romance that time-travel
aficionados will absolutely relish."
—*Writers Write*

"Sizzling! . . . Witty eroticism reaches new heights in . . .
this erotically intense, wildly imaginative romp."
—*Wordweaving*

"Plenty of laugh-out-loud moments . . . if you're
looking for fun and fantasy, you will find it here!"
—*Romantic Times*

AN ORIGINAL SIN

"Ms. Bangs has written a fun comedy of people out of
time. It is a romp and should be enjoyed in large gulps."
—*CompuServe Romance Reviews*

"If you're looking for a funny, heart-wrenching and
truly lovely romance to read, try this one.
You won't be disappointed."
—*All About Romance*

"Nina Bangs has come up with a completely new and
unique twist on the time-travel theme and has delivered a
story that is both
—*R*

TEMPTATION

She had to look up a long way. Past firm calves with a light sprinkling of damp hair clinging to them. Past thighs roped with wet gleaming muscles. She paused to stare at his most riveting feature, because no matter how horrified she was, the corner of her mind in charge of recording historical life events insisted she take note. Like a five-hundred-year flood, or Haley's Comet, you only lived to see some things once.

Yes! She could die a fulfilled woman.

She moved on. If staring at the sun could blind you, Ally didn't even want to consider what staring at Brian's assets would do.

She skimmed over his flat, hard stomach and strongly muscled chest with its damp whorls of hair adhering darkly to his flesh.

Her inspection at last reached his eyes. No shame there. They were bright with amusement. But as she watched, the amusement changed to something else. Something hot, hungry. *Dangerous*.

"You tempt me greatly, woman."

NINA BANGS

Night GAMES

LOVE SPELL BOOKS   NEW YORK CITY

A LOVE SPELL® BOOK

May 2002

Published by

Dorchester Publishing Co., Inc.
276 Fifth Avenue
New York, NY 10001

ISBN 0-505-52480-5

The name "Love Spell" and its logo are trademarks of Dorchester Publishing Co., Inc.

Printed in the United States of America.

Visit us on the web at www.dorchesterpub.com.

For Barb,
Here's to our Dublin years, a magical time
of freedom and infinite possibilities. And
woven through all our memories of
Ireland is its music. May the music
and our memories never fade.

Night Games
GAMES

Prologue

Sex. Rules of the game: play hard, play to win, and play with a passion for the game, *never for the woman*.

Brian Byrne stood in the center of the packed stadium, lifted his face to the artificially generated breeze that cooled his bare body, and saluted the thousands of fans who screamed his name. In the future, experts would agree that 2502 was *his* year.

Why didn't he care more?

Striding away from the women he'd just brought to completion, Brian fought his way through back-pounding teammates, then pushed past the hundreds of robotic reporters hovering around, wanting a piece of him. With a sense of relief, he entered his undressing room.

Alone. Well, not quite. Jupe slipped in as the door slid shut.

He tried to ignore his agent, but it was tough ignoring five feet five inches of lean, mean selling machine. Brian stepped under the cleansing spray and closed his eyes as the liquid sluiced over his body, washing away the sweat and smell of sex.

"You were incredible out there. Wouldn't have believed it if I hadn't seen it. You know, I still think you should try a mask. Add to the dangerous image."

Brian leveled a dark stare at him.

"Okay, okay, so you don't need the mask. But a few chains wrapped around you would play into a lot of women's fantasies."

Brian stepped out of the spray, then rubbed himself dry with a towel. It would've been easier to use the Air Scrubber and Evapo-drier, but he enjoyed the old-fashioned feel of liquid flowing over him and the rough towel on his body. Tactile in all things. If he couldn't touch it, it wasn't worth his time. "I don't *need* to play into women's fantasies."

"Right. You *are* every woman's fantasy. You know why? Because women love the you-can-touch-my-body-but-never-my-heart image. You're a challenge. Women love challenges."

Jupe would never understand. "It's no image. That's me. Take it or leave it."

Jupe ignored him. "I wish you'd let me leak this thing you do for those kids to the Cosmic Network. Soften your image. Let people know you care about something."

Brian shook his head. "You just got through saying that women love the untouchable image. Tell them about the kids and I won't be untouchable anymore." He'd never use the homeless children he supported for public relations purposes. They were a part of who he was, where he'd come from. He didn't have career choices when he entered the league, but he kept playing so his kids *would* have choices. They were a part of himself he shared with no one, not even Jupe.

"Yeah, guess you're right." Jupe glanced at the Experience-the-Thrill pressure pad with a scene of Brian holding aloft the Universal trophy the team had won three months ago. He had only to touch the pad to be drawn into a virtual world where he could relive the glory of his most famous client. He didn't touch it. "I never asked why you chose the name Brian. Great name. Sounds primitive. Women like primitive."

"It's my real name." One of his only links to the parents he'd barely known. Even after so many years he felt the anger, and took it out on Jupe. Jupe who'd seen talent in a raw teen and over the course of twelve years molded him into a face and body recognized on even the farthest explored planet. "At least I'm not named after a big ball of gas."

Jupe paused to study him. "So? Lots of people are named Jupiter. And what's the matter with you? You just won it all. You're the king."

Brian exhaled wearily. "Sorry for the crack about your name. Guess the game took a lot out of me."

Mollified, Jupe rambled on. "Yep, you're every woman's fantasy man." Jupe was practically rubbing his hands together at the thought of how much that fantasy was worth. "This win makes you tops in the universe. When your new contract comes up, infinity's the limit. And the endorsements—"

"I'm tired. Think I'll take a vacation." Brian dropped the towel and started to dress.

Jupe ignored him. "Take a look at this." He motioned, and the image of a cereal container formed in the middle of the room. "ENJOY THE BEST. I like that in big letters at the top. It was a stroke of genius to show you naked with all those women."

Brian narrowed his gaze on the container. "My eyes aren't *that* green. And my hair's black, *plain* black. No gold streaks." He lowered his glance. "I'm not *that* big. What's with the enhancements?"

"Enhancements are good. Keeps you larger than life." He chuckled. "The whole concept's genius, pure genius. Gives you lots of exposure."

"Right. Lots of exposure. Not much dignity, though. Maybe they should lose the women and show me dressed. Fans never get a chance to see me in clothes." Brian was used to Jupe ignoring him when profit was on his mind. And profit was *always* on his mind.

Brian motioned, and the cereal container was replaced by the scene of a grassy hill with a few chunks of stone hinting at an ancient building.

"Uh-uh. Females across the galaxy will relate with the ones on the container. See, it's all about marketing." Jupe moved around Brian to get a closer view of the scene. "And you're not the king of dignity, you're the king of sex." He pointed at the scene. "What's this all about?"

Brian huffed in resignation. "Look, Jupe, *Monday Night Sex* is a team sport, and I'm a team player. The Sex Super Bowl was a team win. They should put all the guys on the container."

"Give me a break, Byrne. You were the MVP of the series. Who was it that brought four women *at once* to screaming orgasms in the final minute of regulation time to win it for the Sex Monarchs? Huh? I still can't believe it. *A fourplay*. Never been done before. You're a galactic hero." Jupe swung his arms wide to demonstrate the scope of Brian's greatness.

"Sure, sure." Brian tried to refocus on the scene. "But that's what the Old One paid for. Capricorn Wilson offered me a lot to stay with the Testosterone Titans another year, but I was a free agent and the Old One offered an incredible package. Plus you negotiate the best contract in the sport. I make more than the world president. More than ten world presidents." He grinned at Jupe. "Remind me to tell you what a great agent you are."

"I get my cut." Jupe's attention returned to the

scene. "A vacation? *A vacation?* You've never taken a vacation."

"Never had the chance. Had to keep busy promoting myself so I could earn more. It takes a lot to support all those kids. Now that I'm on top, I can take a little break." He pointed at an air-chair, and it glided over to him. Sinking into it, he allowed himself to relax. So many women drained him in more ways than one.

"You can't leave now. The Old One has appearances booked solid until the start of training camp. She figures to make a fortune off you."

Brian laughed. "The Old One already has enough fortunes to buy the universe. She just wants to piss off the other team owners."

"You can't—"

"Yes, I can." Brian turned from the scene. "I need to get away for about a month—from the fans, the responsibilities, the *sex.*" He stretched. "I think I'll take a trip back to the ancestral castle. About five hundred years back."

"Five hundred years?" Jupe's expression hinted that Brian might as well be dodging dinosaurs. "Why five hundred years?"

"Something interesting happened between 2002 and 2010." Brian raked his fingers through his still-damp hair. Sometimes he wished it didn't hang past his shoulders, but it was part of his mystique in a society where everyone shaved, polished, and hired artists to paint pictures on their heads. "History's a little vague, but during that time period the whole castle collapsed. Why would a building that had stood for centuries just fall down? I'm curious. I figure it was probably still standing in 2002. Might even use the Constructor to shore it up." He'd rather use his hands. The Constructor made it too easy. Everything in life was too easy. That's why most men had turned into useless Morwin blobs who couldn't even get off their butts to have sex. They'd rather watch it. Viewers not doers. He felt sorry for them. No matter how hard his past had been, it had given him drive.

Jupe paced in a frenzy of denial. "You can't. What if you get hurt where it counts? Whatta we do then, huh? And how're you going to keep your edge without Nebula?"

"I don't need a trainer. I don't think I'll lose any conditioning in three weeks. And don't worry, no sex on this trip. By the time I get back I'll be ready for the season opener." He raised his hand to still Jupe's list of possible dangers. "Look, I'm going to a safe time and a safe part of Earth. I'll go at night so no one will see me arrive, and I'll have the time-travel agent give me authentic identification and plenty of the currency in use. I'll even bone up on a speech pattern that's close to the one I use."

Jupe didn't look convinced. "You want a great vacation? Why not a Canthian Retreat? I hear you come out a new man."

"I don't think you want a new man." Jupe wasn't going to let this go. "I'd guess that five hundred years ago the ancestral castle was already looking pretty grim. Maybe I'll fix the old place up *without* the Constructor's help." It would feel good to use his hands for something besides touching female bodies.

Jupe blanched. "Use your *hands*? Primitive *tools*? What if—?"

"That's it. I'm going and no one can stop me."

Brian watched the white stag move through the trees ahead of him. The thick mist hid much of his surroundings, and it was hard to believe the stag was leading him back in time.

Ironic. Humans had conquered space, disease, and everything else imaginable, but time remained a mystery. Only these magical stags from Sirleen held the secret of traveling through time. Intelligent, willing, and scarce, their services couldn't be afforded by most. He would enjoy himself for a few weeks, but when the stag returned to take him home, he'd probably be glad to go.

He frowned as the castle came into sight. What a mess. Only the keep was still standing. The outer walls and towers lay in ruin. Not much shelter there. Good thing the travel agent had packed him some survival gear. It was dark and rainy; not a great way to start his vacation.

At least he wouldn't have to worry about any females. No woman would be stupid enough to come here on a night like this.

Chapter One

"Horse pooky. Every red-blooded woman would want to meet Black Liam Byrne, the most evil vampire to ever bite a virgin. Bet he's tall, dark, and horny. Heck, at my age, that sounds pretty good." Katy pulled the collar of her all-weather coat more tightly around her ears. "Had a reading done by Mary Jo Clark two years ago. The cards said in 2002 I'd meet a sexy man from far away. Ireland's far away. Black Liam could be the one."

Ally hated to stomp on her great-aunt's vision of sensual nirvana. "Sorry, Katy. From the books I've read, I'd say we're dealing with the dullahan here. Black-robed, headless horseman. Harbinger of death. Vampires aren't big in Ireland, and they don't have discriminating taste buds." She had to shout to be heard above the waves pounding at the base of the cliff. Building a castle with one side backed up to a cliff that dropped hundreds of feet to the sea might make it safe from invaders, but it didn't bode well for sleepwalkers or the chronically clumsy.

"The *dullahan?*" Katy cast her a scathing glance. "Dull is right. What good would a headless man be?"

"None. I know because I married one. All Dave's brains were in his—"

"Can it, Ally. You're a disgrace to the O'Neills. The O'Neills don't give up on romance because they pulled one wormy apple out of the basket. Don't know why the ghosts of your ancestors don't rise up and kick you out of Ireland." Katy peered into a darkened doorway of the ruined keep.

"I'm open to new experiences, but I really don't expect to see any ancestral ghosts rising to defend love. Our family history says most of the O'Neills spent their lives fighting and drinking. That didn't leave much time for anything else." Ally flinched as a large drop of water from a low-hanging branch splattered against her cheek.

"You're here, aren't you? So they must have done something else. Ever since that rotten ex-husband of yours took off with another woman, you've been reading too many books. The wrong books." Katy peered further into the doorway. "Want to take a look?"

"I'd rather eat dirt. Look, it's cold, wet, and dark. Let's go back to the wagon." *And away from comments about my "perfect" marriage.* Dave had been a mistake, but the experience had toughened her. Strength was part of her new persona. "I still don't know why we didn't hire a car to get around Ireland."

"When I was a kid, I always dreamed about living in Ireland. I used to pretend I was one of the traveling people, driving my gypsy wagon from village to village. Used to picture a dark gypsy kidnapping me and having his way with me. Exciting stuff." Katy grinned at her. "Could still happen, you know."

"Katy, we have a horse that's so laid-back I have to keep checking to see if he's dead." Ally smiled. She'd had her own fantasies as a kid. "Excitement is a black stallion, a masked man wearing a black cape. Zorro." Instead she'd settled for plain Dave who'd morphed into rotten Dave.

Katy looked interested. "I could go for a masked man."

A rumble of thunder sounded in the distance. "I still think we should go back to the wagon." Since Katy wasn't into research, Ally had done it for her. Ally knew all there was to know about every Irish fairy, and she'd bet not one of them would show tonight.

"Know what? I think you were switched at birth. Wouldn't be surprised if you belonged to Edna Wilson. She just sits around on that old yellow porch wearin' a sour puss and whining about everything. Whined her husband into an early grave." Katy marched ahead of Ally, her

11

bright orange hair a beacon in the rainy Irish night.

"Give it up, Katy. Black Liam likes virgins. You're no virgin." Ally had been a virgin when she married Dave. Marrying a virgin was important to him. And didn't the "perfect" wife always try to please her husband? Fat lot of good it had done her.

"I could pretend." Katy turned her head to offer Ally a sly grin.

Oh, boy. "This is ridiculous. Let's look at things logically."

"No."

"Any vampire worth his salt would be hitting the streets of Dublin scoping out hot-blooded wenches, *not* wandering around an old crumbling castle at midnight. Face it, we're small change." Ally pushed a damp tendril of hair from her face.

"I want to see a vampire." Katy's tone suggested that if Black Liam knew what was good for him, he'd better appear. "Besides, I'm on to something here. I feel a presence."

"Rain, Katy. It's called rain."

"You've got the sensitivity of a turnip, just like your Uncle George. Wouldn't recognize a spirit if it pinched your bottom." She hunched her thin shoulders and trudged onward. Katy Gallagher, intrepid huntress of all things spooky.

"I've got loads of sensitivity. I'm sensitive to sinus headaches, hacking coughs—things you get from standing in the rain." Ally did some mental fanny kicking. Why had she let her great-aunt talk her into coming to Ireland with her? Okay, so Katy had used the an-old-helpless-woman-can't-go-to-Ireland-by-herself ploy. Hah! Katy was a seventy-year-old Buffy the Vampire Slayer.

To be honest, it wasn't all her great-aunt's fault. When Katy had set her sights on writing about Irish fairies, Ally had thought it might be a fun vacation. The horse-drawn gypsy wagon had sounded relaxing and stress-free. Wrong. She should've known that traveling with Katy would never be stress-free.

"Too bad you take after your mother's side of the family. Don't get me wrong, Ruth's a fine woman, but she doesn't have a speck of imagination. Takes things too seriously. Always too busy fighting with that nephew of mine. Should know by now she's never going to change him. Doesn't pay to get too wrapped up in a man." She cast Ally a meaningful glance.

"Save the lecture. I know I spent too much time on Dave." *Five years too much.* After five years of marriage, Dave had left her for a woman who didn't give a flip whether she pleased him or not. "I vote for heading back to the wagon. It's going to be a no-vampire night, and it can't be too safe wandering around by ourselves in the dark."

"Loosen up, honey. It's fun being scared." Katy peered at her watch.

"The only one who'll be scared is your insur-ance agent. What if you trip and break a leg?

What're you going to put on the claim form? I was chasing a vampire?" Okay, she'd try to think good thoughts about this trip. It would give her time to work on her new book, *Coping with Single Life*.

"You're a depressing person." Katy's stride never faltered. "Remind me to leave you home next time."

Ally sighed. Maybe she was depressing, but negative was where she was at right now. Only one positive in her life at present. She was positive she'd never worry about making a man happy again.

She'd written a string of best-selling books teaching women how to be the perfect wife. *The Perfect Wife in the Kitchen, The Perfect Wife in Bed, The Perfect Wife at the Baseball Game*, ad nauseam, all encouraging women to go the extra mile to please their husbands. She'd been so sure this was the key to a fulfilling marriage.

Ally had watched her mother battle her father over unimportant things from the time Ally was old enough to understand all the screaming and to hide her head under the pillows. She was determined to save other women from a lifetime of constant strife.

Fulfilling marriage. Right. On the way out the door for the last time, Dave had called her boring. He wanted a woman who was more of a challenge, more exciting. Ally narrowed her gaze. He'd wanted bitchy; she'd given him bitchy. The divorce settlement had been more exciting than their marriage ever was.

"It's almost twelve." Katy sounded gleeful.

Black Liam had better protect his most treasured body parts with Katy on the prowl.

"That McDermott guy said if we walk around this ruin at the exact stroke of midnight, we'll meet Black Liam."

Ally rolled her eyes. "The only thing that'll happen if we walk around this place is we'll fall off the cliff. I love Ireland. I might even love this old castle, if I could see it. But I don't enjoy anything while standing in a cold rain at midnight." She hunched her shoulders against the damp chill. "It's raining harder."

Katy stared distractedly into the darkness. "This isn't rain, honey. It's the soft Irish weather."

"Well, some of your soft Irish weather is trickling down my back."

The quiet buzz of Katy's watch signaled midnight. Good. Now they could walk around three sides of this gothic novel reject, nothing would happen, and they could return to their built-by-insane-gypsies-who-hate-tourists caravan wagon.

Ally shivered. As if things weren't bad enough, the wind had picked up. Maybe the breeze would blow the rain clouds away. Was she an optimist, or what?

She turned her back to the strong gusts that whipped strands of hair into her eyes, while the rest of her hair blew in every direction. Lucky that only Katy could see her.

The only comfort in this whole rotten night was knowing she had pepper spray in her pocket. Katy might be looking for vampires, but Ally was ready if something more substantial popped up.

"When I go to the great beyond, tell everyone I'm scheduling hauntings at noon. Midnight is the pits." Ally turned and continued walking, her muttered complaint swept away on a gust of wind that whistled through the myriad cracks and crannies of the ancient building.

Ally was so busy thinking sarcastic thoughts, she didn't even realize Katy had stopped until she bumped into her.

"You go on ahead, honey. Got something in my shoe. I'll catch up. Shout if you see anything." Katy bent down to work at the laces of her running shoes.

Right. She'd just mosey along and see what she could see. Which was nothing. Ally would kill for a flashlight. Katy was wearing a spelunkers headlight on her head, but she wouldn't turn it on. Said the light might scare off a vampire. Now Ally was reduced to feeling her way along the stone wall. At least the sound of the waves would keep her away from the cliff's edge.

"See anything yet?" Katy's voice wafted to her above the wailing wind.

"No." Curse the luck that had sent them into McNulty's Pub. The man who'd spun this yarn for them probably had a tale for every gullible tourist. Well, Ally O'Neill didn't believe in ghosts and ghoulies. She was only here for Katy.

The corner caught her by surprise. One minute solid stone lay beneath her fingers, then nothing. The rain, darkness, and frenzied sea sounds made for a great horror-movie backdrop. What a fun way to spend the night.

Gritting her teeth, she shuffled onward. Besides being wet and windblown, she was bored. Ally was open to a few vampires and demons livening things up. She sure wished *something* would happen.

While a sudden crack of thunder shook the ground, a jagged streak of lightning illuminated the scene for a few seconds.

Ally looked up and froze. *God, cancel that wish!*

The brilliant white flash outlined a massive figure. Huge dark wings floated around the shape as it moved inexorably toward her.

The logical, no-nonsense upbringing of twenty-seven years deserted her in a surge of primitive fear. This was absolutely *not* on her itinerary of things to see in Ireland. Her voice was locked in an off position as she whirled and ran.

She panted and her arms pumped frantically as she tried to put space between *it* and her, but that last slice of banoffi pie at dinner weighed her down. *Please, let me escape, and I'll never whine again.* A sweeping promise she probably couldn't keep, but it was worth a shot. She glanced back to see that Black Liam was gaining. God wasn't bargaining tonight.

"Ally, did you see a vampire yet?" Katy's voice drifted to her on the suddenly still air.

Yep. Been there, done that. Feet, fly. At least she was leading Black Liam away from Katy. They could put that on her tombstone: The vampire didn't get Katy.

"Blood of Boren!"

The husky male voice behind her made her pump even harder. She didn't care how often he mentioned his favorite drink, she wasn't going to be part of it.

She splashed through a stream and scrambled up the steep incline beyond. The thud of pursuing footsteps sounded above the frantic pounding of her heart.

Wait. Human voice. Human footsteps. *Human?* Her logic struggled to its feet and dusted off the footprints her stampeding brain cells had left when they made a dash for the door.

Human. Not a vampire. Some human scumbag was chasing her. She'd allowed herself to get caught up in superstitious claptrap she swore she didn't believe in.

Now she was mad. Her fury stopped her headlong flight with a suddenness that brought the man barreling into her. She crashed to the ground, pinned by his weight.

"You're trespassing, babe."

Ally blinked at the wet blades of grass tickling her nose while she processed the huskily murmured accusation. Where? Where was she trespassing?

"This castle's *mine*." His declaration of ownership warmed the side of her neck.

She tried to concentrate on his words, but the weight of his body, the pressure of his groin tucked against her behind, sort of distracted her from any deep focusing. "Fine. So you own the castle, and I own the Boardwalk. Who the heck cares? Get off me. I can't breathe." The breathing thing had nothing to do with his weight.

His soft chuckle didn't sound friendly as he rolled off her and stood.

"If the vampire's hassling you, you tell him he doesn't want to mess with Katy Gallagher." Katy's voice would have thrown fear into a Viking berserker.

"I'm fine," Ally hastened to assure her. But was she? There were different degrees of "fine."

She thought about her pepper spray. No, he didn't pose *that* kind of danger.

Ally scrambled to her knees, then looked up at him. "If this place belongs to you, why don't you sound Irish?" If she kept him talking, maybe his scary index would go down or her fearless index would rise.

He shrugged. "I don't live here. Just visiting. Couldn't wait till morning to see the old place, so I hiked out here tonight."

"So, you're kind of an absentee landlord." *Keep him on the defensive.* "Sure have let the old homestead get run down."

His laugh was low, not defensive. "It isn't working, babe."

"What isn't working?" *My heart, my lungs?* Seemed like every part of her was either speeding up or slowing down.

"Trying to keep me talking until Katy comes to save you." He turned his head at the sound of Katy's noisy approach, and his long dark hair shifted across broad shoulders.

"That's a lie." *That's the truth, but I'd rather dunk my head in ice water than admit it.*

His all-weather coat flapped open in the breeze. How humiliating. She'd been scared witless by a flapping coat.

Ally climbed to her feet. He didn't try to help her. Carefully, she brushed dirt and grass from her jacket. She needed time to think. "If you hiked out here, where're you staying tonight?"

"I could stay with you." His tone suggested the staying wouldn't be all that unpleasant.

Ally dragged in a deep breath to jump-start her lungs; then the humor in his voice registered. He was only kidding. Relief washed over her.

It was his voice. She knew even if he were reading a grocery list, his voice would carry the promise of danger, sex, and sin. Ally could imagine his murmured whisper, "Don't forget the whipped cream, babe."

Okay, it was his voice *and* his body. He was tall with shoulders that were solid with muscle and maturity; it didn't matter that she hadn't gotten a clear look at his face. Two out of three made for a tempting package. Not for her, of course. But something about his total impact still scared her. She backed up a step.

"Ally, if you've found Black Liam, don't let him get away. I have my digital camera, digital camcorder, and digital voice recorder all packed here in my fisherman's vest. We'll nail this sucker."

"So, did you find him, Ally?" His grin was a slash of white in the darkness.

A clear and present danger to all women? "Yes." No hesitation. Some things were a given.

She had no time for elaboration because Katy burst from the darkness, camera in hand and orange hair flying. "Where is he? Just point me at him and move out of the way."

Ally sighed. This would not be easy to explain. "Sorry, Katy. No photo ops tonight. Just you, me, and . . ." She waited.

"Brian Byrne. I own this keep." End of explanation.

"Maybe it's Black Liam masquerading as the owner. Vampires are tricky bastards." Katy moved closer to peer up into his face. "Are you the dark despoiler of virgins that McDermott guy told us about?"

"You want a dark despoiler, I can be a dark despoiler." He stared over Katy's head at Ally.

Katy stepped back and grinned at him. "I just bet you can. I'm Katy Gallagher, and this is my grandniece, Ally O'Neill."

Katy was way too friendly with this stranger.

21

Fine, so most women would want to be more than friendly with Brian Byrne.

"Guess we missed the vampire. May as well head back to the wagon." Katy paused to give Brian time to fill in any information he might care to offer.

Brian chose to offer nothing.

"Where are you from?" Katy was reduced to direct grilling.

"Philly."

"Tucson," Katy countered. "Where you staying tonight?"

Brian nodded toward the keep.

Katy made a rude noise. "You camp out here, you'll have mold growing on you by morning. Grab your jammies and—"

"No." Ally had never been so sure in her life about a "no."

"—bunk with us for the night. The wagon sleeps four, so there's plenty of room."

Ally blinked. She'd forgotten that Katy could ignore the end of the world if it didn't fit in with her plans for the day. Ally narrowed her gaze. "*No.*"

"I don't wear jammies."

Ally knew he had Katy's undivided attention. He certainly had hers.

"I sleep naked."

Well, that sure cleared things up.

"That won't be a problem. Haven't seen a naked man since Padraic passed on. Sort of miss seeing one once in a while." Katy started walking back toward the wagon. It obviously didn't occur to her that someone else might have a problem with sharing sleeping quarters with a naked stranger.

"No!" Ally's shout would have woken any spirits that weren't already enjoying the show. "No one is sharing our wagon. I'm sure Mr. Byrne brought camping gear with him. Didn't you?" She gave him her death glare, just in case he was thinking of giving the wrong answer.

"Sure will be cold out here."

She knew he was smiling.

"Mmmph. Probably been so long since Ally saw a fine-looking naked man, her woman parts've all shriveled up and dried out. Hormones've stopped flowing. Her ex-husband doesn't count. Wouldn't pay squat to see him naked." With that definitive analysis, Katy strode away, leaving Ally alone with Brian Byrne.

"Bet it'll be cold in the wagon, too." He was still smiling. "But I'm easy. Wouldn't want to embarrass you, so I'll stay here tonight."

Ally sighed. "Katy's used to getting her own way, and her own way doesn't always coincide with good sense." She narrowed her gaze. "You didn't help things any."

"Hey, I did my part. She wanted to know how I slept." He shrugged. "I told her how I slept."

"She didn't ask you." Ally knew she should end this conversation.

"But she wanted to know." Unexpectedly, he moved closer. *"You* wanted to know."

23

"I didn't." Okay, so she sort of wanted to know.

"Afraid of me, Ally?"

"No." Yes. Because she'd finally gotten a good look at his face. She might have missed out on a vampire, but she'd sure as heck found a devil, if you thought of the devil as temptation incarnate. Full sensual lips, knife-edge cheekbones, and his eyes . . . She'd never seen eyes like his. Deep forest green: cool, secret, and shadowed by a thick fringe of lashes as black as his hair. Ally noted the slight slant of those incredible eyes. Yep, definitely a devil.

"Liar."

"What?" She'd forgotten the question. But she hadn't forgotten his closeness. He was close enough for her to feel his body heat, to catch the scent of danger and warm male. Before she could transfer the danger signal from brain to feet, he pulled her into his arms and kissed her.

It was a kiss to build fantasies on. His lips brushed across hers, then settled in for the long haul. They were firm, with a high enough "hot" index to melt her lips and seal them together forever. When his tongue slid along her lower lip, she was relieved to discover her lips weren't permanently bonded. She parted them so he could explore possibilities. His tongue tangled with hers, deepening the kiss, deadening her other senses to everything but the taste, the feel of him.

A sudden flash of lightning lit up the world behind Ally's closed lids. It also awoke her snoozing brain to the reality of an intruder in the house.

But before Ally could move to push him away, Brian stepped back. She blinked up at him. "What was that all about?"

"Damned if I know." He sounded sincerely puzzled.

She couldn't read his expression in the darkness.

"Well, don't do it again."

"Believe me, it'll never happen again." He didn't sound amused anymore.

The conversation was becoming uncomfortable; she should just leave, but she couldn't resist one more shot at all that alpha maleness. "Guess you think all women like to be grabbed and kissed."

"Always have, babe. Always have."

Sensual waves washed over Ally like breakers rolling in off the Atlantic. She fought to the surface and swam for shore. Shore being the safety of the wagon where Katy no doubt waited armed with barbed comments aimed at Ally's non-relationship with men.

She felt his gaze slide down her back, linger on her behind, as she walked away.

She walked faster.

Brian raked his fingers through his damp hair as he watched her practically run away. She was escaping him as fast her legs could take her. Smart lady. She wasn't tall, but those legs went on for a long way. He watched the sway of her bottom until she was hidden in darkness.

Amazing. A woman who didn't recognize him, didn't know what he did and how well he did it. A woman who wasn't waiting for him with legs spread.

Brian Byrne thrived on the can't-be-done things in life. That's why he was tops in the sex game. The league routinely scoured the galaxy searching for females to challenge him. They hadn't found any yet.

But in this new time . . . He was a competitor, and Ally's signals were broadcasting can't-be-had loud and clear. What if he gave her a try? He clamped down on that thought fast.

Brian was a man of his word. He fulfilled the terms of his contracts, and league contracts stated that players could not have unauthorized sex without permission. Besides, sex with females who understood the game was one thing, sex with a woman who didn't realize he'd walk away from her was another. And he'd promised Jupe. . . .

He'd learned the power of a broken promise when he was six years old. His mother had left him in a spaceport with a parting order to be good until she got back. She'd never returned, and he never wanted to be the cause of that kind of pain for someone else. He'd only broken a promise once. That one broken promise had cost a life. He'd never broken one since.

He stared into the darkness where Ally had disappeared. Could've been fun, though. Females hadn't been anything more than hard training and harder competition in a long time. Fun would've been a change.

Brian walked to his pack and pulled out the Constructor. He entered a code, focused his thoughts on a mental image, then watched distractedly as it built his heated shelter for the night.

He smiled, and women in any time would have understood the expression.

"Lucky escape, Ally O'Neill. Because next to me, Black Liam is a hell of a nice guy."

Chapter Two

Ally would still be sleeping. If he were with her now, he could slide his hand under whatever useless piece of cloth she wore and cover her breasts, feel her warmth seep through him, her softness excite him. He'd tease each nipple until it was hard and aching, until she arched her back, even in sleep begging for his lips. He'd move his hand over her stomach, between her legs, stroking her until she opened her legs wide—wet and ready for him. And as she slowly awoke, he'd whisper all the things he'd do to her.

He inhaled deeply. Talk about not being able to leave the job behind. Problem. On the job he didn't get hard until game time, but he was hard now after just a few mental pictures. The reason? She didn't want him, and he was a competitive kind of guy. He didn't really want *her*. He'd react this way to any woman who challenged him.

He didn't need this distraction though. Ally O'Neill was a dangerous woman to his relaxed sex-free vacation. She had to go, and he knew exactly how to hurry her on her way.

Brian continued to sit on the rock wall in the dawn's light, enjoying the fresh sea breeze, the sound of the waves, muted now, and the quiet peacefulness of the old keep outlined against the morning sky. He felt a sense of coming home.

He watched as Ally's horse nudged open the narrow wooden gate and wandered out of the field. He saw it amble over the nearest hill. He did nothing. Time enough later to help Ally find her horse.

Brian glanced back at the wagon. An honest-to-goodness gypsy wagon. He'd seen one in a virtual reenactment of primitive-culture lifestyles. Why would anyone travel in that when motorized transportation was available?

Ally's outraged shout from inside the wagon distracted him from further thoughts of transportation.

"A cat! There's a cat sleeping in my bed. How did it get in? This wouldn't happen at a Holiday Inn."

A short time later, Ally's great-aunt stuck her head from the wagon, glanced at the empty field, then ducked inside again.

He waited.

Ally didn't disappoint. Within minutes, she climbed from the wagon, halter in hand. Her long blond hair was tousled, and her expression didn't bode well for the world. Brian smiled.

"I can't believe the motor to this gypsy's revenge just walked away. A car engine wouldn't do this. That's why we should've rented a—" She saw him. Her gaze narrowed. "Did you let the horse out?"

"Nope." He stood and stretched, watching her glance slide down the length of him then return to his face, feeling the path of her gaze as a sizzle of forgotten sensation. Brian frowned. Women's glances had long ago ceased to trigger any kind of response. How could she do that to him? "He didn't need my help. He just pushed open the gate and wandered away. Probably didn't go far."

Exasperation carried her to where he stood. "Why didn't you stop him?"

Brian shrugged and offered her a smile he hoped would annoy. "I'm a vampire, remember? I don't do the cowboy thing."

"A vampire. Right." She cast him a mocking glance. "Then I guess you didn't have to worry about the heat thing last night."

"Heat's easy, babe." He slid her a glance meant to demonstrate exactly how easy it was.

"Hmm."

She pursed her lips, then walked toward the gate. He noted the pursing with detachment. Okay, maybe not so detached. She had great lips, a sensual woman's lips. Someone should sue her for false advertising.

He followed her to the gate, then watched as

she picked up the lead line from where it was draped over the wall. "Strange. I tied the gate shut last night with this line. No way the horse could have untied it." She narrowed her gaze. "Are you sure that you—"

"I don't do petty stuff just to annoy people." He grinned. "When I do something, you'll know why. I'm a goal-oriented kind of guy."

"Well, someone did. The horse didn't lay the lead line over the wall when he finished untying it."

He watched her as she strode through the open gate, his gaze automatically dropping to the sway of her hips in those old . . . jeans. Brian frowned. It was tough trying to keep the names of things straight. The Language Assimilation Program did a great job of preparing time travelers, but even the best program had gaps.

His grin returned as she quickened her pace. She had enough swing and sway to tempt any man, but he knew if any man grasped those hips and pulled her tight between his legs, it'd be like riding a block of ice. But he wasn't "any man." He was the best because he could read a woman before he even touched her. And that sway said—

"There he is." She pointed down the hill to where the old bay horse grazed near the main road, oblivious to the trouble he'd caused. As they made their way toward the horse, Ally turned her attention back to Brian Byrne. "So what do you do for a living when you're not searching out your roots?"

"Have sex with thousands of women." He slanted her a grin that would've knocked her off her feet if she wasn't already laid out flat by his comment. "Professionally, of course."

"Well, that makes it okay then." A porn star? Her instinct said no. But her instinct had also thought Dave was a great guy when she first met him. How wrong was that? Hmm. What else could Brian be? How about crazy? Sounded logical to her. She was alone with a crazy man. A sexy crazy man, but crazy was still crazy. "Umm, I can do this by myself if you have something else to do." *Please have something else to do.*

"You see, in my time—" he leaned close for an aside—"I'm talking 2502 here—" he leaned away, and she allowed her breath to escape in a relieved whoosh—"there aren't many males with much sex drive. I'm talking zero want."

"Got it. Want is important." If she ran like hell, would he catch her? She remembered last night. He'd catch her.

"So sex has become a spectator sport. Sort of like your football." His satisfied expression indicated everything should be perfectly clear to her now.

She couldn't run, and in hand-to-hand combat she'd be toast, so she had to keep him talking until she could figure out how to get rid of him. No way would she lead him back to the wagon. Katy would probably ply him with a glass of milk and cookies, then make him tell her the rest of his sexual fantasy.

Think. This was 2002 AD. Translation: After Dave. She was a new woman, a strong and resourceful woman, a woman who could cope. This man might be delusionary, but so far he didn't seem violent. She'd just keep him occupied with a meaningful question while she figured out what to do. "Fine. I get the broad picture. How about filling in some details?"

"Sure." He offered her a grin that suggested he could fill in details she didn't know existed.

She paused for a moment of regret. *So beautiful. So flawed.*

They'd reached the horse, and she fumbled with the halter, knowing that he was watching and angry with herself for letting his gaze affect her.

"The game's pretty simple. The teams play every Monday night. Eleven men on each side. Two hours plus a halftime rest. The team that brings the most women to orgasm wins."

She sensed him moving closer, and her fumbling grew worse. "And you do this in front of an audience?"

He shrugged. "About seventy thousand in the stadium plus a few billion in the home audience."

"Billion?" She didn't think she could be shocked by a fantasy, but he was doing it.

"The galaxy's a big place."

"Right. I forgot the galaxy." She continued to fumble with the halter as the horse stood patiently chewing a mouthful of grass.

"You know, controlling large animals with low-level caren waves would be a lot simpler, but I guess you won't have that option for a few years yet."

Caren waves? Time for another meaningful question. "And you perform . . . naked?" Not as meaningful as she'd hoped.

"You have a real problem with naked, don't you?" His soft laugh slid across the back of her neck leaving a trail of goose bumps.

Keep him talking. Don't think about naked. "Uh, how do you know someone isn't cheating, faking a climax?" This was all about being strong and resourceful, and a few deep breaths would slow her heart rate just fine.

"Monitors are attached to the women. Referees can check readouts of blood pressure, pulse, spasms—"

"Okay, heard enough. Don't need to hear any more." She made one more effort to buckle the cursed halter. "Your game seems so . . . cold."

"You're kidding, right?" He reached around her to pull the halter up and buckle it on the horse's head. "Nothing hotter in the universe. Believe it."

His heat surrounded her as her body kicked into automatic anticipation mode. You'd think after one brief contact last night her body would have forgotten his touch. No luck. She dropped her hands from the horse and clenched them at her side. Tried to ignore the press of his chest against her back, the flow of muscle and flesh she could feel all the way to her pounding heart. But no amount of concentration could make her ignore the spread of his thighs hard against her hips, the pressure of his growing erection against . . . Uh-oh, time for another thought-provoking question.

Finished buckling the halter, he stepped back. She turned in time to catch his assessing stare.

"Don't know how you do that, babe. You're lethal."

Ally squashed a twinge of triumph. She wouldn't be drawn into his weird fantasy. "That should be a pretty normal reaction for a man who's had thousands of women."

"Doesn't work that way. *I* decide when to get hard for a woman. Self-discipline. It's important in the game. You have to pace yourself."

She rolled her eyes.

"That's why I was MVP of the Sex Super Bowl." He grabbed the horse's lead line and started walking back up the hill toward the wagon.

She knew it was coming. She knew it was a mistake. She said it anyway. "MVP? Most Valuable Penis?"

He stopped and turned to stare at her. Oh lordy, had she gone too far? She hadn't gotten any danger vibes this morning, but too late she remembered her fear from last night.

Then he laughed, and she *understood*. If Brian Byrne wanted sex with a thousand women, he could have it and still have women lined up. It wasn't about being tall and muscular. It wasn't about long dark hair that lay heavy on his shoulders in the morning mist. It wasn't even about a face with knife-edged cheekbones and a sensual mouth. It was his eyes. There was somebody home in those green eyes. Somebody vital and sexy. The male animal in its most concentrated form. Somebody a woman would want to know and understand, but probably never would.

If she ever figured out the truth about men, maybe she'd write a book, *The Essential Male Animal*. But right now, she was too busy being strong, resourceful, and oh God—she hadn't asked a meaningful question in almost a minute.

He looked away and continued walking, but not before she saw the laughter still in his eyes. "So I guess you'll be eager to get away from here. Hey, a haunted castle and crazy owner can't make for much fun."

She didn't miss the hopeful note in his voice. "That's what this whole story was about, wasn't it?" They'd reached the wagon, and she watched him tie the horse. "Tell me about your life in the future and see me run away."

He shrugged as he caught sight of Ally's great-aunt leaning from the wagon. "It's whatever you want it to be."

"Good to see you didn't freeze to death last night, Brian." Katy Gallagher cast her grandniece an accusing glare. "Come in and have a cup of coffee. Take a look at our wagon."

Brian watched Ally do more lip pursing and eye narrowing. She didn't want him inside her wagon. He smiled. "Coffee sounds great." He'd never tasted coffee, but he'd give anything a try, especially if it irritated Ally O'Neill. There was something about an angry woman. . . . He hadn't met many angry women in his life.

He climbed into the wagon ahead of Ally. Tried to ignore the touch of her gaze on his back, his buttocks, his legs. His awareness of her continued to surprise him.

Brian was a sexual animal, a male who could give and receive sexual pleasure, and as such was valued in his time, where sexual stimulus was at a premium. For most of the population, watching him perform was a vicarious thrill, the closest they'd ever get to the real thing.

He accepted what he was, took pride in what he did so well, but he'd done it so many times that it took more than a woman's glance to arouse him. When he'd first started his career, he'd believed there could never be enough women. Now? He wasn't sure. Lately, arousal had taken a conscious effort on his part, and that was why he needed these three weeks.

So why his response to Ally? He hadn't a clue.

"Cat won't leave the wagon." Katy peered into a mirror as she busily flattened her hair into submission. "Tried to chase him off your bed, but he hissed and swatted at me. Decided to let you deal with him."

"Thanks." Ally moved around Brian to stare at the large calico cat sprawled across the lower half of her bed. "Why *my* bed?"

"Because he knows you don't want him there. Cats are perverse that way." With that bit of folk wisdom, Katy turned her attention to Brian. "Ally likes to think things to death when she'd be better off going with her gut feelings. Like this book she's writing, *Coping with Single Life*. Makes single life sound like a chore. She should be writing a book called *Having a Kick-ass Good Time*. I'm looking to find some Irish fairies—to talk to them, share a few jokes. If Ally ever runs into something she can't explain, she'll analyze every last blessed drop of joy out of it."

Ally's sigh was long suffering. "Okay, what *should* I do if I run into something unexplained, and what does this have to do with that cat?"

"You should say 'yes' and embrace the moment. You don't know if you'll ever get a shot at something that special again." She winked at Brian. "Or if another big old Tom will ever again choose your bed to sleep in." With that cryptic observation, she left the wagon.

"Katy's a little outspoken. Says what she thinks even if she flattens everyone with the saying." The love in Ally's gaze as she watched her great-aunt leave belied her words.

Brian watched distractedly as Ally poured him a cup of coffee then put it on the table. He'd like to know more about Ally's life, but right now there was something else he needed to think about.

Brian narrowed his gaze on the cat. It returned his stare with malevolent yellow eyes. He knew those eyes. They were the eyes of . . .

"Shoo cat." Ally made flapping motions at the cat. It stared at her, unmoved. "Why won't it get off the bed?" Exasperation sharpened her voice.

She sat on the edge of her bed and tried to shove the animal out of her way. Fixing her with an unblinking stare, it hooked its claws into her bedding and stayed put. "Okay, give me some ideas here."

Brian glared at the cat. What did a man have to do to get some peace? All he wanted was to be left alone for a few weeks, to relax away from all the stresses of his job. Was that asking too much? "It's not a *he*, it's a she. This is the Old One. She's my cat. Probably wandered in here because it was warm and comfortable. She's big into comfort." May as well claim her. If he didn't, she'd make his life a living hell when he got back. Probably give Jupe a hassle over the incentive clause they were negotiating.

Ally cast him a puzzled glance. "You brought your cat with you?" She looked back at the Old One. "What a strange name."

"Yeah. I call her Boss for short." He stared into the Old One's self-satisfied eyes as he sat next to her on the bed. He'd have a few things to say to her once they were alone.

The Old One rose, arched her back and yawned, then climbed into his lap and curled up. Great. You couldn't just dump your team owner onto the floor.

"So what other kinds of books do you write?"

He ran his palm across the sheet that separated him from Ally, smoothing out the wrinkles. *Too bad he couldn't slide his hand across her bare stomach, her breasts.* Now that was the kind of thinking he should lose for the next three weeks. He had to learn to think in terms that didn't include sex.

She cast him a thoughtful glance. "I wrote a few successful books on how to be the perfect wife. What's a man's perspective on the subject?"

Absently, he rubbed his aching thigh. "A wife? Haven't thought about it much." He wouldn't marry while he was with the team, but if he ever did marry he'd want a woman who could match his passion. He'd probably have to search the poorer planets to find a woman who didn't have all the sensuality leeched out of her. But there was something more he wanted. . . . "I'd like a woman who'd try to please me." He'd never had a woman who wanted to do little things for him. Not his mother, not the women he satisfied during competition. Maybe a girlfriend would have, but he'd never had time for one.

Her narrowed gaze told him he'd said the wrong thing.

"I wrote books that taught women how to please men, but I was wrong. You try to please men and they leave footprints on your face as they walk out the door. From now on, men will have to do the pleasing." She glanced down. "What's wrong with your thigh?"

"Muscle strain. Championship competition

puts a lot of stress on the thigh muscles. Right here." Reaching over, he laid his palm high on her inner thigh, felt her muscles clench at his touch, felt his groin tighten in response, then felt the agony of red-hot needles stabbing a little too closely to his heavily insured, most valuable asset.

"What the hell!" Instinctively, he stood, dumping the Old One and her unsheathed claws onto the floor.

In a royal huff, she stalked over to the small fold-out table and leaped atop it, settling herself among the coffee cups.

"She's on the table." Ally sounded horrified.

"Yeah, she pretty much goes where she wants." Brian scowled at the Old One. He understood her game now. She was going to run interference with anyone in this time who might mess with her highest paid player. She'd better think again if she thought she could dictate what he did with his free time.

"You should break her of that habit." Ally's expression indicated she was smart enough not to offer her services. "I'll be right back. I need to see how Katy's coming with the horse."

He nodded. Probably he should offer to help, but he had some pressing business right here.

As soon as Ally left, he swung to face the Old One. "Bad choice of forms. Sure, it gives you an inconspicuous way to stick your nose in my business, but it has limitations. Know what I mean?" He grinned, and the Old One's eyes glittered angrily. "For example, you can't talk. Tough."

The Old One swatted at a cup, then watched as it crashed to the floor.

Brian shook his head. "Temper, temper. Everyone knows Serans are powerful shape shifters, but changing shape takes lots of energy." Ignoring the Old one's slit-eyed glare, he cocked his head to study her. "How can I say this without insulting you? Got it. You're into minimal effort and conserving energy. Both of those are great things, but I guess you're stuck with being a cat for the month. Have fun." He didn't stick around to see what else she'd break. He climbed from the wagon to join Ally.

Ally watched him walk toward her, and no matter how hard she tried to concentrate on grooming the horse, her mind insisted on imagining scenes from his fantasy.

"Where'd your great-aunt go?"

Don't pay attention to what he looks like. Remember, he wants a woman to please him. You've already tried the please-your-man thing, and it didn't work. "She walked up to your keep. Says she isn't leaving until she finds a ghost or fairy." Ally cast him a tentative smile. "Got any white sheets handy?"

He shook his head and drew her gaze to his hair. Thick and soft, it invited a woman's fingers. . . . Uh-Uh. She wouldn't go there. No touching any part of Brian Byrne. "Then I guess we're here for the long haul with a few day trips thrown in for variety, unless you decide to throw us off your property."

"You're not bothering anyone out here."

His eyes said "lie" before he shifted his gaze from her. She smiled. Knowing that she bothered him made her feel . . . good. Go figure.

"So tell me about the book you're writing." He sat on a nearby wall, legs spread.

His jeans were tight, but her throat was tighter. She coughed to clear it. "I'm trying to help recently divorced women adjust to single life by sharing my own experiences and my reaction to them."

"And those experiences are?" He rubbed his aching thigh. Probably wasn't even aware he was doing it.

She was aware. "Zip so far. Unless you count meeting a man who's traveled here from 2502."

Ally waited for him to laugh. He didn't.

"No wild sex? Wild parties?" He drew his lower lip between his teeth. Another unconscious gesture.

His lips must ache, too. Overuse. Probably had RKS—repetitive kissing syndrome.

"I'm not a wild sex kind of woman." Not that she was against wild sex. Too bad Dave had been at the tame end of the sex spectrum. Wild would have made for a refreshing change.

"If wild means unplanned, then I don't do wild either. I've had a long career because I think about each move, each word I say. That way, I maximize my results."

Ally knew her mouth must be hanging open. He was seriously into his fantasy. "You sound so . . ." *Insane.* "Calculating."

He shrugged. "To be a success in the sex games, a man has to make sure he has everything in control, timed perfectly. Sort of like your football pass. The quarterback has to know exactly where his receiver is and put the ball right on the money or else no score. It's all about timing."

Right. Ally didn't have a clue what he was talking about, but she couldn't imagine sex being anything but wild with Brian Byrne.

Maybe they needed to get away from this topic. "I'm beginning to enjoy the research for Katy's book. I never knew there were so many varieties of supernatural beings associated with Ireland. I'm keeping a list according to physical appearance so if Katy thinks she sees one we can catalog it. Did you know the O'Neills are one of the few families that have a banshee?"

"Banshee?" He looked puzzled.

Strange. Everyone had heard of the banshee, even people who didn't have a drop of Irish blood. "She's supposed to appear in the guise of a woman, sometimes wearing a hooded gray cloak. According to tradition, she cries to warn members of certain ancient Irish families of their time of death. Let's see, I think they're the O'Neills, the O'Briens, the O'Connors, the O'Gradys, and the Kavanaghs." Just call her Ally, the repository of useless facts. Maybe Dave was right about the boring part.

"That leaves me out." Brian's gaze grew probing. "Do you believe in things you can't see, Ally?" He wasn't smiling.

She shook her head. "Sorry. I don't believe in things that go bump in the night." Distracted, she noticed his cat had jumped from the wagon and was wending its way toward them. It wore a cream mustache that it was leisurely licking off. What nerve. The Old One had guzzled down the cream from their pitcher.

"Things that go bump in the night? I like that." He slanted her a smile that hinted at a secret he wasn't going to share. "So I guess there's no way you'd believe in a time when contact sports don't exist, sex is the biggest game in town, and where white stags can travel into the past?"

"Not a chance."

"Figures." He stood and stared beyond her toward the castle.

She narrowed her eyes. "Exactly what does 'figures' mean? And I've told you a lot about me, but I haven't heard any reciprocal dialogue here." She amended that. "Okay, so I've heard a lot, but nothing too truthful."

He ignored her. "Looks like your great-aunt has brought some company." He didn't look happy about it.

She turned to watch Katy as she hurried toward them with a thin red-haired man in tow. "That's Mr. McDermott. He's the man who told us that if we walked around your keep at midnight we'd meet Black Liam. I didn't believe him. Dumb me."

He knew she expected a reaction from him, but he couldn't drag his attention from Capricorn Wilson as he approached wearing a sly grin.

Brian didn't know why he hadn't been knocked flat and ground into the dirt by the herd of stags stampeding to get their clients here before he arrived. He wondered who else was lurking in the bushes.

"Will you look who I found wandering up by the castle." Katy grinned at Brian. "This here is Sean McDermott. He's the one who told us about this place. And would you believe he's a fan of American football. He's even wearing a Tennessee Titans jersey." She pointed to the blue shirt with TITANS emblazoned across the front. "I told him those Titans should've stayed the Houston Oilers."

"Not the Tennessee Titans, Katy. *Testosterone* Titans." Brian glared at Cap.

Katy didn't miss a beat. "Well, that's okay, too. A man would be a sissy without some of that stuff." She frowned. "Don't recall a team with that name, though."

Cap stepped forward, the grin still pasted on his face. "Ach, sure-and-begorra 'tis himself returned to the ould sod to claim his rightful home. It warms the cockles of me old heart."

"Feel that shaking?" Brian stepped closer.

Cap's grin slipped a little. "No."

"That's every dead Irishman from the beginning of time turning over in his grave." Brian wondered if he could get a stag to take him back home. Since everyone he knew was here in 2002, he'd have peace back in 2502.

Katy wasn't one to be kept out of the conversation for long. "You know, Sean, you talk sort of different from the other Irish people we've met." She cocked her head to study him. "You sound a little like a Saint Patty's day card."

Cap cast her a wary glance.

Ally had been silent for too long. Probably thinking. Thinking was bad. He'd already told her too much.

She stirred beside him. "Maybe I'm wrong here, but I get the feeling you two know each other."

Stupid. He'd let his anger at Cap goad him into saying more than he should have. "Nope. Never met him, but I've seen the jersey in stores around here. The Testosterone Titans are a local soccer team."

Ally cast him a doubtful glance.

Help me here, Cap.

Cap suddenly seemed to realize the value of discretion. "Sure and I've never met the lad, but I knew his father well. 'Tis the spitting image of his father, he is."

Brian didn't get time to feel any deep relief because Cap was off and running.

" 'Tis me prayer the lad'll stay here where he belongs for the rest of his life."

Brian could almost feel the air vibrate as a low

47

growl started behind them. The growl rapidly grew in volume then exploded in a furious feline yowl of outrage.

Great. Just great.

Chapter Three

Ally watched in horror as the Old One launched herself with claws unsheathed at Mr. Mc-Dermott. Every hair on the cat's ample body stood on end, puffing her up to frightening dimensions. A pit bull in feline form.

Wrapping her paws around McDermott's leg, she sank her teeth into the part of his ankle exposed by his too-short pants.

"Get her off! Get her off!" He hopped up and down, doing an Irish jig in fast forward, but the Old One was locked into position.

Ally looked around desperately. "Do something!" It was a generic order, aimed at anyone brave enough to interfere with the Old One and her prey.

Brian rocked back on his heels, his arms crossed over his impressive chest. He grinned.

"The Old One gets upset when someone suggests I shouldn't go home. She's very attached to home. Has a lot invested there."

Ally stared at him. What the heck was he talking about? And what kind of person would stand by while his pet savaged a complete stranger? Okay, so the cat wasn't of mountain lion proportions, but she sure enough made up for it in enthusiasm. One thing was clear, Brian wasn't going to help poor Mr. McDermott.

Frantically, Ally turned toward her great-aunt. Katy jumped up and down like a jackrabbit on too much caffeine. "Grab her by the scruff of her neck!"

Mr. McDermott chose to ignore Katy's advice. He opted for more hopping with occasional wild kicks thrown in for variety.

"Get her off me!" Mr. McDermott's shouts escalated to bellows.

Ally glanced around. "Someone help . . ." Uh-oh. No one else left. Only . . . her.

Ally gulped. She was not a cat person, didn't have the communication skills necessary to reason with an outraged kitty. But someone had to help Mr. McDermott. She'd learned she was capable of a lot of unexpected things once she got over trying to be all things wonderful to Dave-the-Dork. She could do this.

Not allowing herself time to think about consequences, she stepped forward, reached down, then . . . Where the heck was the cat's neck? The

Old One looked like a giant multicolored beach ball with a fur coat.

Aiming for the end where the angry growls were coming from, Ally reached in.

The Old One freed a paw long enough to swipe at the person who dared to interfere with her God-given right to chew the ankle of Sean McDermott.

"Ouch!" Ally yanked her hand back at the same time someone lifted her off her feet and set her aside.

"I'll take care of her." Brian sounded grim as he reached down and pulled the Old One off McDermott.

Ally waited breathlessly for the ensuing cries of pain. Brian would be ripped to shreds.

Instead, he cradled the Old One in his arms while she discussed the situation in a barrage of growls, hisses, and yowls. But she *didn't* try to scratch him.

Ally blinked. "Boy, you must be great with animals. I could've sworn she was ready to tear strips off anyone who touched her."

Brian looked up, his dark gaze capturing her, holding her. "She's female."

As if that explained everything. Ally sank into those green eyes, recognized the sensual knowledge, the truth of his two words, and was suddenly afraid of something she didn't understand. She rubbed her hands up and down her arms, trying to dispel the sudden rash of goose bumps.

"You'll be hearing from my lawyer about this."

McDermott's voice was shrill with anger as he bent down to examine the teeth marks in his ankle.

"Who'd believe it? That cat scared the brogue right out of you." Katy stared at the Old One, new respect in her gaze.

"Ye'll be hearing from me solicitor, ye misbegotten spawn of Satan." His voice was slightly less shrill.

Brian shook his head. "Don't know if that's wise. Isn't there a league rule about interfering with another team's players?"

Funny, Brian was answering him, but Ally could swear McDermott was talking to the cat. Stranger still, McDermott seemed to understand Brian's answer. She had to be imagining it. The stinging in her hand made her forget McDermott. She held it up and grimaced at the bloody scratches.

"Let me have a look at your hand." Brian's voice was low, concerned. He shifted his cat to one arm where she settled in with mumbled cat curses aimed at the rapidly departing Sean McDermott. "Maybe you need to calm down, Boss. The Cosmic Network would love to get hold of a story like this. You know what they'd make of it: Team Owners in Cat Fight Over Player. Not real dignified."

For a moment, Ally thought he was talking to her. Then she realized he was talking . . . to the cat? Nah. The pain in her hand was making her woozy.

Thoughts of the Old One disappeared as Brian held her hand and examined it. His palm cupped hers, his fingers resting against her wrist, and she was sure he could feel the drumbeat of her pulse as surely as she felt the rough warmth of his fingertips.

"I have something that'll take care of this." His voice suggested he had something to take care of almost anything. "Come up to my shelter while I get it." He slid his fingers around her wrist, his thumb rubbing a circular pattern of persuasion over the spot where her blood pounded a frantic warning. He started to lead her up the hill toward the castle ruins. The Old One glared at her over the top of his arm.

She dug her heels in, bringing him to a halt. "I have first aid stuff in the wagon. I can take care of it."

Katy trotted to her side. "Afraid you'll have to go with him. Used the last of the antiseptic on the horse. Figured we'd be going into Liscannor to get some supplies anyway."

"On the horse?" No. Going with Brian Byrne to his shelter was *not* an option. Why? She just *knew*. And if he'd stop touching her, she could think of another reason.

"You need to get something on those scratches. Cats carry germs." Katy was determined.

The Old One made a noise that sounded strangely like a chuckle. Ally shook her head to clear her mind.

"You go on, Ally, and I'll tag along behind."

Katy demonstrated how well she could tag along behind by forging on ahead. "I need to take a look at the far side of the castle. Thought I saw a white deer there yesterday morning. Strange color for a deer."

Ally frowned. She didn't like to have decisions made for her. God knows she'd let that happen enough during her doomed marriage. "I still think I can take care of these scratches here. Why should I hike all the way up the hill?"

Brian didn't release her, and she could feel his thumb smoothing the inside of her wrist as she guessed he usually smoothed away any female resistance. Well, she was one woman who had a whole lot of resistance to him or any man.

"The Old One traveled a long way to get here. Who knows what germs she's carrying that could infect those scratches."

"Traveled a long way. Right." There was something wrong here, just out of reach. "I thought Philadelphia was known for the Liberty Bell and cheese steaks, not exotic diseases."

Something else niggled at her. Something about his cat. "How did you get your cat into Ireland? Isn't there a quarantine?" He was doing the thumb-rubbing thing again, trying to distract her. It wasn't working. Not much anyway.

He smiled at her, and she recognized the expression for what it was, a diversionary tactic.

"I strapped her around my waist, put on a big Hawaiian shirt, and walked on through."

"Give me a break. That's ridiculous. Didn't they

ask you any questions? What did you tell them?" Surprised, Ally realized she was walking up the hill toward the keep with him. And her capitulation had nothing to do with his thumb action. It was her godawful O'Neill curiosity.

"Told them I was pregnant." He shrugged.

That should have been funny, but she wasn't laughing. He wasn't going to answer her question seriously. She pulled at her wrist, and he released her. They walked in silence until she couldn't stand it anymore. "So, I still don't know much about you except that you're from Philadelphia. Thanks to Katy, you know more than I ever wanted you to know about me." It embarrassed her to realize how much this stranger *did* know about her. "Were you born in Philadelphia? What're you interested in? Tell me something."

He stared at her, and she had the uncomfortable feeling he was trying to decide what to tell her.

"I don't know where I was born. If I ever meet my parents I'll make sure to ask." His words were blunt, his lips drawn into a don't-care line. No self-pity.

Ally had enough pity for both of them. "Sorry. I won't pry anymore." Her parents might have fought their lives away, but at least they were there for her.

"It happened. I got over it. I survived."

The bitterness in his voice betrayed him. He hadn't gotten over it. But Ally wouldn't call him on it.

55

"What am I interested in? Kids. I like to help kids."

He paused while she digested what he'd said. "And I'd like to build something, maybe a house."

Brian shrugged, and she sensed the embarrassment behind his admission.

Ally smiled. She might not approve of his desire for a woman who'd please him, but she liked his other goals. She relaxed a little.

He stopped in front of a strange-looking tent tucked behind a corner of the keep. "Wait out here while I get something for those scratches. Won't take a minute."

"Brian. Your cat is running away." Katy's voice wafted to them from the far side of the keep.

"Coran's tail!"

Coran's tail? Ally had heard some colorful curses in her life, but Coran's tail was not one of them.

Brian exhaled sharply. "Look, I've got to get her. Don't leave. I'll be right back." Turning, he broke into a run.

Ally watched him until he was out of sight. He sure was attached to that cat. Of course, that made him a perfectly nice person, didn't it? A man who liked kids and animals couldn't be anything but admirable. Then why did she still have a feeling of unease?

Ally studied his shelter. Talk about state-of-the-art camping equipment. It looked like a square tent, but she didn't recognize the material.

She glanced at her scratches. They were really stinging. Maybe she could slip inside and find his first-aid box. It shouldn't be hard to locate, and surely he wouldn't mind her taking care of the scratches herself. He hadn't said she couldn't go into the tent.

Ally pulled back the flap and stepped inside. Everything looked pretty normal. There was a fancy sleeping bag in the corner and a small box he'd piled some things on.

She walked to the box and glanced at the things scattered on top of it. No first-aid kit. Probably inside the box. She'd just move everything off the box and . . .

A small black object caught her attention. It looked like a remote, but there was no TV, so that was out. Not a cell phone. What was it? She picked it up to examine it, turning it over to see if there was a place to put batteries.

Her thoughts were only half on the object she was examining. She wanted Brian to come back and take care of her scratches. Her stomach was starting to remind her she hadn't eaten breakfast. When she got back to the wagon she'd grab something to hold her until they reached Liscannor.

The object started to slip from her grasp, and she instinctively tightened her grip, pressing several of the buttons. Without warning, the object vibrated violently at the same time the ground beneath her shook.

Ohmigod, an earthquake! Katy was out there.

She dropped the object, then stopped dead. Earthquake? Ireland didn't have earthquakes. But something had shaken the ground. She had to find Katy and Brian.

Brian stared down the narrow winding path that led to the main road, watching helplessly as the Old One trotted out of sight. He wouldn't catch her now, but he knew where she was going. She'd search out Cap and there'd be another battle. He hoped she didn't try to change into her true shape. Earth wasn't ready for the Old One in her real form. Wouldn't be ready for another few hundred years.

He turned to Katy. "Where's the nearest town?" Cap would be staying somewhere close.

"Liscannor. You must've come through it on your way here. Think she'll head for town?" Katy turned to peer at him.

Brian nodded. "You mentioned that you and Ally were going there to buy supplies. Mind if I tag along?"

"No problem. Glad to have a man along." Katy frowned. "Even if Ally isn't. Ever since her husband ran off with that woman, Erica, she hasn't had a real positive attitude toward men."

"Ally." He'd left her standing by his shelter. "I've got to get back to her and take care of those scratches."

Katy nodded, but she didn't pay attention as he strode back toward her grandniece. Something at the edge of a small group of trees held her attention.

Brian was halfway back when he felt the ground shake. He closed his eyes. Kick him if he ever left home again.

Someone had activated the Constructor. One guess who that someone was. He broke into a run.

As he rounded the corner of the keep, he skidded to a stop. Ally stood outside his shelter staring wide-eyed at the Ultimate-Universe McDonald's she'd created.

Okay, this wasn't so bad. It still had the golden arches. She'd recognize those. Familiar was good. Maybe the free-floating planets drifting around the arches weren't familiar, but at least they didn't look threatening.

She turned shocked eyes toward him. "What happened? What is this?"

"Congratulations. You just built yourself a McDonald's." His vacation was finished, but it had been pretty crappy up to this point anyway. Problem was, he didn't know if he could get a stag to pick him up on such short notice. And this was all Ally's fault. "Anyone ever tell you not to play with things that aren't yours?"

She stared blankly at him, then returned her gaze to the McDonald's. "I accidentally pressed a couple of buttons and this happened. What is it? Why is it here?"

"You were thinking of food when you pressed the buttons. The Constructor always aims to please." No use holding anything back now. Might as well tell her the whole thing, then get the hell out of 2002. "Wait a minute." He slipped into his shelter, scooped up the Constructor and the cell-growth cream, then went out to where Ally was still staring at the building.

"It's floating. Why is it floating?" She didn't look at him.

Brian didn't answer. He punched in a set of numbers, pressed the activator, and the McDonald's disappeared.

Ally turned and stared at the Constructor. "What is it? How does it work? Why do you have it? And why was the building floating?"

Brian wearily rubbed his hand across the back of his neck. "It was floating because in 2502 all the buildings float. The greenhouse effect kicked in, all the polar ice caps melted, and there were an increasing number of violent hurricanes. Humans found it more efficient to live above the sogginess. Besides, you can move a floating building. If business is bad in one spot, just move it somewhere else. Floating buildings are cost effective."

"What?"

Brian almost smiled. She looked sort of cute with her mouth open. "Oh, and this?" He held up the Constructor. "This builds things without human effort, and I don't have a clue how it works. Do you know how your cell phone works, or your computer?"

She shook her head as she raised a shaking

hand to push a blond tendril of hair from her face. "I . . . I don't believe you're from the future. I don't know where that 'Constructor' came from, but it didn't come from the future." She was shaking all over now.

He sighed. It was no use. He couldn't let her just stand there and shake. He understood fear. Fear that turned your insides liquid and your legs to boneless jelly. He felt it every time he stood somewhere high and looked down. He couldn't turn away from her fear.

Brian pulled Ally into his arms.

She stood, arms at her sides while he rubbed a circular pattern of comfort on her back. Slowly, her shaking stopped, but she didn't lean into him. She stepped away.

He let her go. "It won't do any good to go to the authorities. They won't believe your story. And I'd be gone before they came to investigate." He grasped her hand and applied the healing cream before she had time to yank it away.

She stared blankly at her hand, then nodded. "I'll harness up the horse, and we'll leave you and your Constructor in peace."

He studied her. "Don't you have the least bit of curiosity? What if my story is true? You're a writer. Are you going to walk away from something like this?"

She cast him an incredulous stare. "You bet. All this is too weird for me."

Brian had no idea why he was goading her. Maybe it was her hardheaded refusal to believe the truth. "And this is the woman who's wandering around at midnight looking for a vampire?"

She straightened her shoulders, and he could almost see the courage oozing back into her. "Katy's hunting for a vampire. I'm hunting for some peace so I can think about my book."

He held up his hands as though it was all very simple. "I don't see a problem. You want peace, I'll give you peace. You won't even know I'm around." What was this all about? He *wanted* her to leave, didn't he?

"I doubt that very much." Her smile was barely there.

"And if you decide you want the story of the century, come to me." *And if you want the sexual experience of five centuries* . . . No, couldn't do that. No sex. His contract was his promise, and he didn't break promises.

"There has to be a logical explanation for that building. There *has* to be." She sounded as though she was trying to convince herself.

"Why? Why does everything have to be logical?" He laid his arm across her shoulders, and she flinched. "Go with what's new and amazing. In another five hundred years it'll be logical."

Ally was confused because no matter what explanation she came up with, she'd seen what she'd seen. And there was no logical explanation for what she'd seen. "Okay, so are you a scientist working on a secret project?" That sounded hokey even to her.

He shook his head.

Since she had no explanation for the unexplainable, she reverted to the mundane. "Katy and I will be going into Liscannor for supplies." *And we won't be back if I can help it.*

"I'm going with you. I already talked to your great-aunt." He cast her a half-lidded stare. "I don't know if you should tell her about what you saw."

"Right. I mean, Katy wouldn't understand, and she's getting up there in years, and I wouldn't want her to be too scared and—" *Lord, stop my babbling.*

"Your great-aunt would love it. She'd build herself a haunted castle." He slanted her a hard grin. "After which she'd ask me to tell her every detail of my sexual technique during the games."

"You're right, she would." Ally felt herself wilting under the burden of what she'd seen. Who to tell? "Katy is a little too gullible."

"Your great-aunt accepts things as the truth until they're proven false." He followed her down the hill toward the wagon.

Ally felt his disapproval like a blow. What the heck did he expect? Nothing he said made sense. *You saw the Constructor at work.* He had to be crazy. *What about the Constructor?* And that was the one thing that kept her from screaming and running away from him. If she walked away now, she'd always wonder . . . because a crazy man wouldn't have the Constructor.

Katy met them at the wagon. " 'Bout time you got back. We need to get started into Liscannor.

Think we should stay at a bed and breakfast for the night so Brian will have time to look for his cat. It'll be good to have my own room for a night." She cast Ally a matter-of-fact glance. "You talk in your sleep. Wouldn't mind if you ever said something good."

Ally chose not to argue with Katy about her talking in her sleep. Katy never lost an argument. She turned to Brian instead. "What makes you think your cat will head for town?" She watched Katy climb into the wagon.

"She's looking for someone." Brian didn't elaborate.

Ally forced a smile. "Oh, come on, a cat wouldn't know where to look for someone."

Brian focused his intense stare on her. He didn't smile back. "She's not a cat."

Chapter Four

Not a cat. Did Ally believe that? Nope. And she didn't believe Brian Byrne was an MVP, future Hall-of-Famer for some solar system sex league. She glanced down at her hand. And she absolutely *did not* believe her scratches were almost gone. Nope. Didn't believe any of it.

She was still feeling shell-shocked as she climbed from the wagon in front of Fitzpatrick's Bed-and-Breakfast.

Brian drove the wagon away to find someone who would let him put the horse in their pasture, while Katy hurried off to do some shopping. Ally slowly walked into the small bed-and-breakfast to register.

She considered calling Dad and telling him they were flying home, but he'd want to know why. Ally could lie to Dad, and she could lie to

Katy, but she couldn't lie to herself. She was running from something she didn't understand, couldn't cope with. The same way she'd run from the truth when she first suspected her perfect marriage wasn't going to make it until "death do us part."

The same way she'd run from the press and readers when they had realized her *Perfect Wife* series was a sham, that it couldn't pass the litmus test of time. She couldn't face all those women who'd believed her, modeled their marriages according to her advice, then watched her fail miserably.

To be honest, it was a relief to be in Ireland. She could concentrate on her coping-with-single-life book while remaining invisible to press and curious readers alike.

She registered, called Mavis her literary agent, and left a brief message telling where she could be reached tonight, then retreated to her room with a sense of letting-go. Flopping onto the bed, she closed her eyes. Just a little nap, then she could decide her course of action.

When she woke, she glanced at her watch. An hour. Katy hadn't knocked, so she was probably still pillaging the local stores. If Katy bought any more souvenirs, they'd have to heave things out of the wagon so the horse could make it up hills.

During her hour's rest, her problems hadn't disappeared. They hadn't even gone away while she dreamed. In her dreams, a packed stadium roared encouragement, waving condoms with their team's colors. Vendors hawked sizzle dogs, and a futuristic version of Queen chanted, "We will, we will boink you."

Horrible. Okay, so one part hadn't been too terrible. The part where a naked Brian Byrne, sleek with powerful muscles and gleaming green eyes, covered her and— She'd never know what happened because she woke up. Her mind probably recognized she wasn't emotionally ready for what came next. Rats.

She'd promised herself she'd never work to please a man again, but if the man was doing the pleasing, hey, that was fine by her.

A hot shower would feel good now, ready her for the face-off she knew was coming: with Brian, with Katy. She'd better do it now before everyone used up the hot water.

Grabbing her towel, washcloth, and soap, she headed for the communal bathroom. The newer places had private baths, but you met more interesting people in an older place like this.

As she walked down the carpeted hallway, she mulled over her options. Stay or run? Each had its drawbacks.

Deep in thought, her subconscious registered an intrusion. Not a sound, but a feeling, a sense that something was wrong. She turned her head to identify the source of her unease and froze.

The Old One padded along quietly behind her. Unhurried, but obviously a cat on a mission. She closed the distance between them. *Not a cat.* Ally didn't know at what point she'd decided to believe Brian's words, but sometime between her nap and now, she believed.

She turned to face the Old One. No way was she turning her back on whatever the cat really was. Carefully, she backed down the hallway, fear catching at her throat. Even if the cat chose to perpetuate the myth that she was just a cat, Ally didn't want the joy of wearing an ankle bracelet with teeth.

"You know, this whole intimidation thing is a waste of your time." She hoped no one opened a door and caught her talking to a cat. "I mean, I'm absolutely no threat to Brian. I don't want him to stay here. Definitely want him to go home. So you can go stalk someone else."

The Old One ignored her babbled plea, lowering herself into a classic cat-stalking-frightened-prey position.

Great. Ally thought about throwing her bar of soap at the cat, but decided the Old One would view that as an aggressive move and pounce.

Ally let out a startled yelp as the bathroom doorknob prodded her sharply in the back. Without thought of consequences, she reached behind, turned the knob, and breathed a sigh of relief as the door swung open.

Never once removing her gaze from the advancing cat, she backed into the room, and a cloud of steam immediately enveloped her. Ohmigod, someone was using the shower. Why hadn't the bather locked the door? *Don't even think about what would've happened if the door was locked.* But she wished whoever it was had taken a minute to turn on the electric heater so she wouldn't be dealing with zero visibility.

Ally could see nothing but the Old One approaching through the cloud, a grade-B horror flick in the making. The Old One was too close to slam the door in her face. A flattened kitty nose would *not* put her in the mood to spare Ally's life. Besides, she'd probably destroy the door as easily as Godzilla demolished Tokyo.

Ally dropped her things and retreated another step, another step that brought the backs of her legs into sharp contact with the edge of the tub and threw her off balance. With a squeak of terror, she teetered for a moment and then, with a thud, fell backward into the tub.

For several endless seconds she sat in bewildered disorientation while warm water cascaded over her and drenched her clothes.

"Coran's tail!"

The familiar husky voice cleared her thoughts, and with dawning horror she raised her head.

She had to look up a long way. Past firm calves with a light sprinkling of damp hair clinging to them. Past thighs roped with wet gleaming muscles. She paused to stare at his most riveting feature, because no matter how horrified she was, the corner of her mind in charge of recording historical life events insisted she take note. Like a five-hundred-year flood, or Haley's Comet, you only lived to see some things once.

Yes! She could die a fulfilled woman.

She moved on. If staring at the sun could blind you, Ally didn't even want to consider what staring at Brian's assets would do.

She skimmed over his flat, hard stomach and strongly muscled chest with its damp whorls of hair adhering darkly to his flesh.

Her inspection at last reached his eyes. No shame there. They were bright with amusement. But as she watched, the amusement changed to something else. Something hot, hungry. *Dangerous*.

"You tempt me greatly, woman."

Something about the intensity of his words, the way his hair fell forward as he gazed down at her, framing a face grown hard, predatory, stirred a growing fear in her. *The face of a hunter.* And his eyes. No longer a forest green that promised comfort from the summer's heat, but a night green, mysterious, perfectly capable of starting a forest fire with one bolt of white-hot lightning.

And Ally knew with every instinct passed down from the first woman, that this was his game face, the face women responded to in 2502, would respond to in any age.

It scared the heck out of her. The Old One was a zero on the scary index compared to the man looming over her. Fear of Brian Byrne drove everything from Ally's mind except the need to escape from the tub.

Scrabbling with all the dignity of a frightened chicken, she grabbed the edge of the tub, prepared to fling herself out and into the waiting paws of Killer Kitty.

But before she could fling any body parts, Brian reached down and pulled her to her feet, slowly sliding her the length of his slick gleaming body. Her blouse and jeans were soaked, so she felt everything as if no cloth separated their bodies. She wished she could strip herself as bare as he so she could feel *more* than everything.

Running her hands along his thighs, she felt them flex beneath her fingers, drew in her breath at the thrust of his arousal against her stomach, and denied herself the pleasure of reaching between their bodies to glide her fingers over the length of his erection.

She splayed her hands across his chest and wondered at the heat, the hard muscles moving beneath smooth skin, the pounding heartbeat that matched her own.

Once standing, Ally leaned into him, allowing the warm water to flow over her, knowing that once she moved away from whatever magnetic force his body exuded, she'd collapse bonelessly back into the tub, never to rise again.

She would become another Irish legend: The Woman Who Sits in the Tub. A tourist attraction to rival the Blarney Stone.

"I wonder what I should do with you, Ally O'Neill." His breath warmed the side of her neck, his husky whisper heated her from the inside out.

So many possibilities, so little time. If he'd just undo the buttons on her blouse and unhook her bra, she'd probably be able to prioritize the possibilities better. All that extra oxygen would help her think.

"I can't have you, Ally. There's a no-sex clause in my contract. Besides, I promised Jupe. And I always keep my promises."

She could feel his lips move against the sensitive skin beneath her ear. What? What was he talking about?

"But I want you."

His tongue traced a path from her earlobe to the base of her neck where her pulse pounded a mad rhythm.

"I didn't think you were a passionate woman. I was wrong. Passionate women please me." He pushed aside the top of her blouse and kissed the swell of her breast.

Please me. She fought her way to the surface through sensual desire and the heavy ache of want. She'd heard those words before. Where?

Remembrance that she didn't intend to *please* any man came at the same moment she noticed a subtle change in their environment. The warm water pouring over them had cooled considerably. Uh-oh. She knew what that meant.

Before she could voice a warning, the aging hot water heater gave up its last drop of tepid liquid, and they were deluged with an icy cascade.

Brian's curses covered planetary and various other unknown bodies. He lifted her from the tub, then leaped out behind her.

She stood shivering on the bathroom rug, watching Brian lean over. With a jerk that made the pipes rattle, he turned off the water. She was treated to an eye-popping view of excellent male buns. Then, still muttering dire threats against outdated plumbing, he raked long fingers through his thick black hair and sat on the edge of the tub.

He looked up at her through a fringe of black lashes and smiled. "Loved your approach. All that enthusiasm was great, but I got the feeling it wasn't a planned visit."

Her attention to what he was saying faded in and out. She was a lot more focused visually.

"What's the matter?" He followed her gaze down. "The naked thing, right?"

"Yes." No use creeping around the point. She picked up a towel and dropped it in his lap. He let it rest there.

"So let's hear your story."

"Your cat was chasing me."

He brightened. "Great. I hope she didn't find Ca . . . McDermott."

"Didn't you hear me? Your cat meant me bodily harm."

His smile softened. "She's trying to scare you. She always plays intimidation games. Where is she now?"

Ally glanced toward the door. Two large round yellow eyes stared back at her through the steam.

Brian nodded. "I'll talk to her."

In the bright light of logic, Ally felt foolish.

She'd let his tale get to her, grow in her mind to gigantic proportions. The Old One wasn't going to rip out her throat and leave her lifeless body sprawled in the hall. Ally glanced again at the cold yellow eyes glaring at her. Okay, she'd admit the possibility existed.

"Fine. Talk to her." Smiling weakly, she turned to make her escape.

"Hi, everyone. Any hot water left?" Katy pushed past the Old One, skirted Ally, and came to a halt in front of Brian. "You are one fine-looking man. Don't know why you bother with that towel. Breaks up the flow. Don't you think it breaks up the flow, Ally?"

"Sure. Breaks up the flow." Brian was on his own. She was outta here. With as much dignity as she could muster, Ally squelched out of the bathroom in her soggy shoes and back to the relative safety of her room.

She could hear the phone ringing even through the closed door. Now what? Flinging open the door, she didn't even take time to shut it as she raced to get the phone before it could stop ringing.

"Yes?" Ally collapsed onto an old overstuffed chair.

"Mavis, sweetie. Got the word from your editor today. She likes the coping-with-single-life premise. Your readers will be dying to know how you're handling single life."

Why did Ally sense a "but" in there somewhere?

"Bunch of voyeurs, really," Mavis offered as an aside. "Anyway, she feels the book needs something more, a hook."

"Hook?" The total collapse of her marriage wasn't a hook? What else did she need?

"Ever had a one-night stand, Ally?" Mavis's voice sounded noncommittal.

Ally knew where her agent was going and immediately went into defensive mode. "No. I had a few long-term relationships, but I didn't do one-nighters. That doesn't have to be part of single life. There're a lot more meaningful—"

"We can talk about your experience later. There's something else we have to discuss."

Ally tensed. Mavis had shifted into her this-is-about-your-career voice.

"Your editor says your proposal's been done to death. Yes, you have a following, but they're not going to follow you into your single lifestyle unless you make it unique and sexy. And the word 'perfect' has to be in the title. It's about the expectations your readership has built up."

"Nothing about my marriage was 'perfect.'"

"Wrong. *You* were the perfect wife, but Dave wasn't the perfect husband. The world sympathizes with you, sweetie. And your editor feels you can turn that sympathy into huge sales. She wants us to go with *The Perfect Wife in Search of the Perfect Husband* for the new series. And since sexual compatibility is part of finding the perfect husband, as well as being extremely marketable, she wants your first book in the new series to be about finding a man who's sexually compatible with you."

"So what she wants is Martha Stewart meets *Sex in the City*."

Mavis chuckled. "Guess that sums it up."

"No."

"Look, you don't have to go from man to man. Just try it once then write about it." Mavis's voice had turned wheedling.

"How about not trying it at all and writing about it from other people's experiences?"

"Uh-uh. The power of your writing is the emotional truth you bring to it. You lived being the perfect wife, and readers picked up on the truth of what you were saying. They believed you. You can't fake it, Ally." Pregnant pause. "Your publisher doesn't want your original proposal, sweetie, and I agree with your editor on this. Women will empathize with what you're going through. Innocent wife dumped by jerky husband. Wife now is thrown into the sex game where the rules have changed since she first played. It happens to a lot of women."

Oh God. Writing was her career. She couldn't imagine doing anything else. But this . . . ? "Fine. I'll find my sexually compatible man and write about my experience. Of course, if he's sexually compatible he'll probably also be a jerk."

"Then that'll be another book, Ally. Look on the bright side. Dave will hate your book."

"Wonderful. Can't wait to write this one. Talk to you later, Mavis." Sarcasm didn't become her, and she really wasn't being fair to Mavis. Her agent and editor had been instrumental in guiding her to where she was today. But what the heck was she going to do about this book?

She leaned back in her chair and closed her eyes. "Sex games." She wasn't going to play. "Mavis is wrong. I can fake this." But would she respect herself in the morning?

The sound of soft laughter spun her attention to the open door where Brian Byrne stood holding her soap and towel.

"Men who hunt never change, babe. You want to know about sex games? I can tell you about sex games."

Chapter Five

"Ye have the look of the Byrnes, lad." Mr. Fitz-patrick paused with his spoonful of oatmeal half-way to his mouth as he studied Brian from the other end of the long table. "It's in the eyes. All the Byrnes had the devil's own eyes."

Brian smiled. Ironic, he knew more about his ancestors who'd lived five hundred years ago than he did his parents. Probably should thank his mother for at least leaving his history chip around his neck when she deserted him. She'd deleted everything about herself, but she'd left information about his father's origins. Not his name, just his family's history. Brian had tried to use the history to track down his father, but no luck. Good old Dad didn't want to be found.

"Aye, and the Byrnes had the devil's own way with the women. Scoundrels, every one." Mrs.

Fitzpatrick harrumphed her way around the table as she served everyone breakfast.

Katy looked interested. "Any more of those Byrne men around here?"

Mr. Fitzpatrick shook his head. "It's been many a year since we've seen a one. Some said they'd all died, but I didn't believe that at all. Ye've come in time to save the place, lad."

Brian frowned. All the Byrnes couldn't be dead. If all the Byrnes were gone, then he wouldn't exist.

"I've never eaten this much for breakfast in my life." Ally pushed the remnants of her meal around on her plate.

"Looks pretty normal to me." Brian glanced down at his half-eaten plate of eggs, sausage, ham, brown bread, and bowl of oatmeal.

Ally stared at him. "You're kidding."

"Team breakfasts are twice this size." He raised his gaze to a roomful of interested stares. Uh-oh. Better watch what he said. Guess he shouldn't mention that in 2502 everyone ate twice as much as this. Gluttony was a way of life ever since scientists invented a stay-thin pill. Eat all you want and never gain weight. "When you train hard you have to eat enough to maintain your energy level."

"Ye play a sport?" A heavyset man at the end of the table stopped eating long enough to ask the question.

"I'm part of a—"

"Football team." Ally looked desperate. "He plays football."

Even Cap seemed to feel a need to change the subject. " 'Tis a fine meal ye serve. Me sainted Uncle Pat would have loved it." He winked at Mrs. Fitzpatrick. " 'Tis no blarney I speak."

The Fitzpatricks stared while Brian winced. As the conversation flowed around him, Brian glanced at the others seated at the large wooden table. Ally still seemed fascinated by her unfinished breakfast, but she didn't fool him. She was probably adding up every speck of evidence he'd let drop and coming to a logical conclusion. He wondered what it would take for her to forget logic, to do something completely spontaneous.

Brian's gaze wandered to Katy. She was busy questioning Mrs. Fitzpatrick about the local ghosts and fairies. And Cap? He'd stopped talking and was staring at Brian while making rapid head jerks toward the door. Cap was a subtle kind of guy. Brian got the message. Cap wanted to talk to him. Alone. That was fine with Brian. He had a few things to say to Cap, and he didn't want anyone else listening.

A prickly feeling between his shoulder blades made Brian turn his head. The Old One sat behind his chair studying him with big yellow eyes. No anger this morning, just watchfulness.

"Is it yer cat now, Mr. Byrne?" Mrs. Fitzpatrick seemed more worried than angry. "Ye might want to put her in yer room. The dog enjoys a good chase, and he'd give the poor thing a terrible fright."

On cue, "the dog" appeared in the doorway. Brian shook his head. When did dogs become woolly mammoths? He'd never seen one this big. In 2502 most large dogs had disappeared, replaced by those that were small and portable. People in 2502 wanted compact in all things.

"Meet Finn. Ye won't see many Irish wolfhounds bigger than Finn. He's gentle with people, but he has a grand time with cats." Mr. Fitzpatrick seemed proud of Finn's cat attitude.

Poor Finn. Brian watched the inevitable happen. Finn saw the Old One. Finn stiffened into cat-alert mode. The Old One stared. Finn turned and skidded on the hardwood floor in his eagerness to escape. His yelps could be heard all the way through the house. The Old One stood, stretched, and quietly followed the dog. She loved to intimidate, and Finn would amuse her until it was time to leave.

Brian ignored Mr. Fitzpatrick's sounds of dismay at his dog's cowardice. Mr. Fitzpatrick didn't appreciate a smart dog when he saw one.

Brian was more interested in Ally's reaction. Her attention was riveted on the Old One, and Brian knew she was making a tally mark in her mental column marked "time-travel story is true." He still wasn't sure whether that was good or bad.

Cap got up and grinned at Mrs. Fitzpatrick.

"Sure and I'd better leave now or the devil will roll me out of here in a soro-tor."

"Soro-tor?" Mrs. Fitzpatrick paused with a fresh plate of sausages in her hand.

Brian savored Cap's look of desperation as he searched for something to explain his mistake. Better save him, though. Cap might not have any power here, but he was still the owner of Brian's former team. Never knew when Cap might get Brian back into the loving arms of the Titans. "The soro-tor is an American brand of wheelbarrow, Mrs. Fitzpatrick."

She nodded, satisfied by his explanation, as Cap hurried from the room. Brian pushed back his chair, made his excuses, and followed Cap. No use putting off the confrontation.

He found Cap waiting in the hallway. "Okay, why are you here?"

"Maybe we should talk in my room." Cap glanced nervously around as the phone rang in the lobby.

"Uh-uh. What do you think would happen if the Old One found out we were closeted in your room?" He lowered his voice for a moment as the Fitzpatricks' daughter hurried into the dining room, then he focused on Cap.

Cap nodded. "You're right. We don't want to involve her in this."

Brian could feel the other man's fear. The Old One did that to people. "So what do you want, Cap?"

Cap ran his hand over his red wig, and Brian

hoped he'd changed the scene from Sex Super Bowl XXXVI he'd had painted on his scalp.

"I know you think I'm just interfering in your business." Cap didn't quite meet his gaze.

"And you're not?"

"I've known you for a long time, Brian. Ever since you first came into the league. And I have your best interests at heart." Cap pulled on his earlobe as he looked directly at Brian.

You're lying. "Okay, so you've come all this way to tell me what?"

"I want to give you some advice. No strings attached." He tried on a fatherly smile.

"No one's ever given me anything with no strings attached. Say what you have to say." He needed to get out of here. Talk to Ally and find out whether she intended to dump him and run, or go back to the keep. And he had to remove the Old One from temptation's way. Eventually she'd trap Cap by himself. If the locals dragged her off Cap, then tried to haul her to the animal shelter . . . Let's just say that would *not* be a shining day for world peace.

"Your heart's not in the game anymore. I can see it. Sure you're the best, but eventually you have to settle down, relax." Cap cast him a searching look. Probably to see how everything was going down.

"Now I've been watching you for a lot of years. You've got a primitive streak. You don't always fit in with life. Like to do things the physical way." He did some more ear yanking. "What I'm saying is you'd probably be a lot happier here. Find a woman like this Ally. Build yourself a little house. Your earnings can be converted to currency in this time. Live however you want for the rest of your life."

Brian leaned back against the wall and grinned at Cap. "And all this for-my-own-good advice wouldn't have a thing to do with you winning the Sex Super Bowl next season if I don't show up to play."

"Of course not." He began to bluster. "I wouldn't think of—"

"Sure you would. I bet you checked my travel schedule to see exactly when I'd be arriving. Then you fed Katy that garbage about a vampire so she and Ally would rush out to the castle at midnight. Ally and I would meet, fall in love, and the Titans would have a fast track to the championship."

Brian pushed away from the wall and moved into Cap's space. "Forget the matchmaking. It won't work. I signed a contract, so I'll be back. And I wouldn't have sex with someone like Ally. It would violate my contract. Besides, I wouldn't have sex with a woman who didn't understand the game. And that's what sex is to me, a game. I never forget it." Brian didn't understand why he was so mad at Cap. While Brian was a Titan, Cap had made Brian's business his business on a regular basis.

Cap started to answer, then stopped, his gaze fixed on the doorway to the dining room.

Brian turned his head, but he already had a premonition of what he'd see. Ally stood not ten feet away. He'd been so involved with Cap he hadn't noticed her. How much had she heard? He wasn't used to guarding what he said. He'd better learn fast.

She stared at him with wide brown eyes. He tried to read her expression, but came up blank. That shook him. He'd always been able to read women. *But only in the sexual arena.* He'd never had to understand women other than in a sexual context, and now he had no weapons except the ones he'd used for the last twelve years.

Brian walked to where Ally stood as Cap hurried away. She didn't back up or show any hint of panic.

He reached out to touch her hand because touch didn't lie. If he could feel the warmth of her flesh beneath his fingers, he'd have a better grasp of what to say to her.

"What will you do now, Ally O'Neill?" He slid his fingers up her arm until the sleeve of her sweater stopped him. "Will you run away or go back to the keep?" He leaned close, inhaling the scent of shampoo and woman.

She looked down at his hand, but she didn't pull away. "I don't—"

Mrs. Fitzpatrick's daughter stuck her head around the corner. "There's a call for you on the line, Miss O'Neill."

Ally nodded, then turned away from Brian

without finishing her sentence. He watched her walk away.

And wondered. Did he want her to stay? Yes. Why? With Cap and the Old One carrying on open warfare, why would he want anyone else interfering with his down time? Sure, sexual attraction was part of it. He wasn't going to deny that. But he could control sexual desire. It was more.

Brian shook his head. The truth? Plain old curiosity. He needed to know more about the woman who could make him desire her when a game wasn't on the line. He wanted to be around her. And if offering to help with her book would keep her around, he'd tell her more about sex than she ever needed to know.

Brian frowned. That sounded a lot like getting involved, and getting involved wasn't wise.

He started back to his room. What he thought didn't matter because Ally would probably be running from him as fast as her horse could gallop. Okay, walk. He grinned. He'd seen Moray slugs that moved faster than that horse.

Ally picked up the receiver. She'd called her parents earlier in the morning so there'd be no reason for them to call her back. And she couldn't imagine Mavis having anything more to say than she'd already said. But no one else had this number. "Hi. This is Ally."

"Ally, thank God I caught you."

Ally closed her eyes. Dave. All the anger and

sorrow rushed back on a wave of memories. "I don't want to talk to you, Dave."

"Don't hang up, Ally. I made a terrible mistake. Erica wasn't the woman I thought she was."

Ally had never met Erica, but she'd gotten great visuals from Dave. Long dark hair, great body, electric personality. According to Dave, Ally's personality was still in the kerosene lamp stage. "Well, poo on me for not giving a damn."

"I know you're bitter, but I'll make it up to you."

Ally held the receiver away from her ear for a moment and stared at it. The jerk actually sounded like he thought she'd want him back.

"Would you believe she got bent out of shape when I told her all the little things you used to do for me? She said some ugly things about a woman who'd put the toothpaste on her husband's brush so he wouldn't have to squeeze the tube. I told her you did that because you knew I was always running late. But I think it was the Cocoa Puffs that really set her off." He paused, and Ally had the feeling he was doing some deep thinking about those Cocoa Puffs. "I told her you put exactly one teaspoon of sugar and a half a cup of low-fat milk in my Cocoa Puffs every morning."

Ally winced. Had she really done those things? "So what happened?"

"She threw the Cocoa Puffs at me. I had to go upstairs and change my suit."

"Good for her."

"Come back to me, Ally. Erica's been gone for over a week. Maybe she won't come back, but if she does I'll tell her we're through."

His betrayal, her disillusionment, pounded at Ally. "What happened between you and Erica doesn't matter to me. It's your life, handle it." She had to know one thing. "How'd you get this number?"

"I knew I couldn't call your parents, so I called your publishing house. They told me you were traveling in Ireland. Someone named Sara gave me the details."

Thank you, Sara. "Katy and I have decided to get rid of the wagon and hire a car. We'll be driving to Donegal and then into Northern Ireland so you won't be able to contact me again." Lying was weak, but she didn't want to field his calls complaining about Erica-the-*not*-boring. She was here to get away from everything and work on that damned book. Dave wasn't going to reach across the miles and mess up her life again.

"No, you have to listen to me. We can make it work again. If only you—"

She hung up, waited for a minute until she was sure the connection was broken, then lifted the receiver from the cradle. It wouldn't take the Fitzpatricks long to discover the phone was off the hook, but by then she'd be gone. And she wouldn't need to call anyone again, certainly not Mavis. Mavis had made it clear what she expected from Ally.

A short while later, she headed across the

street to a sweet shop while Katy and Brian went for the wagon. This morning called for sugar in the bloodstream. Distractedly, she asked for a bag of licorice Allsorts.

"Hey, you're from the States, aren't you?"

Ally turned to look at the woman who'd spoken. "Yes. How about you?"

The woman brushed back a strand of short red hair and grinned at Ally. "Cleveland. Is this country great, or what? Sorry, forgot to introduce myself. Claudia Morgan."

"Ally O'Neill." She felt old and worn beside Claudia. Pretty, young, and enthusiastic. Probably just out of college. Life wasn't fair. If she were kind, she'd warn Claudia never to read any of her perfect-marriage books.

"I love old ruins, castles and stuff. Don't you?" Claudia bit into a piece of chocolate.

"Love them." *Loving them less each minute*.

"Well, if you're sightseeing in the area we'll probably run into each other again." Claudia walked toward the door.

"I bet you hired a car." Ally knew she sounded wistful.

"Yeah." Claudia paused before leaving. "Doesn't everyone?"

Ally sighed as she watched Katy pull the horse to a stop in front of the bed-and-breakfast. "Not everyone."

Leaving the sweet shop, she climbed onto the wagon.

"You go on inside, Ally. I'll drive." Katy clucked

to the horse. The horse ignored her. "This horse is so slow I could take a nap, wake up an hour later, and we still wouldn't be out of town."

Ally grinned. "Feel a need for speed, Katy?"

"Not usually, but I want to get back to the castle as soon as we can. Saw another one of those white deer yesterday. Mentioned it at breakfast, but no one could tell me anything about them." Katy looked thoughtful. "Maybe they're ghost deer."

Ally paused before going inside. "Various cultures have legends about white stags, but I don't know about Ireland."

Katy slid her a warning glare. "Don't you go finding a logical explanation for those deer. I like my idea better."

Ally shrugged and went into the wagon. She paused in the doorway. Brian had folded down the table to make the double bed and was lying on his back studying some pictures. With his dark hair spread across the pillow, his body open and relaxed, Ally could believe him capable of what he said he did in his time. She felt the warm pull of desire, the remembered feel of his bare body touching hers. She coughed to dispel the image.

What she didn't need was one more unwanted emotion. She had enough emotions clamoring for attention: anger at Dave for trying to disrupt her life again, at Sara Somebody for blabbing to Dave. Frustration at the book Mavis was asking her to write, fear that she wouldn't be able to do it. And above and beyond everything else, uncertainty.

"Come here." Brian abandoned his pictures and patted the bed beside him.

Come here. Unwanted images formed in her mind. A hot Arizona night. A light breeze moving the curtain at an open window. The outline of a saguaro cactus, dark mountains, and the excited yips of coyotes in the distance. And this man's naked, sweat-dampened body gleaming silver in the pale light of the desert moon. She frowned. No, that was wrong. Silver was a cool, distant color. Cool and distant would never be words to describe Brian Byrne.

She walked to the bed and sat down by his feet. Ally knew a bed was a dangerous place to be with Brian, but courage was part of her new persona. He wouldn't intimidate her. Not much anyway.

"What do you think, Ally?"

"I think you're a dangerous man." She said the words before she realized he was holding his pictures out to her.

"Don't ever doubt it." His voice was soft with laughter, but behind his laughter was the truth.

What did you say to that? She didn't have to say anything because a low growl interrupted the conversation. Ally turned to see the Old One sitting on the counter top, her designated throne for the moment. The cat's tail twitched angrily from side to side. Her yellow eyes warned Ally away.

Brian exhaled sharply, a clear signal his pa-

tience was at an end. "I'd go out and make sure
Katy isn't having any trouble driving, Boss. Because if you don't, I'm going to talk to Jupe about
the legality of what you're doing. We wouldn't
want anything that could put that multiyear contract we signed in danger."

The Old One's hiss was venomous, but she left.

Still not comfortable with a man who talked to
a cat, Ally busied herself with the pictures. They
showed a castle from several different angles.
"What are these for?"

He sat up in one fluid motion and leaned close
to look at the pictures. "Before I left home, I fed
all the data I had about the original Byrne castle
into a refresher, and it gave me a set of pictures
that simulated the original structure."

With Brian's dark hair sliding across her arm
as he leaned closer to the pictures, and his large
body near enough to touch if she leaned just a
little to her left, Ally decided she needed a "refresher" to simulate her original breathing pattern.

Hundreds of questions fought for supremacy,
hundreds of doubts reared their logical heads,
and hundreds of years stretched between Ally
and this man who sat beside her. *If* his story was
true. It was time to take her head out of the sand
and decide what she truly believed.

"Tell me about your life. All of it. The truth."
She didn't look at him.

"Will you accept what I say?" He carefully took
the pictures from her hand, then used his index

finger to tilt her face toward him. "Will you believe?" His voice was a husky whisper.

*Talk to me in that voice forever, and I'll never
doubt you.* "Make me believe."

As though he'd forgotten his purpose, he slid
his fingers through her hair and gently massaged
the back of her neck. "Afraid of me, babe?"

His touch would end up shattering any com-
posure she'd managed to maintain. She thought
of lying. She didn't. "Yes."

His soft chuckle brushed over her like a promise. "Fear can be erotic when what you fear is
what you really desire."

Oh God. She was losing it. Not only was she
thinking about believing the unbelievable, but
she was contemplating something even worse.

"Brian?"

"Hmm?"

"How do you feel about older women?"

"Older?"

"Five hundred years, give or take a few."

Chapter Six

"What?" Brian leaned back to stare at her.

She sat ramrod straight. Her expression indicated she was steeling herself to meet a solar firestorm.

"I need to know how you feel about older women because once you tell me about your life in 2502, I want you to help me with my book." She avoided his gaze.

"Your book? The one about coping with single life? What does that have to do with older women?" He shouldn't have spent time talking to her. He only talked to women during the game. When the game was on the line, he told women what they wanted to hear, got it done, and walked away. This wasn't a game situation. *Then what the hell was I doing a few minutes ago?*

Ally finally looked at him. "The premise has

changed a little. My publisher wants me to write about sexual adventure in the single life. Sex sells in any time, and my editor hinted sales might plummet if I don't hook up with someone, then write about it. I sort of can't do that, but maybe . . ." She sighed, then shrugged. "Maybe you could give me some ideas. From the sex god perspective."

Brian narrowed his gaze. She was lying. That last part wasn't what she'd started to say. "I'm still waiting for the older-woman connection."

"There isn't one. I almost made a poorly thought-out suggestion, but I changed my mind in time. So tell me about your life." She turned to glance out the back window of the wagon.

Brian had the impression she didn't want him to see her expression. He had a suspicion. . . . "Would that older woman be you?"

"Five hundred years is a sizable maturity gap."

She was now staring out the window in the front door of the wagon where he could see Katy's upper body. When Katy turned her head, he could see she was talking. He smiled. Everyone ended up talking to the Old One. She stimulated conversation.

"Let me guess. The mind-changing thing. At first you were going to suggest that I sacrifice myself on the altar of your one night stand for research's sake." His body tightened at the thought. It must be a reaction to the new environment because he could have sworn that after the season he'd just finished, he wouldn't even want to look at a woman until training camp.

"For just a moment. A mini-moment."

Ally glanced at him, and he could see a flush rising to her cheeks. When was the last time he'd seen a woman blush? Never? Women who came to him wouldn't even think of blushing. They were either too busy anticipating what he'd do to them or determined that they would be the one woman to resist him.

She drew in a deep breath. "I couldn't do that with someone I just met. I'd have to know him better."

"So know me better." He didn't like the curl of excitement that lowered his voice, took his breath away until he spoke in a whisper.

Ally finally seemed focused. "You're playing with me. I heard you talking to . . . Cap, and I know you won't be having sexual relations with anyone." She shrugged. "And I wouldn't want to be with a man who thought of sex as a game. But I do want to know about your life. Then you can tell me what I need to know for my book."

For now, Ally. For now. "I was born on one of the outer planets. Space travel's common in my time, and the haves and have-nots aren't separated by neighborhoods anymore. They're separated by planets. There's an even wider gap between the classes than in your time. Social programs for the poor don't exist."

Ally grimaced. "It sounds pretty grim."

He smiled. "There's still opportunity for someone with drive and ambition."

"And that's you?"

Brian nodded. "Earth is home to the financially secure. No one has to lift a finger to do anything. Machines have come a long way. If you don't feel like thinking, a machine can do it for you. Most of the people who live on Earth inherited their wealth and have never had to do a thing in their lives. Genetic engineering produces humans who aren't susceptible to disease. Medications not only keep you thin, but can cure anything you do happen to get. So why exercise? Sorry to say this, but humans have become do-nothing blobs."

"I want to know about *you*."

He shrugged. "I never knew my parents, or at least not long enough for it to matter. I lived on the streets. I did physical work because on the outer planets people aren't rich enough to afford technology. They're better off in some ways."

She looked away. It made him uncomfortable not being able to see her expression, so he reverted to what did make him feel secure. Touch. He reached over and lifted her hair away from her neck, then curled a strand around his finger. He liked the way her hair curled in the Irish humidity. He couldn't remember the last time he'd stopped long enough to notice what a woman looked like. The only parts of a woman he focused on were the parts that led to a team win.

Ally didn't stop him. "So tell me about your career."

"My agent, Jupe, took me off the streets when I was sixteen. He saw potential. I trained for two years, then was drafted by the Testosterone Titans. Cap owns the Titans. Last year I was a free agent, and the Old One picked me up for her team, the Sex Monarchs." He shrugged. "The Monarchs won the Sex Super Bowl this year."

She nodded. "Go on."

He stopped touching her hair and slid his hand down her back, massaged a circle at the base of her spine. "In 2502 all contact sports are banned. Too violent. But people still crave contact, so the game of sex is the most popular sport of my time. Hey, it's the only game in town. I'm at the top of the heap right now, and I intend to stay there for a long time."

"Aren't you embarrassed?"

She wiggled her bottom into a more comfortable position. One that made him drop his hand from her back.

"Times change, Ally. Attitudes change. In my time, a man's ability to perform sexually is considered a talent to be nurtured and viewed openly. There's no stigma attached to it."

Ally shook her head. "I can't believe that. How could five hundred years make such a difference in what people view as acceptable behavior?"

For some reason, it was important she understand. "Think about what was accepted behavior in your great-aunt's time, then think about now.

Would some of the music videos and movies you have now be allowed in her time? Think about some of the reality shows on your television. It won't be long into your future before *Sexual Survivor* airs to a national audience for the first time. It'll be condemned, but people will still watch. Then when something more outrageous is shown, people will think of *Sexual Survivor* as normal viewing. It'll happen. Soon."

He could feel her mentally shaking off her horror. For the first time in his career, he felt the stirrings of distaste for what he did. Because he was seeing it through her eyes, her perspective, her values. He didn't like what he felt.

"I guess I believe you." Ally didn't want to believe him. She couldn't conceive of the future he described. *Any more than Katy could conceive of MTV when she was young.* "One thing's been bothering me. Why do you speak so much like me?"

Brian grinned. "Contact sports are banned, but I guess humans will always be fascinated by violence. Movies from the past have been preserved. The ones that glorify violent sports are cult favorites. The whole planet tries to talk like the characters in the movies. For the last ten years, fight movies have been popular, especially . . ."

For the first time since he'd started explaining his time, Ally was ahead of him. "No, let me guess. *Rocky.* Everyone in your time talks like Rocky Balboa."

"Yo."

She knew he expected her to laugh. She couldn't. The whole idea of his life was so bizarre, what he was doing in her life even more bizarre.

He shrugged. "I also used the Language Assimilation Program. It scanned this time period's American speech pattern into my mind. When I don't need it any longer, I can have it deleted. I didn't want an Irish speech pattern. It would be too easy to check where I came from."

Thoughts of technology always made her eyes cross. Time to change subjects. "So what do you spend your money on? Big house, big vehicle? Any favorite charities in your time?"

She watched his expression close, his lips tighten, and knew he was going to lie to her.

"I don't do anything with my wealth." His body language said he'd told her all he intended.

Ally prepared to call him on his lie when a car horn blared much too close. The wagon swerved and leaned precariously, then shuddered as something hit it with an ominous crunch of wood and metal. Losing her balance, Ally slid from the bed and landed on the floor of the wagon with a solid thud.

"Katy!" Frantically Ally crawled toward the front of the wagon. Brian reached her in one stride, lifted her to her feet, then yanked open the door.

Ally scrambled out behind him, then paused to

absorb the enormity of what had almost happened.

The wagon was tilted at an unnatural angle against a stone wall while the horse placidly cropped grass.

Katy jumped up and down in place while she shook her fist at a car disappearing around a curve. "Come back here and fight like a man, you scumbag. Where'd you get your license, out of a cereal box? You want road rage, come back and I'll show you some road rage." Katy in full voice could shatter a whole set of Waterford goblets.

Brian's muttered curse distracted Ally from Katy's tirade. She followed his gaze to the top of the wagon. The Old One crouched on the wagon's roof, every hair on end, her mouth opening and closing on soundless snarls.

The Old One's fear touched Ally, and she wanted to pull the cat into her arms. Even as she reached up, she realized it was her automatic comfort response.

Brian put his hand on her arm. "Don't. She's trying to change forms. This is not a good thing, believe me." He turned his attention to the cat. "Calm down, Boss. Everything's okay. You don't need to do this."

His voice had become a husky purr. Ally sure enough would want to do whatever that voice asked. But then Ally wasn't an ancient shapeshifter.

"Don't change. We're not in danger anymore." He reached up to touch the Old One, but she backed away from him, then started to shake.

Ally had seen enough. And what she saw wasn't the interfering owner of the Sex Monarchs, but a cat. Just a cat. She stood on the wagon seat and reached for the Old One. "Come on, girl. Women should stick together. I don't blame you for being scared. Whatever happened scared me too."

And to the shock of everyone, probably including the Old One herself, the cat crawled to the edge of the roof and allowed Ally to scoop her up. Ally held the cat in her arms until the shaking stopped. Ally didn't have the courage to pet her. It would probably offend the Old One's sense of dignity anyway.

Climbing off the seat, Ally turned to her great-aunt, who was making internationally understood finger signals toward the departed car. "What happened, Katy? God, look at the wagon." This was directed at Brian, who'd leaped to the ground and was inspecting the damage.

"Lots of bent and crunched stuff on this side. Afraid we won't be going anywhere with the wagon in this condition." Brian walked to the other side of the road to peer down at a steep drop-off. He stopped well back from the edge.

Ally and Katy climbed off the wagon and joined him. Ally gulped. The rocky cliff dropped straight down to where the sea churned far below. Suddenly, the condition of the wagon paled in comparison to what *their* condition might have been. The Old One took a glance, then with a plaintive meow, crouched lower in Ally's arms.

Surprised, Ally stared at the cat. "She's terrified. And she's certainly not terrified of humans."

"She can control humans." He shrugged. "Everyone fears something." There was nothing mocking in his statement.

"Even you?" Ally realized his answer was important to her.

"Even me." His tone warned Ally that his fears weren't open to discussion.

He put his arms across both women's shoulders, then turned them away from the road edge. Ally felt a sense of security that she couldn't explain, didn't want to dissect.

"What happened, Katy?" His tone was grim.

Katy drew a deep breath, then was off and running. "I was driving there on the other side of the road, next to that cliff, just relaxing, when here came that car from behind me like a bat out of hell." She paused for an editorial aside. "Stupid jerk."

"Did you get the plate number?" Brian walked over to inspect the horse.

Katy stared at him askance. "You're kidding, right?" When he didn't answer, she continued. "I thought he would zip on by, but he didn't. He got right behind me and laid on his blasted horn." Time for another commercial break. "Stupid pea-brain."

"And?" Brian carefully checked the harness and shafts.

Ally wondered how he could be so calm. She

was still working on her pounding heart and erratic breathing.

"That horn scared the crap out of me. Thought it would do the same to the horse. I looked over the side of that road and thought I was about to take a shortcut to heaven." Katy walked over, pulled the horse's head up, and kissed it soundly on its surprised nose. "I'll never complain about a laid-back horse again. I figured when he heard the horn, the horse would jump and take the wagon over the edge, but he kept right on walking."

Katy sighed and looked uncomfortable. "The horse had more sense than I did. I was scared and not thinking straight. All I could remember was that you turn the wheels into a skid."

Okay, Ally was officially confused. "What's that have to do with anything?"

Katy glared at her. "Nothing. Anyway, I steered the horse to the right, and that damned driver wasn't expecting us to swerve into his path. He tried to go around the wagon, but he clipped us." Katy's expression dared her to make a comment. "Knocked us against the wall."

"Are you sure the driver was a man?" Brian patted the horse and turned to Katy.

"Well, I'm not sure. Everything happened so fast. But he drove like a man."

"We're not going anywhere without a new wagon." Ally glanced at Brian while Katy walked to the back of the wagon.

She didn't say it, but Brian knew they'd

reached a proving ground. Ally wanted him to use the Constructor. "Is this what you really want? Katy will find out. We could just wait until someone comes by, and you could go back to Liscannor to call the office. They'd bring out a new wagon. This accident wasn't your fault."

Ally offered him a half smile. "Getting cold feet, Byrne? Katy will find out eventually anyway if we park at your keep while you help with my book."

"So you've made a definite decision to stay?" The logical part of him reasoned that if she stayed there'd be no relaxing vacation. But a part of him that had never spoken up before said having Ally around would be fun. Fun? Women had never been fun. They'd been nothing more than a number on a scoreboard. Maybe it was time to explore the fun concept.

Her smile faded. "I need to write a blockbuster book about sex and the single life without going through the field-testing stage. I need to consult an expert so I can write a reasonable facsimile of the real thing. I've never tried to fool my readers before, but look where writing from the heart got me."

She meant it as a joke, but he didn't laugh. He wanted to touch her, but he didn't. A milestone in his life. It was the first time he'd ever wanted to touch a woman and hadn't.

Ally drew a deep, steadying breath. "I guess I've found out something not so admirable about myself. I value my writing career more than my integrity."

Brian couldn't let that go by. He shook his head. "Not true. You simply realize your limitations and are consulting an expert. The audience you're appealing to will expect wild and sexy. Can you deliver wild and sexy?"

Her smile returned. "Wild and sexy isn't in my experience bank. How about logical and informed?"

"Won't sell books, babe."

She nodded. "That's what I thought. Anyway, the up side of this is you're the perfect consultant. You know your subject, and you won't be around later to write a tell-all book about me. Oh, and you don't want sex or money in return. All in all, you're the perfect one-night stand."

Her intense stare told him she'd just defined the parameters of their relationship. No sex.

Brian glanced at the Old One, still nestled in Ally's arms. "What do you think, Boss?"

The Old One's eyes gave nothing away. She was evidently opting for a wait-and-see approach.

"You have a deal." His common sense groaned at the complete idiocy of those words.

Ally visibly relaxed. "So what about the wagon?"

Brian reached into his pocket and pulled out the Constructor. Closing his eyes, he visualized the outside of the wagon. Then he thought about the interior. Hmm. He remembered seeing the interior of an ancient building through a Virtual Viewer a few years ago. It had fascinated him.

Brian smiled. He hadn't promised to restore the wagon to its exact pre-accident state. Ally needed some fun in her life. Not take everything so seriously. He could probably use a laugh, too. After he saw Ally's reaction, he could change the wagon back to its original interior.

Opening his eyes, he punched in the appropriate code. The ground shook, the wagon shimmered, changed, and Ally whispered a particularly interesting oath he hadn't run across when he was learning the slang for this time period. He'd have to ask her to repeat it later.

Ally's face paled, and Brian realized how hard it was for her to face the physical proof of who he was. She could write off what he'd told her as the babbling of an idiot, but she couldn't explain away what the Constructor did.

Ally slid her fingers over the wagon's side, a side without a mark where a moment before it had been scraped and dented. Her fingers shook as Katy reappeared around the side of the wagon. "If the horse had spooked, or you hadn't steered away from the cliff, Katy, we probably wouldn't be here. The driver didn't even stop to see if we needed help."

Katy ignored her. She was staring transfixed at the wagon. For the first time since Brian had met her, Ally's great-aunt was speechless.

Katy moved closer to the wagon, but didn't reach out to touch it. "Godalmighty, what the hell did you do to that wagon?" She turned her astonished gaze toward the Constructor, then slowly raised her eyes to Brian's face. "I came to Ireland to see ordinary stuff like ghosts, leprechauns, or the pooka. Not weird stuff like this. This I'd expect in California. How'd you do it, and what's that thing in your hand?"

Brian frowned. Had he scared her? She was old, and he hadn't thought ahead to what the shock could do to someone Katy's age. "Sorry if I frightened you."

Ally intervened. She put her arm around her great-aunt's waist and steered her away from the wagon. "I'll explain everything." Her comment seemed as much for Brian as it was for Katy.

Brian walked to the horse's head and absently stroked the animal's neck. The confidence his sense of touch usually brought him was absent this time. When he'd first met Ally, the thought of having to cut his vacation short and return to 2502 didn't bother him much. It was just an annoying inconvenience. But now? He wanted to stay. He wanted to know Ally better, help her write her book, even help Katy spot a few Irish fairies. Surprisingly, his desire to fix up the castle wasn't at the top of his list anymore.

This wasn't entirely good. He'd never gotten involved in any woman's life. Didn't know how. And he wasn't used to being uncertain where a woman was concerned. Besides, his time here was limited to a few weeks. It wouldn't pay to care too much about Ally's life.

No matter what his logic said, the rest of him was damned glad to see Ally and Katy returning with smiles on their faces.

Katy sidled up to him and pointed at the Constructor. "Lend me that when we get back to the castle. Got to build something."

"What?" He hadn't expected Katy to be so unaffected by what Ally had told her. But then again, this was the same woman who sincerely believed she would meet a vampire. So he supposed a man from the future wasn't such a big deal.

"I want a john."

John? Frantically, Brian scanned his memory for the meaning of this bit of twenty-first century slang. "You want a prostitute's client?" The beginning and end of that sentence definitely did not go together.

Katy stared at him, then grinned. "You've got a lot to learn, good-looking. I want to build a toilet. The wagon's great for traveling from town to town, but it doesn't have a toilet. Since I want to stay at your castle and find some spirits, I won't be close to any facilities. Got to have facilities."

Brian thought about modifying the wagon but decided a toilet would take up too much space. When he got back to—

"And I want you to sit down and tell me all about your job. How does a passionate woman get to play your game? Your league have any openings for mature women? Bet they're equal opportunity employers." Katy looked way too hopeful.

"Come on, Katy. Let's get into the wagon."

Brian rubbed the back of his neck to relieve the tension. *Thank you, Ally O'Neill.* He didn't think the league would survive Katy.

Ally glanced at Brian. "Thank heavens these Irish roads aren't busy or we would've been zapped a dozen times by now. I forgot that the wagon is sitting on the wrong side of the road." She moved toward the wagon.

Brian felt anticipation building. Surprised, he savored the feeling. He'd never played a trick on anyone before. Maybe before his mother had left, but that was too long ago to remember. Definitely not after. But now? He could hardly wait. "You go into the wagon. I'll drive. But first I want to check everything one more time."

He watched the women climb onto the wagon, then open the door to go inside. He saw the exact moment they peered inside. He wasn't disappointed.

"Ohmigod!" Ally swung around to stare at him, dropping a disgruntled Old One onto the seat.

Katy disappeared inside. "Well, isn't this nice? Looks just the way I picture *The Best Little Whorehouse in Texas.*"

Chapter Seven

"You have a warped sense of humor, Byrne." Ally grimaced as she stole another quick glance into the wagon. Yep, it hadn't changed. The new décor was still overwhelmingly scarlet, reeking of sex and sin. "Change it back." She would *not* live in a bordello on wheels.

Brian settled onto the driver's seat, picked up the reins, and clucked to the horse. The Old One slipped past Ally to join Katy inside. Ally grasped the edge of the door as the wagon rolled slowly toward the castle. "Why change it? You have to write a sexy book, so it makes sense you need a sexy environment to put you in the mood."

"I don't need a mirrored ceiling to put me in the mood. What's sexy about waking up in the morning and seeing your hair standing on end? Sounds scary to me." She would control her temper. She *never* lost her temper. Even when Dave the Dork announced he was abandoning her for young-and-exciting Erica, she'd discussed the situation in a calm voice. Ally smiled. Calm didn't mean she wouldn't get even, though.

Brian shrugged. "Sleep on your side. But if anything exciting ever happens in your bed, you'll have a front row seat." He didn't sound like a man who intended to do any redecorating soon.

Ally looked into the wagon again. Katy and the Old One had their collective noses glued to one of the many paintings that covered every bare space. "Don't worry, Katy. I'll make him get rid of those paintings."

"Why would you do that?" Katy never took her gaze off the painting. "I like this one." She cocked her head to the side. "Don't know if two people could do this, though." She finally looked at Ally. "At my age, the body don't bend real good anymore." She sounded regretful.

Ally rolled her eyes. No help from Katy, so she turned her attention back to Brian. "We have to return this wagon when we're finished with it. I can't return it looking like a pleasure palace, a . . . bordello in a barrel."

"Guess I can understand that. Let's compromise. I still think you should wallow in sexy surroundings to get the old creative juices flowing. When I'm ready to leave, I'll change it back to the original."

Ally's gaze narrowed. He was enjoying this way

too much. "Do you need a sensual environment to do *your* work?"

He turned his head to grin at her.

Hmm. Maybe that hadn't been a great question. She didn't need to know any more than she already did about his job.

"I can perform anywhere, sweetheart." His soft insinuation was that wagon seats were not beyond his abilities. He returned his attention to the horse as he guided it along the dirt lane leading to the castle.

"Then why would *I* need this . . . this . . . ?" Her powers of description failed her.

"I'm a lot more talented than you are, babe." He pulled the horse to a stop, then jumped from the wagon.

And didn't realize that he'd just put his life in grave danger. *More talented?* What an arrogant, egotistical—

"Come in and see this place, Ally. I want to fix my place up like this when we get home. Get myself a hot granddaddy and a sexy nightgown. . . ." Until now, the only thing that got Katy this excited was The Home Shopping Channel.

Ally would kill Brian Byrne for this. "Coming, Katy." She glared at him, letting him get a foretaste of how his life would end.

He didn't seem intimidated. "Go in and look around. It'll grow on you. I'll build your bathroom before I go back to my place."

Grow on you? Right. Sort of like scarlet mold. Sighing, she went inside the wagon.

It was worse than she'd imagined. The Old One was lying on her back, all four legs waving in the air as she studied herself in the ceiling mirrors. Katy was engrossed with the sink. What was so interesting about the sink? A sink was a sink. She'd just draw Katy outside where she could talk some sense into her and . . .

Ally saw the sink. She closed her eyes. She opened them. Nope, still there.

"Never saw anything like this before. They don't have stuff like this at Braddock's Hardware. Look at this. The knobs are boobs, and the faucet is a man's—"

"I can see what the faucet is." She'd discovered a new talent. She could talk through gritted teeth.

Air. She needed pure asexual air. Ally hurried from the wagon and climbed down. She noted that Brian had finished the bathroom. On the outside it was a square nondescript building, but Ally now knew how Mr. Byrne's dark mind worked. The building was suspiciously large for just a toilet. Thank heavens it wasn't floating.

She turned her back on whatever new horror he'd created and started taking the harness off the horse.

"Want to see the bathroom?" He walked over to help her.

"Nope."

Brian squatted to remove the strap from under the horse's belly, and as Ally glanced down at him she had the impulse to slide her fingers across his tangled hair . . . then grab a huge hunk and yank. She'd almost given in to her impulse when he looked up at her.

"Not a good idea, babe. Wouldn't want to force me to physically restrain you." His eyes promised that physical restraint could involve a number of exciting sensations.

Ally stared into his eyes, watched them darken with a sensual promise she didn't believe, knew he didn't intend. Because Brian had made two things clear: Sex was simply a game, and he wouldn't have sex on his vacation.

Fine. This was exactly what she wanted. A man with sexual expertise who didn't want to practice on her. *And when did you become such a liar, Ally O'Neill?*

Ally turned away, trying to ignore him as he took care of the horse then turned it out into the walled paddock. It was time to come to grips with the truth. *Brian Byrne was from the future.* She couldn't refute the proof of her own eyes. She was a writer, so she'd store as much information as she could before he left, not for her present book, but for a future book. One she'd write years from now. One the rest of the world would believe was fiction.

Years from now. Something about the thought saddened her.

She stopped thinking as the air seemed to shift and heat around her. Brian had moved into her sensual monitoring area. Every atom of awareness in her vibrated and hummed when he approached. Amazing phenomenon.

Katy stuck her head out of the wagon. "I'm making soup and sandwiches. Should be done in about fifteen minutes. You want mayo on your sandwich, Brian?"

He frowned. "I guess so." Mayo? Wasn't that a county in Ireland? The Language Assimilation Program he'd used for this trip had a lot of gaps in it.

But right now he wasn't thinking about food. "Let's walk up to the keep, Ally. I came a long way to see where my family began. Maybe we can start talking about your book." *Maybe we can start talking about you.*

She seemed distracted as they turned toward the hill in silence.

Katy's yelled order caught them before they'd taken a few steps. "Keep your eyes peeled for that white deer. Saw it again yesterday morning. Probably stays around here." She shouted into the wagon. "You want mayo on your sandwich too, Boss?"

Brian bit back an oath. The white stag had brought another meddler to poke his nose into Brian's down time. And Brian could pretty much guess who it was. Maybe he needed a new agent, one who didn't interfere in his clients' personal lives.

"It always amazes me how Katy adjusts so easily. Nothing fazes her." Ally avoided one of the many rocks littering the hill as she glanced up at him and smiled. "I mean, she's already accepted that your cat isn't your cat at all. The Old One still looks like a cat to me."

Brian returned her smile. "Katy hasn't seen the Old One in her true form. Believe me, she'd be fazed."

"Tell me about the Old One. Tell me about *you*." She held up her hand to ward off his argument. "And I don't mean just the surface stuff you've told me. You'll be helping me with this book, and I'll bet you'll do some in-depth digging into my psyche, so I deserve some info in return."

He shrugged. "I'll tell you about the Old One. Not much to tell you about me that you don't already know."

Her expression said she didn't believe him. Maybe he shouldn't have offered to help her. He didn't need anyone digging up his past. He'd stopped thinking about his early life a long time ago. Okay, so he'd *tried* to stop thinking about it. He must still need a sense of family if he'd decided to come here for his vacation. He pushed the thought away. "The advent of space travel opened Earth up to a whole new type of immigrant. Some were easier to accept than others. The Old One settled on Earth about 2200. No one really knows how old she is. She's accumulated massive wealth and has investments that span the known universe."

"The shape-shifting concept is hard to believe. Does she have a . . . mate?"

Good. He'd turned Ally's attention away from

117

him. "She doesn't need a mate. The Old One can be a he, she, or it. For the last hundred years or so, she's chosen to be female. In her true form she's an 'it.' Doesn't need a mate to reproduce. She's chosen not to. Too busy making herself rich."

Ally looked horrified. "No relatives?"

"Not that I know of."

"She must get lonely." Ally's gaze was warm with sympathy.

Brian had never thought of his boss in personal terms, had never thought of her as anything more than the owner of his team. He was uncomfortable with personal. Brian shrugged. "She gets by."

"Like *you* get by?"

Where had the conversation taken a wrong turn and ended up back at him? "I have people who take care of my needs." *That's what I pay them for.* "I have friends." *As long as I stay on top.* He hadn't brought any friends from his old life, didn't *have* any friends in his old life.

She cocked her head to study him, and he felt like a Marwin subspecies under a thought-scan.

"What would you have if all your fame and wealth were taken from you?"

He knew his smile didn't reach his eyes. "I'd have myself, babe."

"And that would be enough for you." Her whispered comment wasn't a question, so he didn't answer.

"Let's talk about your book." He came to the

spot where he'd left his shelter and reached for the Constructor.

"Where's your tent? It's gone." She swung in a circle looking for it. "It was here yesterday. Do you think someone took it?"

He pressed a button on the Constructor and the shelter materialized. "It was still here. I put it in sleep mode while I was away so no one would stumble across it."

"That's amazing. How does—?"

"I don't know." He was relaxing now that the conversation had shifted away from him. "I'm not into technology enough to want to know."

"More into touch."

"Right." He caught the teasing sparkle in her eye and momentarily lost his train of thought. Women never teased him. They were focused on only one thing during competition. And his contract discouraged friendship with females outside of the game. The team owners didn't want players expending energy randomly, then showing up at training camp out of shape. "I have to change. Wait here and I'll be out in a minute."

Ally turned to study the castle while she waited, tried not to think about Brian sliding his jeans down over lean hips, muscular thighs. Did her best to block out pictures of him stripping his shirt off, baring all that warm skin and . . .

She took a deep breath and forced her thoughts to the castle. The number of years represented in this spot was mind-boggling. The castle had stood for untold hundreds of years, while a few feet away a man from five hundred years in the future changed clothes.

Ally had never believed in ghosts or the paranormal, but a few days ago she wouldn't have believed in Brian Byrne either.

She wandered over to what must have been an entrance at one time. There wasn't much of the building left, but as she stepped inside, darkness enveloped her. A chill that had nothing to do with the temperature made her shiver, and she clasped her arms across her chest.

Silly reaction. It was just an old building. She'd let Katy's stories get to her. Ally eyed a winding stone staircase that disappeared into the gloom and thought about seeing what the view was like from the top of it. On the outside she'd noticed narrow openings placed at regular intervals all the way to the top. An icy breath of air touched her. Well, maybe not. She'd just wait here for Brian—

Strong arms circled her, warm breath moved over the skin at the base of her neck, and she screamed loud enough to convince the people in Liscannor that the banshee was alive and well.

"I've waited for ye, I have, Ally O'Neill. Many a long cold night I've called to ye, and now that ye've come I'll never let ye leave me."

Brian. She couldn't help it, her legs shook and she slumped against him. His arms tightened around her, his soft laughter echoed off the ancient walls, fading into the blackness.

"Don't do that again. If I were the Old One,

eight of my lives would've been gone. Poof."

"Ye've wounded me sorely, lass. Do ye not remember?" he slid his hands down her arms, her sides, and when he reached her hips, he pulled her tightly against him. Slowly, he rotated his hips in a sensual rhythm no woman could ignore.

"I . . . would've remembered that." It was getting more memorable by the second.

"It was a fine summer eve with the moon full when I first saw ye." He paused to glide his tongue along the side of her throat, then placed his mouth over the spot where her pulse pounded madly.

"Got it. You really *are* Black Liam, the evilest vampire in all Ireland. Katy would want to know about this." Her breaths came in short gasps. Must be the humid Irish air and damp stone walls causing her respiratory problems. Made perfect sense.

His soft chuckle sent an anticipatory shiver down her spine. He raised his head, and cool air touched the spot where his mouth had been.

Ally knew if she turned her head she'd see the wicked slash of his smile, the predatory gleam of his eyes in the darkness.

"I watched ye stop yer gypsy wagon at the bottom of yon hill. Ye climbed down, then lifted yer long golden hair away from yer neck. . . ."

"How long?" She was into details. Specifics were important.

"It hung long and heavy all the way to yer round bottom." He cupped her bottom in his

large hands just in case she couldn't remember
its location.

Long and heavy. Pause for mental picture de-
velopment. Ally smiled a feline smile. If he didn't
want her thinking about him, then he shouldn't
use such provocative adjectives.

"I never had hair that long." She was really
having a concentration problem as he moved his
hands deliberately over her stomach until he was
cupping her breasts.

"Ye were a gypsy, and gypsies have hair to their
bottoms." He sounded firm in his conviction.

"If you say so." His thumbs lightly skimmed
her nipples, a pattern of seduction that forced
her to bite her bottom lip to keep from crying
out. She'd agree to hair sprouting from her toes
as long as he kept touching her.

"Ah, then came the greatest joy."

There *was* no greater joy. Ally closed her eyes
and focused her complete attention on her nipples. Who cared that this could lead to clinical
nipple fixation? So she'd have to deal with nipple
withdrawal, nipple rehab, then avoid nipple
temptation for the rest of her life. Who cared?
She was into the moment.

"Ye flung off yer gown and danced naked in
the moonlight." He paused, and she sensed he
was having some difficulty with the humid air
and damp stones, too. "Yer breasts gleamed pale
in the moonlight. Yer body tempted a man to—"

"To *what?*" He couldn't stop now that he was getting to the best part.

She felt him draw a deep breath. He abandoned her breasts, let his fingers glide down her stomach and hips once more, then stepped back.

Damn and double damn. She didn't know which amazed her more: the fact that she really wanted him to finish what he'd started, or her desire to touch him. When it came to sex, she'd done everything for Dave. He'd made a few generic passes at her lips and breasts, but she'd done the grunt work. After all, the perfect wife was supposed to be an enthusiastic, engaged sex partner. She'd sworn if she ever let a man touch her again, she'd lie back and let him do all the work. While he was slaving away, she could do her nails, finish a book . . .

"Was that a seduction attempt?" Ally swung to face him.

He turned and strode out into the sunlight. "No."

"It sure felt like a seduction attempt." He'd given her a one-word answer. He needed to explain what had just happened. "Okay, you can at least tell me what happened after the naked dancing was finished." Did he stride from his castle, pick her up, then carry her into the wagon where their passion rocked the bed and scared the horse?

Brian shrugged and narrowed his gaze on a donkey cart wending its way up the road to the castle. "The lads and I went back to our drinking and fighting."

"Lads?" This was so *not* what she wanted to hear. "How many watched me dance naked?"

He began striding down the hill toward where the donkey cart had stopped next to the wagon. She trotted along beside him.

"About twenty. The others had passed out below from the drink. Or it might have been the fighting." He slanted her an appreciative glance. "Ye were fine entertainment."

They were close enough to see that three people sat in cramped discomfort in the cart. The donkey didn't look too happy either.

"You know, Byrne, if that's the kind of fantasy you feed women during competition, I don't know how you became the MVP of anything."

Startled, he stopped to stare at her. "I don't 'feed' fantasies to women during a game. It's against the rules. I can talk to the women, but I can't use a fantasy. If I do, the team is penile-ized."

"*Penile-ized?* I hope that's just a strange pronunciation of 'penalized.' What else is against the rules?" She was sick, sick, sick, to want to know about this. But hey, after her dull, dull, dull marriage, this was hot stuff.

The people were climbing from the donkey cart as Katy left the wagon with the Old One trotting behind her.

Ally could almost feel the waves of anger coming from Brian as he continued toward the three strangers. At least he didn't seem angry at her. "No one can wear any kind of scent to gain an advantage, and the women can't touch themselves to hurry along their climax."

Now he was getting into her embarrassment zone. "Fine. I have the picture now."

He paused one last time and slanted her a grin that would have curled all her appendages if they weren't already in permanent crinkle mode from his gypsy fantasy. "I don't think so. I can use only touch and a few words to bring a woman to orgasm, and I can do it in two minutes. I call it my two-minute drill, and no one does it better."

"From a cold start? That's impossible."

"You haven't tried me, babe."

He turned toward the visitors, while she worked at closing her mouth. "Meet two of my business associates. This is Jupe, my agent, and Nebula, my trainer."

For the first time, Ally really looked at the visitors. Well, one of them anyway. Her gaze slid over Jupe and fixed on Nebula. Her eyes widened. Katy spoke for both of them.

"Holy hell, would you look at that? Stay right here while I get my digital camera."

Chapter Eight

Brian allowed the stunned silence to drag on for a reasonable amount of time before he spoke. It always took people a while to recover from their first encounter with Nebula.

The moment of shock ended with the click of Katy's digital camera.

Brian checked to make sure the driver of the donkey cart had wandered toward the castle, out of hearing range. "You'd better have a good reason to be here, Jupe, because—"

"Wait." Nebula held up her hand, and all movement ceased.

Brian hated to admit it, but she intimidated even him.

"Your friends have questions. They are not speaking because awe has closed their throats and frozen their tongues. It is the usual response." She nodded regally in Ally and Katy's direction. "I will tell them only what they need to know about me. Their primitive brains could not fully grasp what I am."

"I never saw a woman as tall as you." Katy aimed her camera for a second shot. "The leather jacket and pants are real cool, especially with all those studs. Turn around so I can get a shot of that skull and crossbones on the back of your jacket. Bet you could get your picture on the cover of *Bad-ass Bikers and Their Old Ladies*." Katy frowned. "Don't know why those women put up with being called old ladies."

Nebula looked insulted. "I am *more* than a woman." She turned for Katy's shot, then took off her jacket. "You will probably want to take a picture of my tattoo." She flexed a massive arm. "I chose a heart with the word 'mother' inside so that I might lessen the fear of the masses by making them believe I have a sentimental side."

Katy looked thoughtful. "Don't think that itty bitty heart is going to lessen anybody's fear. Why'd you wear that outfit if you didn't want people to be afraid?"

Nebula cast her a dismissive glance. "I chose clothes from your time that would enhance my status as more than a woman."

Ally glanced up at Brian. "Just like the Old One is more than a cat. You have a lot of more-thans in your time."

Brian didn't react to her teasing because he was so pissed off at Jupe. "Okay, Nebula, I know

127

you've concocted some story to throw off suspicion. So let's hear it. Then I want to know why you and Jupe are here."

Katy shook her head. "Hate to break it to you, but it'll take more than a story to make Nebula, here, inconspicuous." She cocked her head and studied Nebula. "Maybe if you cut off some of that green hair. All this humidity makes it puff up a lot."

"Why would I want to be inconspicuous? And I chose this wig because it is memorable, as am I." Nebula sounded sincerely puzzled. Evidently feeling there was no reasonable answer to her question, she launched into her speech. "I am seven feet five inches tall and weigh three hundred fifty pounds by your measurements."

"Bet I know where at least a hundred of those pounds are. Must be hard to exercise without bouncing and jiggling." Katy's gaze turned wistful. "I always wanted to be one of those well-endowed women. Tried a Wonderbra, but you can't push up what isn't there."

Nebula forged on. "I have told everyone that I play for the WNBA."

"You'd be a real hit with the World Wrestling Federation. Stone Cold Steve Austin would be toast." Katy seemed excited by the prospect of Stone Cold getting squished.

Nebula ignored her. "Of course, I would never play for the WNBA. Those puny women would provide no challenge." She brightened. "I would rather test my skills against Shaquille O'Neal, a man worthy of my talent. It would be amusing to dunk over Shaq Daddy in front of his LA Fakers fans."

"Wouldn't call them that to their faces," Katy advised.

"Okay, now why are you and Jupe here, and why the hell did you come in that cart?" Brian could feel Ally shaking with laughter beside him, and it made him even angrier. "Your wig is slipping, Jupe. Wouldn't let it fall off if I were you."

"Fat lot of good the cart did. We walked most of the way because the old guy said his donkey couldn't drag all that weight." Jupe glared at Nebula as he straightened his wig.

Jupe's gaze drifted around the group and settled on the Old One, who didn't seem particularly interested in the new arrivals. "Thought maybe the Old One could discuss your incentive clause with me. Need to get that straightened out before the season begins."

"She's a cat, Jupe. Cats don't talk." Let Jupe slither out of that one.

A puzzled line formed between Jupe's eyes. "That was a stupid form to take."

The Old One unsheathed her claws.

Nebula felt the need to insert her comment. "We were forced to travel in that primitive conveyance because all the males who had more modern vehicles were unavailable. It was obvious they feared me."

"Bunch of wusses," Katy offered in sympathy.

Nebula shrugged. "Men are the weaker sex. It

is to be expected." She turned away. "I will take our things from the cart and build a shelter near yours, Brian."

Brian felt his explosion building, threatening to blow Jupe, Nebula, Cap, and the Old One all the way home to 2502 without the aid of a white stag. Jupe was here for the same reason as the Old One: to make sure nothing interfered with the return of their main moneymaker to the safety of his own time.

Jupe knew him well enough to be nervous. "I know what you're going to say, Brian, but you can't send us home. There won't be another stag until the one comes to take you home. We'll have to go with you." He glanced at Brian to see the effect of his words. What he saw evidently didn't reassure him. "We'll stay out of your way."

"Why did you bring Nebula?" His anger simmered and bubbled, his quiet words fooling no one.

"You could probably use some toning . . ." Jupe held up his hands. "The truth? She makes me feel safe. No one will mess with us while she's around."

"Got that straight," Katy offered.

Jupe seemed to notice Ally and Katy for the first time. "They know about you, Brian?"

Brian nodded. "Ally and Katy are staying in the wagon while I help Ally with a book." He narrowed his gaze, daring Jupe to say something.

"Nice." *Uh-oh* was in every worried crease of Jupe's gnome-like face.

Ally interrupted. "Don't worry. This is strictly a business consultation." The flush rising to Ally's face proclaimed that the rest of her body didn't believe a word she said.

Brian exhaled sharply. He didn't believe it either. Something had gone terribly wrong. Back in the keep, it had taken every bit of his self-control to back off, to keep from sliding his hands between her legs, touching her through her jeans. He wanted to feel the cloth grow damp with her desire, wanted to turn her into his embrace and press his erection against her until . . . No, he couldn't let it happen.

He had to be the strong one. He'd had a lifetime of practice. Ally didn't need a man who'd enjoy sex with her, then walk away just like her husband. That's why she'd asked for help with her book. She shouldn't have to go through an actual night of meaningless sex. No, Ally didn't have to go through the experience. She had an expert on meaningless sex.

He closed his mind to the bitterness of that last thought. His career had pulled him from a cycle of poverty and crime that would have eventually destroyed him. He was a survivor. And the money he made helped other kids break the cycle. So he'd continue doing his job until he couldn't anymore, then retire. He'd probably be voted into the Sex Hall of Fame, and they'd retire his number 69. Somehow he couldn't work up a lot of enthusiasm for any of that.

Jupe's worried look didn't fade. "Remember

your contract. Page fourteen, clause fifty-eight."

No sex. "Sure. How could I forget?" *Especially with you here to remind me every ten minutes.*

He glanced at the Old One. If a cat could smile, she was smiling. For once, she and Jupe were on the same page.

Brian tried to slow his heavy breathing, control his rapidly expanding temper. Suddenly, he felt Ally wrap her hand around his clenched fist.

"It's okay, Brian. Don't let them get to you. Katy and I can run interference for you. I'd take odds on Katy over all of them, even Nebula." She slid her fingers back and forth over his knuckles until he opened his hand.

Brian didn't even notice when Jupe scuttled away or when Katy climbed back into the wagon followed by the Old One. His attention was completely on Ally.

She probably had no idea why he was staring at her. He glanced down at his hand where her fingers still lingered, and she lifted her hand from his. *No, touch me again.*

Women rarely touched him, except in passion. And they were paid well to do it. The bottom line was that even then, they didn't technically do any touching. They weren't allowed to.

And he avoided friendships with women outside the game. Those friendships could slide into the physical, endanger his career. Besides, he'd learned early that most of the women who showed interest in him didn't have kindness on their minds. He was famous and wealthy, incentive enough to try to convince him to break his no-sex clause.

He smiled. Ally hadn't a clue she'd pleased him in a way she'd never expect. It would probably irritate her that she'd done even this small thing for him when she was so determined never to do another thing for a man. "Thank you."

"For what?" Ally controlled the urge to shake the hand she'd used to touch him, to get rid of the connection in the same way she'd return circulation when it went to sleep. But this time the tingles were sensual and not the result of renewed blood flow.

"For being on my side. For touching me."

His gaze warmed, his eyes moving with emotion she'd never seen there before. And it scared the hell out of her. Give her aggressive, sardonic, infuriating. Those were things she could deal with, battle. *Nonthreatening* things.

She shrugged. "I was just trying to calm you. No big deal."

His voice softened, heating her from the inside out. "Your fingers do a lot of things, babe, but calm me isn't one of them."

She inhaled sharply. "Remember that next time you run a fantasy by me like you did in the castle. You had your fingers on a lot more than my hand, and it wasn't a calming experience."

"No kidding." He grinned. "One thing I don't understand, though. You said you were finished trying to please men. So I should be the perfect man for you. I do all the work, you do all the enjoying."

Ally frowned. Logically, he was right, but something sounded off. "Fine. So you're the man of my dreams."

Brian shook his head and offered her a wry grin. "We're arguing abstracts here. It's not going to happen. My sexual life is under contract for five more years."

She narrowed her gaze on him. Funny how every time he reminded her she couldn't have him, he made her mad. Ally got the same feeling when she went on a diet and told Mom not to bake any fudge brownies. Then when Mom didn't bake the brownies Ally felt . . . deprived. "Sure. I forgot. You're dedicated to the endless accumulation of wealth."

"Don't sound so ticked off, sweetheart." He'd stopped smiling, but she could see the laughter in his eyes. "You only want me as a consultant, not for a hot night of sex."

A hot night of sex. Ally pushed and shoved the words into different corners of her mind, then stood back to see how they looked. They didn't look bad. She might be able to live with the arrangement.

You've come a long way, baby. Just a few days ago she would have laughed at the idea of a man in her bed, a man she'd want to touch and . . . The *and* was still out there.

"I'm not angry." And her nose *wasn't* growing. "Let's walk up and see what's so interesting to the owner of the 'primitive conveyance.' "

He nodded, then started up the hill. Ally dropped slightly behind, caught up in the beauty of the vivid green hills, the starkness of the old castle, the motion of marvelous buns. Strange, but she didn't remember much about Dave's buns. Probably because he didn't have any. He was bunless.

But Brian . . . During competition a woman could hold on to them, feel their strength with each thrust. Hmm. He'd said the women couldn't touch him. That was poor planning by the rules committee. Every woman should have one moment in her life when she clasped the perfect buns.

Perfect. Ally's flight of fancy crashed and burned. Perfect didn't exist. She'd found that out the hard way. She hurried to catch up with him.

They found the donkey driver standing in the large opening at the front of the keep. Old, bent, and wearing rumpled tweeds, he turned to stare at Brian.

"Ye're a Byrne, lad. No one would be missing those eyes." He peered closer at Brian. "Odd, but I've lived near the old place since I was a babe and never knew that Kieran had a son."

Kieran? Brian thought about his history chip. Yes, he remembered a Kieran who'd had a son, Brian. In fact, the time-travel agent had listed Kieran Byrne as his father on his identification papers. He hoped Kieran and the other Brian didn't show up until after he left. "My mother raised me. Never knew much about my father. Does Kieran live around here?" He hadn't brought the information with him, but he could have sworn Kieran had died sometime before 2000. And Brian hadn't shown up on his history record until 2003. He'd thought he was safe.

"Kieran's been dead these twenty years." The old man cast him a sly glance. "He died in Boston."

Brian allowed himself a moment of relief.

"He was a priest. So ye understand why I was after thinking he had no sons."

"Hmm." He offered the old man a weak smile. "Even the holiest of us can lapse." Brian figured Father Kieran would be waiting at the gates of the beyond to punch him out for that one.

The old man returned his attention to the castle. "Aye, the sins of the flesh were a weakness with all the Byrnes." He glanced at Ally. "Ye have a fine caravan wagon. It be a calm way to travel."

Ally looked doubtful.

"Did yer family come from Ireland?"

She nodded. "The O'Neills."

His gaze softened. "It's home ye've come. The O'Neills be a fine old Irish family, one that has the *bean-sidhe*, the banshee, to mourn their passing."

Ally smiled at him. "My great-aunt is searching for Irish fairies. The O'Neill banshee is one family member I hope we don't meet."

The old man nodded, but seemed to have other things on his mind. "There be many stories about the castle and grounds. On moonlit nights many have seen the pooka, a dark horse with yellow eyes and a long wild mane. Those who've seen him say he roams the countryside around the castle tearing down fences, opening gates, and scattering livestock. A grand mischief maker he is."

"Opening gates?" Ally looked thoughtful; then her expression cleared. "Nah, not possible."

The old man looked offended. "Ye have not spent many nights here. Wait, listen, and when the chill of the night wraps itself around yer soul, and the waves pound against the cliffs, calling ye, *then* tell me ye don't believe."

Brian shifted his gaze to the large opening in the keep's wall. The old man sure made *him* believe.

Ally looked doubtful. "I've never—"

"Ye have nothing to equal this in America." He spat on the ground for emphasis. "Ye have no castle that has stood for eight hundred years, that has seen murder, treachery, and worse."

Brian shifted uneasily. This wasn't helping him to bond with his ancestors.

Ally was starting to look interested. "Tell me one of the stories about the castle. My great-aunt wants to write a book about Irish spirits and fairies."

The old man seemed mollified. "It was in the time of Cromwell when Donal Byrne ordered that the huge boiling pots the kelp gatherers used be covered with the hides of Tyrone oxen to make drums. They used the beasts' thighbones to sound the drums all along the coast when Cromwell's fleet sailed into sight." His gaze turned distant as he looked toward the cliff that fell to the sea below. "On a stormy night ye can still hear the drums warning of invasion."

Ally looked thoughtful. "Couldn't that just be the sound of waves hitting the air holes and caves in the rocks?"

Immersed in his story, the old man ignored her. "It be said the ghosts of Cromwell's victims haunt the castle. The devil's own slaughtered them as they slept."

The old man turned his gaze back to the large space where once the main entrance had stood. He touched the keep's wall, sliding his fingers over the rough stone, and Brian had a feeling the old man wanted to enter, but couldn't. That didn't make sense. He was probably imagining it.

"Donal Byrne escaped, but all others in the castle died." His voice grew soft. "There was a serving woman in the castle that cursed night. It was only to take the place of her sick husband that she had come from the village to work."

Brian took a deep breath, trying to dispel his unease. This was simply a story told by an old man.

"Her husband drove his cart to the castle when word came of the massacre, but none would let him in to claim his wife's body." The old man turned from the castle and started hobbling down the hill. "His heart failed while he waited by the gate for her body to be dragged out so he could take her home."

Mesmerized, Brian followed while Ally walked beside him.

The old man stopped when he reached his donkey. "They piled the bodies in the great hall. There are those who say on a moonless night ye can hear Bridget's body being dragged from the hall. The chill of it will freeze ye as it passes ye by."

"Thank you for sharing your story." Ally looked as uneasy as Brian felt. "You never told us your name."

He nodded. "Eamonn Clancy." With no other words, he drove away, and they watched until he disappeared from sight.

Ally glanced up at Brian. "Do you believe in ghosts?"

"Yes." Both kinds. The ghosts of those who'd died and the tortured ones who lived in his soul. But Ally didn't need to know about the second kind.

"Why? I'd think the further into the future you traveled, the less people would believe in the supernatural."

He smiled down at her. "Not true. The more we've learned, the greater our belief in possibilities. Take the Old One and me. Once you accept that I've traveled through time and the Old One is a shape shifter, then you have to believe in things you can't explain."

139

She sighed. "I guess that makes sense."

He laid his hand across her shoulders. "We ought to get our soup and sandwiches before the Old One decides to eat our share. She's never had a delicate appetite."

Ally refused to be led toward the wagon. "I need to take care of something first. You go inside, and I'll be there in a minute."

Brian stopped, puzzled. "I can wait for you."

She turned an exasperated glance his way. "What I was trying *not* to say was that I have to use your bathroom."

He grinned. "I'll walk you over, show you how everything works."

"I think I can figure it out all by myself." Every word was a shard of ice. "I don't for a minute believe you want to help. You just want to see my reaction."

Brian nodded. "That too, but—"

. "So you don't feel cheated, I'll give you my reaction *before* I see it. Because I *won't* see it with you." She offered him her I-know-how-your-mind-works glare.

"You know, you're not a whole lot of fun sometimes, babe."

She ignored him. "Okay, here it is. I'll open the door. I'll look inside. I'll cover my mouth to keep from screaming. I'll pick my way through the statues of naked cherubs, sunken marble tub, and fountains in the shapes of various erotic body parts. I'll sit on the john while trying to ignore the paintings of naked women in need of six months at Weight Watchers. Maybe I'll take a minute to peek at your magazine that tells me what men want and how they look when they get it. I'll flush, then fight my way back to the door past red velvet drapes and strategically placed hanging plants. When I get outside, I'll take a huge gulp of fresh Irish air to clear my nasal passages of the scent of sin." She smiled up at him. "There. You have the whole experience. See you in the wagon."

"You're a cruel woman, Ally O'Neill," he murmured as he watched her walk to the bathroom door and open it. When she'd closed the door behind her, he sauntered over and leaned against the wall. To listen.

Chapter Nine

"What the . . . ?" Ally scanned the room. White. Everything in the room was pure, shiny white.

Talk about unexpected. She paused for thought. She raised her voice. "I know you're listening, Byrne, and this is too weird." This *wasn't* Brian Byrne. Brian was color: intense, brilliant. Colors that soaked into you and played in your memory long after they were gone. She took a deep breath. When had she learned so much about him, and why did she care?

She focused on the only thing in the room that could possibly be a toilet and ignored the antiseptic quality of the rest of the place. This was not somewhere she would come for a long, sensual soak.

Ally walked over, sat down, and thought longingly about the bushes. She gazed at the phalanx of buttons beside her. Which one would flush, and which would change her into a spider? Taking a deep breath of courage, she pushed one.

A scene materialized on the walls, surrounding her. For a minute, Ally didn't realize what she was seeing. A strange-looking stadium with thousands of people. Something about those people . . . She blinked. They were all bald. Every single person in the stadium was bald and . . . She peered more closely. They had pictures painted on their heads. If she could only get a close-up she could see . . . Something else caught her attention. They were waving things. At first Ally thought it was the large numeral one that fans waved to indicate the hoped-for position of their team. But it didn't quite look like . . . Ohmigod, it was a—

Ally hit the button and the scene disappeared. Just in time. Probably the next scene would be the competition. She didn't want to see that. *Yes, you do.* Okay, so she did, but she wouldn't. She wouldn't even take a peek at Brian's workday. *Because it would bother you.* And that was the biggest shock of all.

Scanning the bathroom, she realized something else was missing. No toilet paper. Oh boy. First she'd find the flush button, then shout for Brian to get the roll they kept in the wagon. Katy could hand it in to her.

She heaved a sigh of defeat. No way would she push another button at random. Time to yell for help. "Where's the flush button, Byrne?"

"The one at the top." His shout sounded muffled.

Ally narrowed her gaze on the door. If he was laughing at her . . . She pushed the button and wondered why there wasn't a flushing sound. Her eyes widened. With a startled yelp, she leaped from the seat with enough forward momentum to carry her to the door. Pulling up her jeans, she tore open the door, then pushed past a laughing Brian.

Ally found her courage halfway to the wagon. She turned to face him. "You will build a new toilet, or I'll never go in there again."

He shrugged, but his eyes still glittered with laughter. "It's the future, sweetheart. In my time, we don't need water. We vaporize and sanitize everything. Air pulses combined with robotics do the rest. Humans don't have to do a thing anymore."

Ally realized her face must be neon red. "No one touches my bottom except me, Byrne. Remember that."

"Hmm." He still sounded way too amused.

"Why the white? After what you did to the wagon, I didn't expect white."

"Earth's gotten a lot warmer in 2502. White's cool. Everything is white." He stopped and leaned against the side of the wagon. "I like it here. The crisp air, the colors."

Ally could feel his gaze on her.

"It's special." His softly murmured comment incorporated her in its specialness.

Ally clasped her arms across her chest to dispel her shivery reaction to his words. He didn't mean anything by them. She smiled up at him. "Must be hard to be bad when you're surrounded by pure-and-chaste white."

He didn't smile back. "Earth is perfect. No war, no violence, not even games that might result in injury. There're regulations for everything. No smoking, no drinking. All discomforts are gone. In your time, scientists learned how to clone allergy-free cats. We don't even sneeze anymore." He smiled, but it didn't reach his eyes. "It's a different story on the outer planets. There it's every man for himself. Violence, hunger. Earth doesn't worry too much about them. Maybe in time . . ." He shrugged.

Ally tried to keep it light, afraid if she looked too deeply, she'd care too deeply. And she wasn't ready for caring on a large scale. "So everyone on Earth lives a saintly life?"

His smile hinted at dark, warm places. "I'm the only sin in town, babe."

Gimme a double scoop of sex with some hot sin on top. No, she had to modify her thinking. He'd help her with her writing, but he'd made it perfectly clear he wouldn't make love to her. The only heat would be between the pages.

Something about his determination bothered her. She was a competitive person. He teased her with his sensuality, but then said hands off. What would it take to make him forget about his almighty contract and go for the gold? Thought-provoking question. Might be worth investigating.

One thing she had to know before they went into the wagon: "I pushed the wrong button in there, and a scene flashed on the walls. I saw a stadium, and people were waving oversized . . ."

"Penises?" He frowned. "Oversized? What made you think they were oversized?"

She blinked.

He grinned.

Damn, she'd forgotten her question. She scrambled into the wagon before he could expand upon oversized penises.

Katy met her with hands on hips and nagging ready. "Took you long enough. I had to put the sandwich stuff away, and the soup's cold."

Ally looked at the Old One, who sat on a chair beside Katy. She wore the same expression as Katy, in a whiskery kind of way. "Don't tell me you're making the Old One into your clone."

Katy and the Old One exchanged meaningful glances. "Females of a certain age have a better understanding of things. It's all about experience." She walked toward the door, the Old One by her side. "Think I'll try out Brian's fancy new bathroom. The Old One can show me the ropes."

Ally didn't comment as she retrieved the ham and cheese from the fridge, then made herself a sandwich. Maybe she should warn Katy, but Katy loved surprises. Wouldn't want to spoil her first experience with a space-age toilet. She'd just started to heat up the soup when Brian entered the wagon. He looked fresh, and she surmised he'd used his bathroom to clean up.

"Your great-aunt just went into the bathroom. I told her to use the top button, but I have a feeling she'll be in there a while pushing them all." Sitting on the plush red velvet bench seat, he watched her work.

"How about a sandwich and some soup?" When he nodded, she made an extra sandwich, put it on a paper plate, and handed it to him.

His fingers slid over hers and remained there as he took the plate. She started to smile. Present and future connected by a ham sandwich. Was that deep, or what? Her smile faded as the heat of his hand seeped into her, made her consider the connection she'd feel if the rest of his body covered her.

"Thank you." His voice indicated a level of appreciation that seemed too intense for a mere sandwich.

"It was nothing." She felt like fidgeting under his intense stare.

"Sure it was." He looked away, and she felt a sense of release. "No one ever made me a ham-and-cheese sandwich before."

She smiled. "Probably because no one eats ham-and-cheese sandwiches in 2502."

He glanced back at her, but he didn't return her smile. "That, too. But I meant that people do things for me because I pay them to. We're not talking random acts of kindness here."

She sat down next to him, but didn't bite into

her sandwich as she thought about what he'd said. "You can't tell me there aren't thousands of women who'd do things for you free of charge if you gave them a chance." The thought made her frown.

Brian shook his head. "Women would always expect to be paid, either with my body or my wealth."

Now Ally was really looking at him. "For someone who's king of the universe, you don't have a high level of self-esteem."

He shrugged. "Just being realistic. Everyone wants something." His smile returned. "Except you. You had no ulterior motive with that sandwich."

Wouldn't count on it. She didn't want to dwell on that last thought. Time to get serious about research for Mavis's idea of the perfect night of single bliss. "Katy's gone for a little while. Maybe we should talk about the book."

"Right. The book." He took a bite of his sandwich and chewed while he thought. Beside him, Ally did the same. He noted the small gulping sound as she swallowed. Brian smiled. The old ham and cheese wasn't going down too easily. She was nervous. Good. Because he was working in virgin territory himself. He knew the two-minute drill, but that wasn't what Ally wanted. "So what we're looking for is the perfect night of sex."

She nodded. "This has to be *New York Times* spectacular. It has to be erotically perfect, but still something the reading public can believe I actually experienced."

"Hey, no pressure." This "experience" would obviously have to last more than two minutes. Well, hell. "You know there is no 'perfect' sexual experience."

Ally frowned. "Of course there is, and I'm going to write about it." She bit her lip in concentration as she stared at him. "If you don't know what the perfect sexual experience is, then who does?"

He shrugged. "I give great orgasms, but I don't spend any extended time on foreplay. Just guessing here, but I think your reading public will be looking for the complete package. And everyone has a different idea of what makes for perfect sex."

"Really?" She looked like the thought had never occurred to her.

Leaning over, Brian closed his lips on her earlobe, then gently nipped it.

Her sudden intake of breath encouraged further experimentation. He blew into her ear, and she jerked away.

He straightened and smiled at her. "You like the nipping but not the blowing. The blowing excites some women." He shrugged. "Different women find different things erotic."

She still looked uncertain. "What about men? Not in your time, but mine. Do they find different things erotic?"

"Grass growing is erotic to men in your time,

149

babe." Hey, he was excited sitting here eating a ham-and-cheese sandwich.

She tightened her lips and straightened her spine. Every tasty inch of her said she'd come to a decision. "Okay, I can deal with this. I'll have to put every possible erotic detail into this book so no one feels left out."

"You'll run out of consulting time, sweetheart. I have three weeks. You'll need a lifetime."

Ally widened her eyes. "I don't believe that. Bodies have a limited number of parts." Her gaze turned thoughtful. "I'll have to figure out a way to keep readers engaged so they'll finish the book. It can't read like a how-to manual. It'll have to have emotion. *Heart.*"

Brian didn't know about the heart part. He'd done just fine without all the emotional stuff. But then, what did he know about women in this time? He was a quick learner, though. It might be fun finding out. *From Ally.*

"It's not just about body parts." Did he say that? His whole adult life had been dedicated to the premise that it was *all* about body parts. During competition, nothing else mattered. So why did he think it would be different with Ally? And this *was* about Ally. When he discussed her book, he'd be picturing her, not a faceless reading public. "It's about what comes before. The preparation." What would come before? He'd never had to seduce a woman with fantasies, with any senses beyond touch. What would a woman in this time expect from him? He'd have to think about this.

A line of concentration formed between Ally's eyes. "You're right. We need preparation. Okay, so we have the usual foreplay, and there's always some generic sex talk. But we have to come up with something that goes beyond the same-old-same-old." Her gaze turned thoughtful. "Do *you* need any preparation?"

At the beginning of his career he'd needed nothing but the sight of a woman. Lately? He'd had to resort to fantasies. Interesting sidebar. He sure didn't need any fantasy with Ally.

Brian shook his head. "I'm a hot talent, babe. But believe me, the rest of the world needs preparation." He waited expectantly for her reaction.

"Hot talent? Try huge ego. I don't know what kind of women you have in your time, but women in 2002 are tougher. It takes more than two minutes to satisfy us." She almost vibrated with outrage.

Brian shifted his gaze to her breasts, waited hopefully for some outraged heaving. Too bad. No heaving, just vibrating. "Sure sounds like a challenge to me. Are you including yourself in the collective 'us'?"

Caution crept into her eyes. "No. Well, maybe." Her expression cleared. "Why am I arguing with you? This isn't about life in your time. It's about one fictitious night in the life of a woman from 2002. So use your imagination. What do you think would happen first? Run some ideas past me, then I'll choose one I like and enlarge on it."

Tough. Since he had no point of reference, he'd go with what would make sense in his time. "I'll leave the initial small talk to you. Small talk isn't a high-level skill with me." He closed his eyes, concentrating. With his eyes still closed, he could feel Ally's gaze moving over him: warm, *hungry*. And he allowed himself a moment of complete truthfulness.

He wanted to have sex with Ally O'Neill, but he wanted it to last a lot longer than two minutes. And for once in his life, he wanted to explore all his senses, steep himself in the full spectrum of sexual enjoyment. *Without a scoreboard in sight*.

Brian opened his eyes, and she shifted her gaze from him. He wouldn't do it, because nothing had really changed. He was still going home in a few weeks. But maybe he'd come back each year during the off-season. Something about this time felt more like home to him than 2502 did.

He still had kids depending on his support. But he had investments that would support all his kids for quite a few years.

What in the blood-of-Boren was he thinking about? Staying in the year 2002 and having sex with Ally O'Neill? Abandoning everything now that he was at the top of his career? Making an incredibly stupid mistake because he'd found a woman who attracted him more than just sexually?

He still had a contract. But the no-sex clause only specified the complete sex act. There were other avenues to fulfillment. Maybe that would be enough.

"You're awful quiet, Byrne. Is that good or bad?" She stood, then peered out the back window. "I think I see Katy coming." She glanced at her watch. "I didn't realize how late it was. It's almost dark out there." She returned her gaze to the window. "Strange. I thought I saw someone go into the keep. This is pretty late for tourists to be wandering around."

"Probably Jupe." He took a deep, cleansing breath. *Think straight.* Staying in this time with Ally O'Neill wasn't an option. And even though he wouldn't have sex with Ally, he could enjoy being with her, touching her, because he was the complete master of his sexual impulses. No woman could make him lose control. He felt better now.

"I like the idea of starting with a warm shower. Together. It relaxes muscles, loosens inhibitions. What do you think?" Just the thought loosened a lot of things in him. Namely his brains. And now that they were loose, they were doing a free fall to his groin, where they'd probably set up a command post.

"Okay, I can go with that." She still didn't turn from the window. "Um, maybe we could experiment. See if it really works. I have to make this book as honest as I can. Within limits." She finally turned to face him, and he silently saluted her for letting him see her flush.

Brian smiled and hoped it wasn't too predatory. "Thought we already had, sweetheart. Don't know about you, but the shower we shared at the bed-and-breakfast is still fresh in my mind."

Her flush deepened. "That was *not* relaxing."

Relaxing was way overrated.

"Besides, I still had my clothes on."

"You're right. Maybe we should explore the whole skin-to-skin thing." *Imagine.* Warm, smooth skin moving over his body from chest to groin. Hot water sluicing down his back. Ally reaching between their bodies to slide her fingers the length of his erection. What would it feel like to have a woman touching *him*, exploring *his* body?

He pulled his thoughts from his groin, which was now totally engaged in the conversation. "Maybe it's just me, but I could've sworn your original plan was for a hands-off consultation. Aren't you afraid this will degenerate into an unplanned sexual experience?"

She offered him a cool smile at odds with the heat in her gaze. "No. I have complete trust in your ability to control the situation. You're a sexual expert, remember."

Something was wrong here. Somewhere along the line she'd changed her game plan, and he wondered why. "Watch out for misplaced trust, babe."

She nodded. "So what would come next?"

"You might—"

Katy flung open the door and swept into the wagon. The Old One squeezed in beside her.

"Haven't had that much fun in a bathroom since Padraic locked me into the one at the hotel we stayed at for our honeymoon. Had his way with me in a tub full of bubbles. Almost drowned me, but we were young and the hormones were ragin'. Ragin' hormones make you do silly things." She peered at Ally. "Ever let your hormones jump any fences?"

"No." Ally turned away, but not before Brian caught a glimpse of her smile.

"Hmmph." Katy's expression said what she thought of people who had repressed hormones. She glanced at Brian. "Don't have to ask about your hormones. A little redirection would probably do them good."

"Redirection?" Brian glanced down at the Old One, and she looked back at him. Neither had a clue what Katy meant.

Katy didn't give them time to figure it out. "Saw that championship game you just won. How do you stay hard all that—"

"I'm sure Brian would love to explain everything for you, but I bet he's tired and wants to get some sleep. In fact, I bet he's leaving right now." Ally's pointed glare suggested that life as he knew it would end if he didn't leave.

For once he agreed with Ally. He scooped up the Old One and headed for the door.

"Wait." Katy grabbed his arm. "When I was getting ready to come in, I saw something moving up by the castle. Bet it's Black Liam. Maybe he appears earlier because of daylight saving time." She paused. "Do they have daylight saving time here? Anyway, I want to take a look. I'll walk you up to your place, and you can explain about what you do to those women to make them—"

"I'll go with you." Ally looked frantic. "And I think you should wear your headlight, whether Black Liam likes it or not."

Katy nodded, giving Ally a small victory.

Brian left the wagon first. He smiled into the darkness. Ally wasn't being too subtle about why she was coming along. But he didn't think anyone would have much luck in shutting Katy down. Her curiosity was like a light-absorbing black hole.

Brian watched as Katy climbed from the wagon and turned on her headlight. Ally climbed down behind her.

He knew his smile had turned wicked. Maybe he should satisfy Katy's curiosity and tell her all about the game.

Chapter Ten

"Brian thinks you probably saw Jupe, Katy." Ally trudged through the darkness beside Brian and decided she was conflicted. *Conflicted.* A nice precise word that meant she couldn't decide whether she was tagging along with Katy because she wanted to deflect conversation from Brian's work or because she wanted to learn every sordid detail. *Fine, so I want sordid details. Sue me.*

"Nope. He's in his tent over by those trees. The Old One wanted to take a listen to hear what she could hear, so I kept her company. Didn't hear much of interest except that Jupe figures he's smart enough to out-negotiate the Old One." She cast a sly glance down at her furry calico shadow.

The Old One's rumbling growl sounded suspiciously like a chuckle.

Katy grinned. "I know. We're two nosy old biddies." She turned her attention to Brian. "Now tell me about your game." She held up her hand to stall Ally's interruption. "I want to know."

Ally subsided. There was no stopping Katy. She could either stay and listen or go back to the wagon. Ally frowned into the darkness. She wanted to listen, didn't she? A few seconds ago she'd definitely decided she wanted to hear everything. So why the sudden doubts?

Brian stopped to stare up at the keep, then scanned the area beyond it. Ally knew he couldn't see far. It was as dark as only a moonless night could be, and the cool air had the feel of rain in it. Ally tried to control a shiver. It reminded her of her first night here. Only now instead of hunting for a dark and dangerous vampire, she hunted for answers to the riddle that was her very own dark and dangerous time traveler.

He began walking again. Ally didn't. She gazed down at her shoes. "You guys go on. I have something in my shoe. I'll catch up with you."

Ally's decision surprised her. She'd really thought she wanted to know everything about what Brian did. But a wiser part of her knew better.

"*Penile-ized?* No kidding?" Katy's voice drifted back to her.

Ally started walking again, keeping a space between Brian and herself so that she couldn't hear, couldn't picture *him* on the playing field. And that was the crux of the matter. As long as she could imagine faceless players, as long as she could keep the games impersonal, everything was okay. But her thoughts of Brian had gone beyond faceless and impersonal.

The wiser half of Ally O'Neill suggested this was not a good thing. Ally sighed. Her wiser half must be getting tired of her ignoring its advice where Brian Byrne was concerned.

Glancing up, Ally realized Brian and Katy had stopped to wait for her.

"A *feel-goal?* You're the *man*." Katy had found a new hero. "That's an excellent game." Katy turned to Ally. "Isn't that an excellent game?"

"Excellent." Rotten. Even though she hadn't heard any details, she hated it. She hated the thought of Brian on the field, doing things to all those women. She was glad she didn't live in his time. *Why are you so hot and bothered?*

Brian's lips tilted up in a knowing smile and his gaze said "coward." But Ally didn't care. For once she'd made the right decision.

Hot and bothered. She continued to hang back a little, thinking about that last thought.

But it was hard to do much deep thinking as Katy continued her endless stream of questions.

The clip-clop of hooves drawing near distracted Ally from Katy's questions. They all turned to watch Eamonn Clancy pull his donkey to a halt near the keep. The old man ignored them as he climbed down from his cart and walked slowly to the gaping hole that had once been the keep's entrance. He stood staring into

159

the blackness, but, as before, he didn't enter.

Ally didn't blame him. She'd never feared ghosts and ghoulies, but she was a lot braver out here than she'd be inside the keep on a dark night.

His passenger stepped out of the cart, lifted a suitcase and shopping bag to the ground, then strode happily over to them. "Sure and it's a fine evening to be hunting the wee fairies—"

Brian's irritated grunt said it all. "Lose the brogue, Cap. They know everything."

Cap heaved a sigh. "Good. I was getting tired of talking that way."

"Not as tired as everyone else was of hearing you." Brian didn't sound sympathetic.

"I probably need to reintroduce myself." He smiled at Katy. "I'm really Capricorn Wilson. I own the Testosterone Titans. Brian was the best player on my team for a lot of years." He cast Brian an accusing stare.

Katy nodded. "Got it. He was your star stud."

Cap chose to ignore that. "Guess I can get rid of this for a while." He pulled the red wig from his head.

"Bend your head." Katy stood on her toes and craned to get a look. "It's about time I saw one of these head paintings. Got a glance when I was in the john, but no close-ups. Well, look here. Is that your daughter?"

Cap nodded. "Oriona. She's ten years old." His chest expanded and his grin widened.

Ally smiled. Evidently, parental pride had survived everything time could throw at it.

"Heard in your time some people have a male member problem. How'd you have her if your Mr. Wizard doesn't work?" Katy looked suspicious. "Maybe yours still works."

Ally winced. "You're getting too personal, Katy."

Katy cast her a belligerent glance. "I'm old. When you're old you can ask questions like that. It's one of the perks of getting wrinkled and achy." She offered Cap her brightest smile. "I bet yours still works."

Cap studied Katy as if she were a particularly puzzling new life-form. "Let's keep it a mystery. But reproduction has come a long way. There's more than one way to produce a child."

"Yeah, but only one way is fun." Katy left them to join Eamonn Clancy.

"Why're you here, Cap?" Brian didn't sound like he had much patience left. "And why did you come with Eamonn?"

"I had a little accident with my rented car. Met a herd of sheep and thought they'd give me the right of way." His expression turned sour. "I thought wrong. Had to steer into one of those blasted rock walls. I walked to the nearest house and called the rental people. They'll have a new car out to me tomorrow."

Cap glanced at Ally, and she smiled at him. She should walk away and give them some privacy, but the O'Neill nosiness was terrible and compelling.

Cap turned his attention back to Brian. "I want to win that championship next year. I can't do it if you're playing for the Monarchs. So I'm going to do my best to convince you to stay here. I think this is your time period. You fit here." He sounded dead serious.

"And what will you do if I decide to go back?" Brian's voice was soft, danger disguised beneath a thin layer of civility.

Cap met his stare. "I'll try something else."

Ally watched the exchange with unblinking fascination, until a movement near Cap's feet caught her attention. Her eyes widened. "Uh-oh."

Her warning came too late. The Old One was squatting on Cap's shoe and calmly urinating. A Stealth Feline expressing her anger in time-honored fashion.

As everyone stood frozen, watching, she carefully scraped a small pile of dirt over the shoe. A tidy cat even in moments of great duress.

Cap hopped and cursed. "Just wait until the next time you want to trade for one of my players. You can take a flying leap into a Sindian mud sea before my people will talk to your people."

"Show's over, Boss." Brian scooped up the cat and strode to where Katy was still talking to Eamonn.

Ally would have followed him, but Cap put his hand on her arm to stop her. "Wait, I think you and I have some things to discuss." His glance was full of sly suggestion.

Curiosity held her in place. "I can't imagine what."

"You want him, and I want you to get him. We have a common goal, so it only makes sense we should work together." His voice was tight, intense.

Ally wondered why she had never seen the real man beneath his red wig and exaggerated brogue. She wouldn't underestimate him again. "Why would I want him?" What a big fat, stupid question.

Cap's smile held no humor. "Because I've never met a woman who didn't want him. It's not just the way he looks. It's something deeper." He shrugged. "Brian came from a hard background, and women see that hardness and respond to it. He's the best because he taps into women's primitive subconscious, the part that wants to mate with the dominant alpha male."

Ally swallowed hard. Was her attraction to Brian so simple? "How do you know so much about what women feel?"

"Lady, it's my business to know what women feel. And until I was stupid enough to let Brian get away, I'd never made a mistake. I'm going to fix that mistake."

She shivered. There was something scary about his determination.

Suddenly, he smiled at her, and once again he was the man she'd first met. "I brought my stuff with me, and I'm going to stay with Jupe and Nebula. This is where the action is."

Her gaze was doubtful. "I don't think they'll be happy about that."

He shrugged. "Doesn't matter. Jupe's an agent. Some of my players are his clients. He won't say anything to make me mad."

Ally could see Brian looking her way. "This has been fascinating but—"

"Here's some advice. Get Brian to open up about his childhood. Make him think you care about him as a person. Get beyond the sex stuff, and you'll have him." A sudden rustling made him turn. He stared into the darkness for a moment, then shifted his attention back to her. "Guess it's nothing. Oh, and I picked up something in town you might be able to use."

He pulled a small book from the pocket of his brown pants. "Bought this from a gypsy." He frowned. "At least she said she was a gypsy." He handed the book to Ally. "She said this was a book of ancient gypsy love potions. Aphrodisiacs have been around forever. Wouldn't hurt to try. I have all the ingredients you'll need."

Ally looked blankly at the small book. He was kidding. No one could be that desperate. She glanced up at his narrowed gaze. Maybe they could. Opening the book, she skimmed the first potion. "Hmm. Looks like the recipe for McDonald's secret sauce. Maybe you should hang on to this. I'm not into gourmet cooking anymore."

Pushing the book back at him, she walked quickly to join Brian before Cap could say anything else. But his innuendo followed her like an evil shadow. Was she attracted to Brian because she sensed his hard inner core, and it excited her? Was the hard inner core all the substance of the man? Would she look for softness and never find it? And did the substance of Brian Byrne matter in the grand scheme of things? He would only be here for a few more weeks, and in that time all she really wanted was his help with her book. *That's not all you want.*

Suspicious, Brian studied Ally's face, watched her bite her lower lip, felt his body respond to the temptation of her lip's promise. He shook his head to clear his thoughts of Ally and her lips. "What did Cap have to say to you?"

Ally blinked. "He was just telling me how he planned to move in with Jupe and Nebula." She smiled up at him. "They'll be so busy fighting with each other they might leave you alone."

"Don't count on it." He didn't believe that was all they'd talked about, but Brian wouldn't push her. He turned back to listen to what Eamonn was saying.

"It'll happen again this fine dark night. They'll drag her body from the great hall while her husband waits to carry her from this accursed place. But he'll die too soon, too soon." His old voice cracked and faded into silence.

The blackness of the night was a living, pulsing thing. Brian felt it. And as Ally edged closer, he put his arm across her shoulders and pulled her to his side.

"Will it ever stop, Eamonn?" Katy's voice was hushed.

The old man's nod spoke of endless weariness. "Aye. When the keep topples, never to rise again, then he'll take her home forever."

While they stood watching, he spoke softly to his donkey in Gaelic, then donkey and cart disappeared into the darkness.

No one spoke for a few moments. Finally, Katy broke the silence. "Well, wasn't that interesting? I bet there're a lot of bloody things that happened here. Next time Eamonn stops by I'll ask him. Bet I could find a lot of discontented spirits in this place."

Ally moved away from Brian to stand beside her great-aunt. "Why do we only hear about discontented spirits, Katy? Some laughter and cheeriness would sure brighten up this place."

Katy shrugged. "You'd be discontented too if you had to stick around this old ruin. Can't be much fun on a cold dark night. Guess the only ones who stay are the ones who died violent deaths and have to settle some issues before moving on."

Brian thought about that. "I suppose spirits keep on reliving traumatic events. The question is, why would they want to?"

"If it were me, I'd want to do it until I got it right, until it came out the way it should've come out in the first place." Ally's grin was wry. "Forget I just said that. I've never come close to seeing a ghost and probably never will. But I've got to hand it to your keep, Brian. If I were going to believe in spirits, I'd believe in them here."

Katy glanced around. "Looks like Cap's gone." She turned on her spelunkers headlight. "Let's get this show on the road. I'm going up those stone steps to the top and see if I can spot whatever it was I saw hanging around earlier." She frowned. "Too bad Cap made up that stuff about Black Liam. Sure would've liked to have seen a vampire. But maybe I can see a banshee since the O'Neills have one."

Katy paused to look at the Old One, who hadn't moved and was busily grooming her whiskers. "Coming with us, Boss?"

The Old One kept on grooming. "Scaredy-cat," Katy grumbled.

Brian smiled at Ally's sigh of resignation as she walked with Katy toward the stone steps spiraling up into darkness. He brought up the rear.

"The banshee only cries if an O'Neill is about to die, Katy."

"Hmm. Guess at my age I don't want to see her then. Maybe I'll spot . . . Tell me again what I could spot. You're the one who loves all that research stuff." Katy adjusted her headlight and started up the worn steps.

Ally stood at the bottom of the steps and watched Katy. "Okay, let's go with something not so well known as a pooka or leprechaun."

"Don't want to hear about that dullahan guy either." Katy paused at the curve of the stairs.

"How about the gancanagh? You'd like him.

167

He's sort of like a leprechaun, but he spends his time making love to shepherdesses and milkmaids." Ally peered into a large opening in the wall that had been a doorway at one time.

"Don't know about a milkmaid, but I could be a shepherdess. What do you think my chances are of meeting up with this gancanagh?" The pool of light from Katy's headlight bobbed across the stone walls with every word.

"Not too good." Ally sounded distracted as she gazed through the opening.

"Hmmph." Katy turned back to her climb. "Why don't you stay here and see if anything shows up. I'll go on up to the top, look around, then come back down. And no, I don't want you trailing after me. Any spirit that hears a mob clattering up the stairs isn't going to stick around."

"Okay, but be careful." Ally still seemed distracted as Brian joined her at the opening. "This might sound crazy, Brian, but something about this spot feels . . . strange."

Brian glanced through the doorway and tried to recall the pictures of what the keep would have looked like whole. "This would've been a doorway into the great hall." Now it opened into nothingness. All that wasn't stone had long ago disappeared. He looked up at the overcast night sky, clearly visible where the roof had once been. Below, everything was shrouded in darkness. *Shrouded.* Maybe that wasn't a great choice of words. "On the night they died, I wonder if they were sitting in there drinking and eating, a roaring fire in the fireplace, talking about ordinary things. Never suspecting that this night would be their last."

Ally shivered and moved closer to him as the wind picked up. It moaned and whistled through the cracks and crevices of the ancient building. Funny, there hadn't been any wind when Katy started up the steps.

Then he heard it. A distant booming that settled into a slow rhythm carried to him on the wind's currents.

"Drums? They sound like kettle drums." Her voice quavered.

Brian pulled her into his arms and wrapped her in whatever strength he could offer. He held his breath: waiting, listening. His heart echoed the hollow pounding of the drums as the sound of something being slowly dragged across a floor reached him.

"No. This is *not* happening. I can't believe they starred this place on the map. Tourist-friendly attraction. Hah! Tell the Irish Tourist Board to lose the star. Tell them those were my last words before I keeled over from fright." Ally's voice was a shaky whisper.

He felt a powerful surge of an emotion that caught him by surprise. Protectiveness? He hadn't needed to protect anyone during his whole adult life. Before that? He'd always taken care of himself, and everyone else could go to hell.

But something in Ally's brave attempt to joke

about her fear reached him. He understood fear, a silent predator that couldn't be fought because it couldn't be seen, any more than the drama being played out in the great hall could be seen.

The sound drew closer, and he ran shaking hands through her hair, making soothing sounds that had no meaning. He should grab her hand and run like hell. But where? Away from the keep? They couldn't leave Katy alone. Up? They'd be trapped with no escape. Besides, he felt incapable of movement, frozen against the stone wall by a force that seemed determined they witness the castle's ancient agony.

He took a deep, steadying breath. "We'll be okay, Ally. This isn't about us. This is about something that happened a long time ago."

"They're coming this way." She burrowed her head into his chest. "I never watch the scary parts of movies."

Coming this way. The door. They'd have to drag the body past Ally and him to reach the door.

No way out now. The wind shrieked and whipped in fierce swirls, coming from everywhere and nowhere, pulling at them with insistent fingers. A jagged streak of lightning lit the scene for a moment. What had once been the great hall remained eerily empty. Thunder rumbled, punctuating the warning of the distant drums, a warning that Cromwell was coming, a warning that had come too late.

As the bumping and scraping sounds grew closer, other noises intruded. Shuffling steps, heavy breathing. Brian pushed Ally against the wall, then placed himself between her body and whatever horror was approaching. He flattened himself against the wall as best he could without crushing the life from her. She wrapped her arms around his waist and held on.

They were with him now, moving past him on their torturous reliving of that terrible night. Their harsh breathing sounded in his ear, the unspeakable emotions they felt, blood-lust, terror, horror, filled *him*. He wanted to scream into the gale, rid himself of the stench of blood and death that seemed to cling to him. *And the cold.* Frigid air skittered down his spine, seeped into his blood, and chilled him from the inside out.

Just when he felt he couldn't stand another second, it ended. The wind died, the drums faded, and silence closed in.

He shut his eyes for a moment, feeling the pounding of Ally's heart slow, giving himself time to recover before he pushed himself away from the wall.

Drawing in a deep breath, he stepped back.

She dropped her arms to her sides and stared up at Brian. "I feel so sorry for them." Her voice was soft, raw emotion in each word.

That was absolutely the last thing he'd expected her to say. "Sorry?"

She nodded. "I don't know which they were, the good or bad guys, but to have to relive the horror over and over . . . That's the true meaning of hell." She offered him a shaky smile. "I'd end it for them if I could."

"Yeah, I know." He now knew more than she'd want him to know. He knew that Ally O'Neill had been the giver in her marriage. He knew that no matter how hard she denied it, she'd always be a giver, of her emotions, of her sympathy for others, even if those others lived centuries ago.

Brian smiled into the darkness. He wouldn't tell her what he knew.

"On that night, maybe there was a man and a woman like us, hiding in the darkness, watching the bodies being dragged out, wondering if they'd be next." She shook her head. "Okay, so I'm a writer. I like to deal in what-ifs." Her gaze grew distant. "What would they do, think, as they saw their world collapsing around them?"

Her words triggered his own imagination. What if there was no contract, no promise? What if he was free to do what he wished with Ally O'Neill? His thoughts were no longer with the lost spirits who'd touched them only moments ago. He could only think of what he wanted, *needed*.

"The man would've lain with her on the cold stones and covered her with his body. He would've pulled her gown down to her waist, then put his mouth on her breast, warming her flesh with his, feeling her nipple harden as he teased it with his tongue. He'd hear her groan as she arched her back, wanting more. Then he'd push up her gown, slide his hand along the inside of her thigh, feel her legs spread for him. When his fingers touched her, he'd find her already wet for him, open. He'd touch her there, and she'd buck beneath him. And as he slid his fingers in and out of her, he'd cover her mouth with his to smother her cries. At last, when he couldn't stand it anymore, when his arousal became painful, he'd move between her legs and thrust deeply, completely." He moved closer, bracing his hand against the stone wall, absorbing its coldness to remind himself that *this* was reality, not the fantasy he wove.

"Then what?" Ally's voice was a warm whisper, fanning his need.

"She'd wrap her long legs around him as he found his rhythm. With each thrust the wire holding them in time would stretch tighter and tighter until it snapped, freeing them from all the horror that surrounded them. At that moment, it wouldn't matter if heaven or hell came for them. They wouldn't be there." Surprised, he realized his breathing was hard and fast.

"*Why?* Why would he do that?" Ally's question was a harsh whisper.

His control restored, he gazed at her. And answered for himself. "Because there'd be no promise to keep him from her." He smiled. "Because it would be the right memory to hold in their minds."

Silence stretched between them, and Brian felt that something important needed to be said, but he wasn't sure what it was.

173

The sound of Katy descending the steps broke the tension.

"Can't believe I climbed all those steps to see nothing. Must've been a thousand of the damned things. Sure didn't build these places for senior citizens." Her words echoed off the stones, proclaiming her dissatisfaction ahead of her arrival.

Ally glanced at Brian. "I'm not going to say anything to Katy. She'd camp here every night if I told her what happened. It could be dangerous. She could fall down the steps or . . ." She looked away.

Brian nodded, aware of what Ally *hadn't* said. These hadn't been friendly spirits. They'd scared the hell out of him.

Katy huffed down the last few steps. "Can you believe it? A clear starry night, not a breath of air, not a ghost in sight. I can't write a book if nothing happens." She continued past them down the steps.

Ally smiled weakly and followed her great-aunt. Brian cast a last glance out the doorway to where the great hall area was now bathed in moonlight.

Could he travel back to the time of Cromwell? Would he be allowed to change history? He shook his head to clear it. It was a moot point. The white stags never went to a time where they might be injured. They were too valuable. If a stag was threatened or injured during a visit, they never traveled to that time again.

He followed Ally and Katy out of the castle.

Katy strode over to where the Old One waited patiently for them.

Brian walked to Ally, who stood in the moonlit shadow of the keep's wall.

Ally sighed. "She's bending the Old One's ear. Telling her that she didn't miss anything. Why were we the ones, Brian? Katy's the one who wanted it to happen."

He shrugged. "Who knows? Eamonn would probably say that one of us has the power to end it. I don't believe that."

The night was suddenly split by a feline cry. It wasn't a cry of anger, but of terror. *And warning*.

Startled, Brian glanced at the Old One, then followed her gaze to the top of the keep.

And froze.

Chapter Eleven

A huge chunk of stone from the top of the keep was hurtling toward them. Instinct took over as Brian shoved Ally away from the wall, then as she fell, clasped her to his body and rolled away from the point of impact. The thud of the stone burying itself in the damp earth where they had stood a moment before gave his heart a mega-shot of adrenaline.

Ally lay beneath him, her breaths coming in quick gasps, her eyes wide with shock. "Tell me this castle isn't cursed."

Katy rushed over with the Old One beside her. Brian rolled off Ally, but remained flat on his back in the damp grass. Ally sat up and brushed grass from her jeans with shaking fingers.

"How did that happen?" Katy put her hands on her hips and stared up at the keep. "I was just up there, and I didn't see anything loose. How could that big chunk of wall just fall like that?"

"No sign of the person you thought you saw earlier?" Brian narrowed his gaze on the Old One, who determinedly crawled onto his stomach, then plunked her furry behind on his groin. She glared around her, daring anyone to damage "The Franchise." "Get off me, Boss. It's my head you need to protect. Understand?"

The Old One's expression made it perfectly clear she knew exactly what she should protect.

Katy shook her head. "Didn't see a soul up there. Of course there were lots of shadowy corners I didn't look into. Figured a spirit wouldn't be hiding in a corner. It would be up-front about wanting to scare the crap out of me."

Brian rose to his feet and helped Ally up. "Did anyone see where Cap went?" He didn't want to acknowledge the tiny suspicion lurking in his mind. But two accidents so close together made him uneasy. He took a deep breath. Maybe his imagination was working overtime. Who could blame it? This whole night had been bizarre. He should go up and check, but if there had been someone, he'd had plenty of time to escape down the steps on the other side of the keep. Besides, Brian didn't want to leave Ally and Katy alone.

Ally rubbed her eyes. "Don't go there, Brian. They were just accidents. We're tired. Everything will look different in the morning."

Absently, Brian reached out and massaged the back of her neck, felt her muscles relax, and felt rather than heard her sigh of enjoyment.

"That feels great." She dropped her head to give him more access.

No kidding. Even after tonight's events, his body was still focused on its own priorities. Neither ancient spirits, nor lethal accidents, nor contractual obligations could stay his sexual interest from its appointed target. He sighed a resigned sigh. It was going to be a long few weeks. "We all need to get some sleep. I'll walk you back to your wagon."

Ally nodded. "Ready for bed, Katy?"

Katy took a last long look at the keep. "Can't help thinking there's a secret here. I love solving mysteries, but I don't think I'll go poking around at night by myself."

Brain thought of the ancient tragedy played out in the great hall tonight. *More of a secret than you know, Katy.* He walked back to the wagon in silence and watched the women climb inside. Then he headed back to his shelter with the Old One at his heels.

"Look, Boss, I don't think all this togetherness is good for anyone. I appreciate that you want to protect your investment, and I'm really grateful for your warning about that falling stone, but I can take care of myself." He stepped into his shelter. The Old One settled down by the entrance. She obviously didn't believe him. His thoughts drifted to Ally. The smooth slide of her hair through his fingers, the warmth of her body pressed to his. He recalled the anticipation of his erection hard between her thighs. He took a deep breath. Maybe the Boss wasn't keeping danger out, but keeping her prize player in.

Ally opened her eyes to a bright clear morning. She pushed aside the hot-water bottle she'd tucked in beside her last night for warmth. She also pushed aside her thoughts of how much better a hot-blooded man beside her would be. Glancing out the wagon window, she dispelled the shadows from the night before. When the sun shone on Ireland, no sky could be bluer, no grass could be greener. She couldn't wait to get outside to smell the fresh air.

A banging on the wagon door interrupted her communion with nature. Katy paused in her morning ritual of making a bowl of instant oatmeal to open the door. Cap stepped in. He held a covered paper plate.

Ally climbed from the bed to see what he'd brought. She wasn't worried that she hadn't dressed yet. She didn't think he'd be driven to lust by her tangled hair and flannel jammies with the feet in them.

Cap glanced around. "This is really unusual. Very colorful." He bent closer to study a painting. "Very explicit."

Katy lifted the foil covering the plate. "Now this was really nice of you, Cap. Haven't had any hot cinnamon rolls in a while. Look what Cap brought us, Ally."

Hot cinnamon rolls. Every bit of misplaced lust

she felt for Brian riveted its attention on the rolls. If she couldn't have a hot man, hot rolls would do for the moment.

Taking a roll, she bit into it and almost groaned with pleasure. Definitely orgasmic. "These are wonderful. Where'd you get the recipe?"

Only then did she glance into his eyes. Their eager glitter woke her sleep-fogged brain. The last bit of roll slid down her throat with a loud gulp. She glared at him. "You didn't."

He nodded happily. "My sainted mother's Unleashed Passion cinnamon rolls. Page sixteen."

Katy licked her fingers. "Strange name for cinnamon rolls, but these are a lot tastier than my oatmeal. You'll have to give me that recipe." She headed for the door. "I'll get the horse some grain and water. Then I'm going to visit Jupe and Nebula. Bet they have some great stories about those sex games."

Ally hardly noticed when Katy left. She narrowed her gaze on Cap. "There'd better not be any eye-of-newt stuff in these."

Cap frowned. "What's a newt?" His expression turned calculating. "Never mind. So, do you feel any different?"

"No. And I don't intend to feel any different. Give it up, Cap." She almost pushed him out the door.

Alone at last, she closed her eyes and looked within herself. Nope. She felt like her ordinary before-coffee sluggish self.

Ally cleaned up at the small sink, did the minimal-makeup thing so she wouldn't scare all the fairies out of Ireland, then brushed her hair. She could have done a lot better job in the bathroom Brian had built, but she only used it when she had to. It still felt too . . . white for her.

Changing into her jeans and a sweatshirt, she poured herself a cup of coffee and went outside.

Ally stood beside the wagon, savoring the hot coffee and crisp sea air. She gave Katy a hard time about the castle, but there was something magical about this place.

She glanced toward the cliff and realized that the "something magical" was standing several yards from the edge staring out at the sea. His jeans showcased his long muscular legs and tight buns, and he had his hands jammed into the pockets of a short windbreaker. His long hair blew away from his shoulders. She wanted to bury her fingers in that hair and . . .

Hmm. Okay, so what she wanted was a normal, healthy female response. Nothing special about what she wanted to do. And it certainly had nothing to do with Cap's cinnamon rolls. But she should really check her response out to make sure it wasn't even the tiniest bit abnormal. No way did she want Cap to be able to claim her response was induced by his love potion.

Feeling supremely self-righteous, she strode over to join Brian. Glancing over the cliff edge, she felt the cinnamon roll churning in her stomach. "That's a long way down."

He turned to smile at her, and Ally drew a deep breath at the power of that smile. Its wicked slant spanned centuries, suggested dark secrets in hot places that needed no words, made her want to trace its shape, taste its sweetness, then wipe it from his face and replace his grin with serious desire.

Nope, Cap's cinnamon roll wasn't affecting her at all.

Brian turned toward the castle. "It doesn't look so threatening in the bright light of day."

You look threatening in any light. He was a threat to her promise to herself. The one that said she'd never again be the one to do things for a man. She wanted to do any number of things for Brian Byrne.

A threat to her newfound strength and self-discipline. She'd sworn the only contact she'd have with men would be on a need-to-have basis. She'd enjoy a physical relationship, but she wouldn't care about any man's life, his past, his future. Oh, she wanted the physical with Brian, but she also wanted, no *needed*, to crawl inside his heart, his head, and learn everything there was to know about him. There, she'd admitted it.

You're a failure, Ally O'Neill. The first man who'd strode into her life since her divorce had made her forget all the vows wrenched from her heart during the endless tear-filled nights after Dave left her.

"Looks like Cap's new car is here." Brian nodded toward the road. "Let's take a look." His expression turned thoughtful. "I'd like to know what his first one looked like and if the sheep story is true."

Something about Brian's suspicions troubled Ally. "You can't think Cap would really try to hurt us. The bottom line is that you play a team sport. We're talking entertainment here, not mob hits."

His expression told her he wasn't quite sure what "mob hits" meant, but he got the general idea. "The game is everything to Cap. He might not show it, but he never got over how the Old One managed to lure me away from the Titans. And he never forgave me for taking her offer."

His suspicion was an uncomfortable facet of Brian's personality. "You really don't trust anyone, do you?"

He shrugged. "I trust myself. And I trust my instincts. That's all I had to trust until I was sixteen. And I survived." He started walking toward where the car was parked. "I guess I don't really think Cap is behind what's happened, but I never close the door on possibilities."

Possibilities. The word conjured other things for Ally that had nothing to do with Capricorn Wilson. "We need to talk about the book today. I can't keep putting it off."

Brian nodded but didn't answer as they reached the car. Jupe, Nebula, Katy, and the Old One had gathered to listen to Cap. Ally only half-listened to what he was saying. She was busy trying to figure out how she could get some uninterrupted time with Brian to discuss the book.

"Thanks for bringing the car out so early, Mr. Doyle." Cap was all jovial goodwill as he turned to his audience. "I'll have to drive Doyle back to town. I wouldn't mind if someone wanted to go with me. We could stay a few hours and do some shopping." Cap's pointed glance at Ally said he was doing his best to make sure she had some time alone with Brian so the effects of his gypsy potion could play out.

Doyle smiled at everyone. "I'll be wishing ye a fine day then." He climbed into the rental car, slammed the door, rolled up all the windows, then cast Nebula a fearful glance.

Ally watched the by-play. Jupe glanced at the Old One, then nodded. "Guess I'll tag along."

She knew the Old One would stay here to make sure no contract breaching took place.

Katy nodded eagerly. "Sign me up. Shopping's the second best thing in the world." She frowned. "I used to know what the first thing was, but it's been so many years since Padraic passed on that I can't remember."

Great. More souvenirs. After the terrible and very real haunting of last night, Katy's plastic shamrocks and leprechauns seemed an insult to the memory of Ireland. But then, Katy didn't know about last night.

Ally glanced at Nebula. Even at this early hour, she looked focused, a woman warrior planning the day's battles.

"I will stay here. I must commune with my inner self."

Ally figured that Nebula didn't think there was anyone else worth communing with.

"Afterward, I will look at this ruin so I may tell everyone I saw something meaningful in this time." She frowned. "Although I cannot see what interest a poorly built structure holds. I would have built it to last longer than a few puny centuries."

Nebula had a certain fondness for the word "puny."

She pinned Brian with her gaze. "Then I will work with you for several hours so that you may maintain your thrust power and lower-body strength."

Katy couldn't let that go. "My Padraic could've used some of that thrust power. Didn't know there was anything you could do about it. I'd like to see how you get some of that. Maybe I could assist a nice granddaddy who'd like to be hot, but he's not." She glanced at Ally and thought better of what she'd said. "Guess Brian wouldn't want anyone standing around and staring, so I'll go shopping." Her expression turned thoughtful. "Problem is, I'm still young and hot to trot inside. But all the men I know are old farts inside and out. It's tough on someone who still has womanly needs."

Ally's inner self was aging rapidly. And she'd never admit it out loud, but she'd like to see Brian's workout, too. "You'll probably enjoy the shopping more." Ha! "Besides, watching something like that would destroy the mystery of the sensual experience."

Everyone stared at her like she'd gone crazy. They were right. That line sounded like something straight out of her Perfect Wife books.

Brian smiled. "No one will ever accuse Nebula of fostering sensual experiences, but it sounds intriguing to me."

Ally cast Brian a grateful glance. *Thank you for saving me from foot-in-mouth disease.*

Nebula looked unconcerned. "Sex is an enjoyable bodily reaction, nothing more."

Katy grinned. "What a woman."

Nebula looked offended. "I am more than a woman. I have told you this before."

"Sorry. I forgot." Katy climbed into Cap's car. "Let's get this show on the road."

Cap and Jupe climbed in after her.

Ally watched silently as the car bumped down the rocky path onto the paved road. Nebula had clarified something for her. Ally would die before she'd write a book where sex became a diverting but meaningless act. She had felt like squirming with distaste at Nebula's words. Which reminded her . . . the book.

Nebula and the Old One wandered away as Ally turned to Brian. "I need to get some solid ideas for this book."

He nodded. "Let's go into the wagon."

They climbed into the wagon, and Ally watched as Brian shut the door and locked it. He quickly pulled the scarlet-sin velvet curtains across both windows.

"That should keep out any unwanted visitors." He sat on the bed and patted the space beside him. "This is more comfortable than the bench seat."

Something about the closed-in feel of the wagon made Ally edgy. "Nebula could just rip the door off its hinges, you know."

Brian nodded. "She won't, though, because she works for the Boss, and the Boss is a little more circumspect." He smiled, remembering the Boss's last two confrontations with Cap. "Most of the time, anyway."

Ally retrieved a pad of paper and a pen, then sat down beside him. She raked her fingers through her hair. "Where do we start?"

He thought about that. Brian had always been a realist. He wouldn't pretend to have expertise that wasn't his. "Your book will have to deal with foreplay. I don't do foreplay." He smiled and suspected his hunger showed through. "But I can fantasize with the best of them."

Ally glanced down and fiddled with her pen. "I wrote a book, *The Perfect Wife in Bed*, while I was still married to Dave. It was pretty tame and dealt with sex in the context of a loving relationship. The relationship was the main focus." She looked up. "This book has to be different. I want the emphasis to be on the sensual enjoyment, the complete pleasure sex can bring. But I can't divorce it completely from what I am. On some level I have to care about the imagined man in my book."

Imagined. Brian knew his gaze was mocking. "Don't play games, sweetheart. We both know I'll be the man in your book. And when I'm fantasizing, I'll sure as hell be picturing you."

He watched her cheeks turn pink.

"Fine. Now that the gloves are off, I'd like to suggest something else. I'd like to actually try the foreplay stuff, to get a clear focus on my feelings. I can do a lot better job with the emotions in my book if I've really experienced them."

"You must have a lot of faith in my self-control, babe." He hoped it wasn't misplaced.

She cocked her head to study him. "From what I've heard, your control is legendary. But one thing puzzles me. I'm playing devil's advocate here, but what would be so terrible about breaking that one clause in your contract? No real harm would be done, and I don't think the Old One would throw you off her team. You're too valuable. In fact, she wouldn't have any way of knowing if you broke the clause unless you told her."

"The contract is a promise. I never break promises." *Leave it alone.* Brian knew he shouldn't say anything else, but something drove him on. "My mother left me in a spaceport when I was a little kid. The last thing she said to me was that she'd be right back. She broke her promise. I lived on the streets until I was sixteen. I lied, stole, and did things you don't need to know, but

I never broke a promise." *Except for that one time. And I've paid for it. God, how I've paid for it.* He felt a moment of despair. How could she understand where he was coming from? Now she'd ask a lot of questions he didn't want to answer.

She glanced down at her pen again, hiding her expression. "Is there anything that would make you break a promise?"

"It would have to be something more important than anything else that's ever happened in my life." And nothing had ever been more important than what happened in that spaceport so many years ago. *Except for his one broken promise.*

Ally nodded, but she didn't ask another question. When she raised her head he saw tears glittering in her eyes.

"Hell." His comment was succinct and expressed his feelings exactly.

Her smile was a little watery. "Okay. Blinking madly so I won't embarrass you any more than I have already." Her smile faded. "Look, if you think acting out the foreplay will threaten your control, we don't have to do it."

Brian's face relaxed into a smile. He had enough male ego to reject her doubts about his self-control. "My control is in good shape, babe." And he'd prove it even if it killed him. "Maybe we could start with a sensual massage."

Ally nodded. "Sounds good, but I want it within the context of a sexual fantasy." She bit her lip as she thought. Then her expression brightened. "A harem. That's it. Harems have sensual connotations."

Brian lowered his lids on his mental picture. He smiled. "You're sure you really want to act it out?" He didn't want to think about his disappointment if she said no. He'd never given a massage, but anything that got his hands on Ally's bare body had to be good. He stopped smiling. Painful, but good.

"Yes. This is something I need to do. I'll write down my impressions as soon as we're finished." She glanced around the wagon. "I guess the bed's the only place with enough room. We—"

She was interrupted by wild scratching on the door accompanied by feline yowls that began as guttural expressions of outrage and climbed the scale to screams that threatened eardrum damage.

It was now Brian's turn to drag his fingers through his hair. "She won't give up. I'll have to talk to her."

"Sure." Ally glanced at him, then let her gaze skitter away.

No wonder Ally looked uncertain. He was steamed, and he didn't bother hiding it. Striding to the door, he flung it open.

"We need to talk." Without breaking stride, he scooped the angry calico fur ball into his arms and leaped to the ground. Brian stopped when he got far enough away from the wagon so Ally wouldn't have to listen to a grown man yelling at a cat. He plunked Her Bossiness onto a rock wall, then sat beside her so they could communicate eye to eye. "When Jupe comes back, I'm having him add something to that incentive clause he's negotiating."

The Old One's gaze turned cautious.

What the hell had he said? He exhaled sharply. Fine. Time for complete honesty. He wanted to have sex with Ally O'Neill. And the only way his personal code of honor would allow it was if he changed the no-sex clause in his contract. *What about your other reasons for not having sex while you're here?* Brian pushed the thought aside. He wanted Ally enough to ignore anything that would stop him. And that was scary because he'd never wanted a woman so badly.

"Here's the deal, Boss. I'm taking the no-sex clause from my contract and putting it into the incentive deal. If I have sex outside the game, then you don't have to pay me any bonuses. It's a win-win situation for you."

The Old One blinked her big yellow eyes at him. He could almost read her mind. She liked the idea of not having to pay him, but still feared that sex with someone from this time could lead to him wanting to stay here.

"Don't worry. I give you my word I'll be back with the Monarchs next season. I don't belong here." Then why did he feel so at ease, so alive in this time?

But he really wasn't considering staying here. He had too much going on in 2502. *Like what?* His kids. The wealth he channeled into supporting his kids was important, but he liked touching their lives in other ways. A placement in a loving home, a start in a good career . . .

Why was he even having these thoughts? He just wanted to have sex with Ally, get her out of his system, then move on. "Accept this, Boss. It's the way things are going to be."

She turned her head to study a bird that showed really bad judgment in landing on the rock wall not far from her. Brian knew she wasn't thinking about the bird, but his ultimatum. He didn't underestimate the Old One for a second. She'd accept his terms because she wanted to hang on to him, but that wouldn't stop her from trying to make sure he didn't stay here. He'd leave, all right, only not before he had sex with Ally.

But that wouldn't happen today. First, he wanted to work through her foreplay fantasies. Slowly. Savoring all the senses, the things he'd never allowed himself to enjoy before. Right now he felt freer than he had in years. But if he wanted to move slowly, he would need to do something physically draining. If he went back to the wagon now, he might rush Ally into something she wasn't ready for.

Glancing toward the castle, he spotted Nebula seated lotus fashion doing her communing. She'd just have to finish later because he was ready for his workout.

Ally watched Brian walk toward the keep. Why

hadn't he come back to the wagon? What had he said to the Old One?

The Old One turned her head to study Ally, then leaped from the wall and padded over to look up at her. The cat turned toward the space-age bathroom, then glanced over her shoulder. When Ally only blinked, she walked a few feet then stared back again.

"Okay, you want me to follow you. I get that. But why?"

The Old One wasn't answering questions.

Curious, Ally followed her into the bathroom. Ally used the bathroom when necessary, but she'd controlled any urge to explore. She felt like a coward, but she didn't want to face any more evidence of Brian's life in 2502.

The Old One led her to a corner where there was something that looked like a waterbed enclosed in glass. Even as Ally watched, she could see the surface of the bed undulate. She forced her gaze away . . . and saw the sign. Reality experience: Sex Super Bowl.

Drawing a startled breath, Ally glanced at the Old One. The cat's yellow eyes gleamed with a challenge Ally knew she didn't want to accept. Where had this come from? It hadn't been here the last time she'd visited. She couldn't have missed this.

Jupe? Of course. He had a Constructor and could modify this building if he chose. But why?

The Old One fixed her with one last hard stare, then padded from the room. The door swung shut behind her.

Leaving Ally alone with her decision.

Chapter Twelve

To wimp out or not to wimp out? This was Ally's chance to glimpse the future. If it hadn't involved Brian, she wouldn't hesitate.

Ally took a deep breath. She should see this. If it turned her off Brian, so be it. Wouldn't that be better in the long run? She could get his help with her book and still maintain her emotional distance. She didn't want any regrets when he returned to his time.

How real would it be? Could she handle it? *Give me a break, I'll still be wearing clothes.* Anyway, how long could it last? Two minutes? Ally smiled grimly. No matter what Brian did to the women of his time in two minutes, it wouldn't affect her. Women in 2002 expected a little more.

Opening the door, she stepped in before she could think of more reasons to run the other way.

The quiet click of the door behind her seemed ominous.

Get real. She'd been to an IMAX theater. This would feel like that.

Gingerly, she lowered herself onto the bed, then frowned. She didn't feel physical movement in the bed, but it was almost as if there were waves of energy. . . . She glanced around. Where the heck were the buttons to . . .

Ally's eyes widened and her breath caught as everything around her changed. The bed still remained, but now it rested in the center of a playing field with many similar beds. Screaming people packed the stadium, and along the sidelines male cheerleaders wearing what looked like cellophane briefs in their team's color urged on the fans. Sunlight poured through a clear domed roof. It bathed her body, touching her breasts, stomach, and thighs with warmth.

With a sigh of enjoyment she spread her legs to let the warmth touch her everywhere. Her nakedness didn't surprise her, and she felt no embarrassment. Only anticipation.

Her gaze drifted over the field. She felt satisfaction that today she'd be pleasured by the best. For a few brief moments Brian Byrne would cover her. Her orgasm would be intense, more powerful than anything she'd ever experienced, even though she came from an outer planet where men were still sexually alive. She never doubted her expectations would be met.

The crowd hushed, then broke into thunderous applause as Brian strode toward her from the tunnel. The other players on the field seemed invisible when Brian was in the competition.

Out of her peripheral vision she could see the other players pouncing on their women, arms and legs tangling in a frantic groping they hoped would end with a climax.

But then she thought no more of the other players. Brian stood beside her bed, his powerful body thrown into shadow as he blocked out the sun. His muscular torso glistened with a damp sheen, drew her gaze to his legendary sexual assets, his tools of the game. His erection was as impressive as the man, and as she stared he ran his finger along its length, touched the head with its beaded moisture.

"Look what you do to me, woman." His voice was soft, a male's admission that she had the strength to command his sexual reaction.

She felt powerful, primitive. The heated scent of a predatory male stirred her own hunter's instinct.

With a lithe, unhurried movement, he knelt on the bed and straddled her hips. Then he just looked at her. "Feed me with your passion. Take my body in payment." His order was a harsh whisper.

She lifted her hips convulsively, her unexpected surge of emotion shaking her. She was dominator and dominated, every woman who would ever know these feelings.

Leaning forward, he touched her lips with his

tongue, traced their outline. She opened her lips to him, and he took her mouth with a hunger born of man's darkest need to plunder, to take all that a woman could give. She understood the need, welcomed it.

Too soon he lifted his mouth from hers, but before she could moan her disappointment, he lowered his head to her breasts and touched the tip of each nipple with his tongue.

She held her breath, waiting. But instead of drawing her nipple into his mouth, he shifted his hips, then touched each nipple with his erection. Caught in his erotic web, she couldn't tear her gaze from her nipple bathed in the proof of how much he wanted *her*.

Only when he put his finger beneath her chin did she lift her gaze to his.

"Look into my eyes, woman. Know that whatever happens for the rest of our lives, this time was ours. There can never be another woman to fill this exact moment in my life. It will always be yours."

Sitting back on his heels, he put his hand between her legs, touched the part of her that seemed to be the center of every sensation she'd ever feel. And in her last moment of coherent thought, she wondered how he'd known how much she needed to be the "only one," if only for this short time.

He wasn't a gentle lover as he moved between her thighs and spread her legs farther apart. Lifting her to meet his thrust, he plunged deeply, burying himself in her.

This was how she wanted it. Hard, with each powerful thrust filling her body as well as something far more elemental. Each new plunge renewed her womanhood.

As she clenched her muscles, tightening her flesh around his, her gaze followed the path of a single drop of moisture that slid down his neck and chest, then clung for a moment to his right nipple. She wanted to touch his nipple with her tongue as he'd touched hers, but it was against the rules.

How many other women had suffered this way, denied themselves the joy of sliding their fingers over his warm, slick flesh? She gritted her teeth. She wouldn't think of other women. This was *her* time.

The drop glided lower, across his hard stomach, down to his groin. Gazing at their joining dragged a moan of pleasure from her.

"Yes, I like the way you watch me moving inside of you." The grate of his voice was pure animal enjoyment. "It excites me."

Her body tightened in response, the hot heaviness building, expanding. She wrapped her legs around him—the only motion she was allowed—and met each of his thrusts with her own in an attempt to drive him deeper, force him to touch more of her.

Suddenly, the spasms started, pushing her toward an explosion of pleasure she frantically tried to force back. No, it was too soon.

She stared into his eyes, pleading with him to make it last longer. But beneath lowered lashes, his green eyes glittered with heated focus. Despairing, she gave herself over to an orgasm that lifted and battered her with its intensity, wrenched wild sobs from her, then . . .

Slowly, everything faded. The bed rested once again in its glass enclosure, and Ally rested once again in her own body. She knew as certainly as tears coursed down her cheeks, she had been someone else. Felt what that other woman had felt, experienced what she'd experienced.

By Ally O'Neill's standard of sexual behavior, she ought to have been embarrassed by her nakedness, the crowd, her uninhibited reaction, *Brian.* Ally closed her eyes. *That wasn't me.* But no matter how she denied it, honesty forced her to admit it *had* been her.

She opened her eyes and stared sightlessly at the closed door. The scariest part? It had been the most spectacular sexual experience of her life. After this, what could compare?

She'd learned something important, though. Brian Byrne would not be a man to love. Shaped by his childhood, he was a hard man. During the game, she'd looked into the eyes of a sensual animal and seen no softness, no caring about her as a woman beyond his calculated words to make her more open to him. His game plan. He was totally focused on his drive to mate with her and drag an almighty orgasm from her body.

Rats. Now why was she crying again? None of it mattered. She was just thankful she didn't live in a time when machines manipulated minds and when men manipulated women's bodies in the name of the game.

Something else bothered her. Brian's speech pattern had been different during the game, more formal, *sexier*. It was almost a distancing of himself from what he was like off the field. Ally sighed. She was grasping at straws. During the game, he was an actor, performing in a way that would draw women to him. His speech was part of his performance.

With eyes still blurred by tears, she stared through the glass enclosure. Had anyone noticed she was missing? Would they come trooping in here . . . ? Her gaze swept past a digital readout flashing on the clear wall behind her. She blinked, stared at the readout, and blinked again.

Reality experience time lapse: 2 minutes, 30 seconds.

That couldn't be right. Something so intense had to have taken hours, days. Standing, she glanced once more at the flashing message. Nope, it hadn't changed. Her only consolation? It had taken His Sexiness more than two minutes with her.

Gathering her dignity, she walked from the building. The Old One waited outside the door for her.

Ally met the cat's gaze. "Fine. Mission accomplished. What happened in there was enough of a turnoff to keep me from getting physical with your MVP."

For a moment, Ally could have sworn that regret flickered in the Old One's eyes. Nah. She was reading an emotion into a being who probably reserved all regret for her occasional poor business decisions.

Ally glanced at the wagon. She didn't want to go there yet, didn't want to picture what might have happened on that bed during the course of their sensual massage, didn't want to imagine Brian using his hands to manipulate her. Most of all, she didn't want to turn over and see the hard, calculating gleam in his eyes, her own eyes heavy-lidded with desire reflected in the ceiling mirror. She didn't ever again want to be *stupid* for a man.

Her decision made, Ally climbed the hill to the keep. She didn't feel threatened by this place during the day. She stared at the top, where the stone had somehow become dislodged. Maybe she could work off some of her disquiet by walking up there. Not giving herself time to argue the pros and cons of climbing all those steps, she started up.

By the time she stepped out at the top, she was huffing and puffing. Brian wasn't the only one who needed to work on lower-body strength.

Drawing a deep breath of sea air, she gazed past the opposite side of the keep to the Atlantic, then turned to glance across rolling hills of patchwork green fields framed by rock walls.

Lord, but it was beautiful. Worth the sore leg muscles she'd have tomorrow. Would she be sore from her *other* experience? No, she wouldn't ruin this great view on thoughts she should have left at the bottom of the steps.

Sighing, she stepped back from the edge of the wall. Wonderful or not, she didn't want to take a shortcut to the bottom.

"Wow, this is great!"

Startled, Ally turned to see who had walked up behind her, then relaxed when she recognized the girl she'd met in Liscannor. Claudia?

Ally smiled. "Incredible." She took a last look at the view before turning her full attention on Claudia. "So how're you enjoying your sightseeing?"

Claudia's red hair whipped in the wind, and her eyes gleamed with excitement. "Oh, I love old buildings. They're sort of a passion of mine." She moved up beside Ally, blocking Ally's view of the steps.

Ally backed a little closer to the edge of the wall to make room for Claudia. "You like visiting them?" Ally could hear footsteps echoing up the stone keep. She must have been really involved in the view not to have heard Claudia coming.

Claudia grinned at her. "No, I like destroying them. I'm a demolitions expert."

"Oh." What did you say to that? "I'm impressed. Not an ordinary job."

Claudia moved a little closer to get a better view, and Ally moved back a little more.

"But I'd never destroy something like this." Claudia turned her head, probably hearing the steps approaching too. She frowned. "I only destroy things that aren't needed anymore, things that're in the way."

The conversation came to a stop as Brian appeared in the opening. Claudia smiled at him, then turned and started back down the steps. "Well, it's been nice seeing you again. I'll be hanging around the area for a few more weeks, so maybe we'll meet." With a small wave she clattered down the steps.

Claudia had certainly been much quieter coming up. Ally smiled. And she hadn't even reacted to Brian. What normal woman wouldn't do some heavy-duty gawking at a man like Brian?

Brian. She remembered who stood watching her, and her smile faded. "I thought you were working out."

"I stopped." He moved closer. "Who was that?"

"Claudia. A tourist from the States. I don't remember her last name." Ally backed away from him, then glanced behind her. Wouldn't do to lose her balance and go splat. Of course if she did fall, the keep would be a much more compelling starred attraction for the Irish Tourist Board. The great hall spirits and the clumsy American author's ghost could haunt in counterpoint. Scrape, shriek, scrape, shriek, with the O'Neill banshee joining in for an occasional chorus.

Trying to think of other things was *not* distracting her from the proximity of Brian's muscular body, from memories of what it had looked like during competition.

Okay, why was he just staring at her? "What? What's the matter?"

"You look different." He started to move even closer, then stopped to cast a wary glance at the wall behind her.

"Heights make you nervous, Byrne?"

"A little." He didn't step back.

Ally had nowhere to go, physically or mentally. She resisted the urge to put her palms flat against his chest to ward him off. Closing her eyes wouldn't do any good either because the warm clean scent of him, the *male* scent of him disturbed her as much as looking at him did.

She knew of only one thing that might stop him from invading her space until she came to grips with what she'd experienced: the truth.

"You want to know why I look different? I'll tell you." She was enough of a wuss not to want his hard gaze on her while she told her story. Turning away, she gazed toward the ocean, where gray mist was moving in, signaling the end of her sunny day. She knew when the mist reached them it would touch everything with cold damp fingers. She shivered.

She knew him well enough already to know he'd be narrowing those green eyes on her.

"So what happened?"

"There's something new in your bathroom. I guess Jupe built it. A reality experience of your

Sex Super Bowl win." She shrugged. "I couldn't resist."

The silence behind her grew ominous. The mist reached them, blotting out the scenery, enclosing them in a gray cocoon. Ally could very well believe they were the only people on earth.

"*Salont!*" His one word was a harsh expletive.

"What does that mean?" She rubbed her hands up and down her arms to dispel the goose bumps.

He ignored her question. "Did I disgust you?" Brian didn't know why he'd asked that or why her answer mattered. In his time, the question never would have occurred to him. But in this time . . .

"No." She still kept her face turned from him. Was she lying? "Tell me what you felt."

She shrugged. "While I was involved in the game I felt like any woman would in that situation."

What had she felt? "And afterward?"

Finally, she turned back to him. "Afterward? I felt embarrassed." She offered him a brief smile. "Embarrassed because I'd enjoyed it so much. It doesn't help to remind myself that I was someone else during the game."

He nodded. "There's more."

She met his gaze. "I realized I'd never want you to look at me like that again. I didn't see any softness in you, no caring, no concern for anything but sexual release."

He felt suddenly weary. "That's all the games

are supposed to be about. I can't care for any woman during competition."

"I understand that. But I guess I'm greedy. I want more than just mutual enjoyment."

He knew his smile was bitter. "Right. You gave everything to your husband, so now you want a man who'll do all the giving." *I need you to give to me.* "Just think about this. You took your pleasure out on that field. I'm not the only taker."

"You're twisting my words." She seemed determined that he believe her. "Besides, that wasn't me."

"No, it wasn't. I bet the woman on that field was passionate, wanted to give enjoyment even if the rules said she couldn't. You don't want to give anything." He didn't try to hide his anger. What right did she have to judge what he did in his time?

"You're right." Her voice was soft, and her eyes had taken on a suspicious sheen.

He exhaled deeply. If she started crying, he'd lose control and take her in his arms. That wouldn't be good. It wouldn't solve anything. He raked his fingers through his hair. "Let's give it a rest. Maybe you need to rethink whether you want my input for your book."

She edged past him to the steps, making sure she didn't touch him in the process. He wanted to trap her against the wall, press his body to hers, make her face her feelings for the real man, not the one in the reality experience cubicle. The problem? The man in the cubicle *was* him.

207

Ally stopped before descending the stairs. "What will you do now?"

His thoughts were grim. "I'm going to get rid of Jupe's reality experience toy. Then I'll add to the castle's violent history as soon as my agent gets back."

She gave him the first real smile since he'd climbed the steps. "Go easy on him. The Old One and Jupe are trying to protect you in their own way."

"Sure. And the fact that I'm making them rich doesn't have a thing to do with it."

"Not everything." Her words were tentative.

He had the feeling she wanted to add something but changed her mind.

"Oh, you'll have to tell me what 'salont' means sometime." She didn't wait for a reply as she hurried down the stairs.

He listened as the sound of her footsteps faded. Then he slammed his open palm against the stone wall. What the hell was wrong with him? Before coming to this cursed time he'd been perfectly secure in what he did. Maybe everything had gotten a little old, but he was proud of what he'd accomplished.

Now he was busy wondering about foreplay and meaningful relationships and how the hell he looked at women during sex. Things were getting too damned complicated. This vacation was great, just great. He tried to relax and unclench his jaw, then slowly descended the stairs.

Chapter Thirteen

Brian used the Constructor to get rid of his MVP performance, then stood looking down the road. The mist had really settled in. Not much to see. He could hear waves crashing against the rocks at the bottom of the cliff, but he couldn't see the ocean. Fingers of mist wove in and out of the ruins, giving the whole scene an alien look. It fit his mood just fine.

He might as well be an alien to Ally. She didn't understand the game. How could he explain that he had to put the game in a box, separate it from his emotions? How could he make her understand why he still played the game when the joy was gone? Had there ever been any joy? He'd felt challenged, sexually satisfied. But joy? Afraid not.

Maybe she'd sympathize if he told her about

his kids, but he didn't talk about them with anyone. He'd never even told Jupe what those kids really meant to him. They *were* him. Or what he'd been twenty years ago.

He'd always told anyone who asked that his life on the streets had made him stronger, made it seem a positive. That's what he wanted. He'd never tell what it was really like because that would be the same as standing naked in the street. First truth of the streets: Never get caught without weapons. He'd survived because he'd never stood with his emotions bared.

He shook his head to clear his thoughts. No use thinking about his other life. Even while he'd stood here, the mist seemed to have thickened. If Jupe and the others were smart, they wouldn't take a chance on the cliff road tonight. If Jupe were really smart, he wouldn't come home at all. Because if the mist didn't get him, Brian would. His agent had messed with his life once too often.

Brian had one more thing to do. He walked to Jupe's shelter, where Nebula waited with folded arms.

"You did not finish your lower-body exercises. Since I am more than a woman, I have no difficulty maintaining muscle tone. But you do not have my advantage. If you do not exercise, you might collapse on top of a woman during competition. This would humiliate your team, your owner, your agent, your—"

"I have *never* fallen on a woman." *Relax.* Keep it light. He took a deep breath. "You're right.

Don't want my thrust to go bust." He narrowed his gaze on the shelter. "Let's start with some weight-bearing exercises. Help me get everything out of here. I'm moving it."

"Why? I chose this spot because it would be close to your shelter." She watched as he strode inside and started heaving Jupe's stuff out.

"I've decided I want it over there." He walked to the other side of the castle with Nebula in tow and quickly rebuilt the shelter.

"I do not understand why you put it here." She helped Brian move everyone's things inside.

He grinned at her. "I want privacy to meditate so I can be more than a man."

Nebula nodded her understanding. "Ah, you wish to impress this Ally."

Brian cast her a searching glance. "What makes you think that?"

"I have seen the way you look at her. She is puny and will never be more than a woman, but perhaps I could enhance her skill level so she will be worthy of you."

And for the first time in the history of Nebula's stint as his trainer, she smiled.

Brian narrowed his gaze on her. "Don't mess with her skill level, Nebula. I like it right where it is."

He walked to the wagon, then paused. Would Ally still want him to help with her book? Probably. She'd convince herself she had the strength to resist him, that she didn't want him sexually after what she'd experienced. He tightened his lips. He'd just have to convince her he could be an invaluable resource for foreplay information and everything that came after.

Brian climbed onto the wagon and reached for the door. *Eyes.* He'd make sure he didn't look at her the way he looked at the women in competition, whatever way that was.

Thinking sex-free thoughts that he hoped would translate into sex-free gazes, he opened the door.

As Brian entered, Ally glanced up from what she was writing. He brought the scent of cool mist and excitement with him. Her heart automatically ratcheted up a beat when he entered her sphere of awareness. Pathetic. An adult should be able to control one small organ.

The Old One lay on the bed beside Ally, indicating in her unique way her thoughts on Ally's foreplay brainstorming. Taking a look at Ally's latest effort, the Old One yawned.

Ally cast her an irritated glance, then turned her attention to Brian. "She hates everything. What do I have to do to please her?" She slapped her pad down on the bed.

"Make her richer." He sat down on the bench seat rather than next to her.

"You must make her very happy then." Okay, she was being bitchy. She smiled. It felt good.

"I could make *you* happy, too."

He shifted his gaze to the naked-woman-in-need-of-cellulite-removal painting, but not before she saw the gleam in his eyes.

"You have that look in your eyes, the same one you had during the game. I hate it." Fine, so she didn't hate it. She wanted to hate it, though. It was pure sex and sinful desire. And it put her in a sinning mood, too. If she were going to sin, she wanted to do it with a man who met her criteria, a man with caring eyes. Brian didn't come close.

He looked back at her. Anger had narrowed his eyes.

Hmm. She liked the other look better.

"Give me a break, woman. I'm here to help you with your book, not to pass some eye-expression test. Who cares what my eyes look like? My eyes can't do anything to you."

"Don't call me woman. That's what you called me during the game." And his eyes could do lots of things to her. They could strip her bare of clothes and resistance. They made her heart pound too fast and her breathing work too slowly. They made her hands sweat and her stomach churn. He was *not* a positive influence in her life.

Suddenly, he relaxed and offered her a slanted grin. "Okay, now that you've laid down the ground rules, let's get started with the book."

Ally frowned. Maybe she should add that smile to her list of banned facial expressions. Maybe she should make him wear a mask. "Well, since I'm now totally immune to you . . ."

He laughed softly.

"I guess we could start with the massage." She cast the Old One a meaningful glance.

The Old One stood, stretched, then jumped from the bed. She was headed for Brian.

Brian stood. "Uh-uh. No lap to sit in, Boss. You're out of here."

The Old One jumped onto the counter and planted her ample bottom among the clean plates stacked there. Her yellow eyes gleamed. The lines of battle were drawn. This was war.

Brian moved to the counter, leaned his hip against it, then crossed his arms. "Remember our little talk, Boss? The win-win thing? Make my life tough, and that incentive clause could get expensive."

Expensive. Brian had touched a hot spot. The Old One hissed her disgust with his below-the-belt tactics and leaped from the counter.

He walked to the door, opened it, then watched as she stalked out with tail twitching angrily. "How about a visit with Nebula? She's lonely. Doesn't have anyone worthy to talk to." Brian closed the door behind her, locked it, then leaned against it. "So let's talk about your night of perfect pleasure."

"Sure. Perfect pleasure." Ally heard the doubt in her voice. After what she'd gone through in her reality experience, she didn't know how much help Brian would be. Except for the perfect orgasm part. "Umm. What do you know about foreplay?"

"I told you, I don't do foreplay."

"Foreplay is very important to women in this time." They'd start with the massage; then she'd have to think of something else creative.

"Never needed it. Why can't we go directly to the orgasm?" His smile had irritating written all over it.

Now she was getting steamed. "Because I can't write a book with four hundred pages of orgasms."

"Why not?"

He didn't do dense well.

"Because foreplay is *fun*. Women in 2002 are about *fun*." Her voice rose with each word. "Didn't you ever have *fun* with sex?"

He looked sincerely puzzled. "Fun? The orgasm is fun."

"Five hundred years of male evolution, and what hath time wrought?" She glared at him. "Nothing."

Then she saw the laughter glittering in his eyes. With a sigh, she released her anger. Anger would not make this a successful collaboration, and even though he knew squat about foreplay, he knew loads about the female body and how to wring a response from said body.

Ally also needed a real male body to practice foreplay on so she could write her book with all the required emotion. Brian's was the only acceptable male body in sight. Okay, more than acceptable. Lord, she was starting to sound like Nebula.

"Listen up. Here's the scene." She glanced at Brian. "We've come back to my place—"

"*My* place. I'd bring a woman to my place. Definitely." He moved to the fridge, pulled out a Coke, then took a few gulps.

Fascinated, Ally watched his neck as he swallowed. He had a great throat. She'd love to put her mouth right there where his blood pulsed—

"We're at my place. Now what?" He left his drink on the counter and sat down beside her on the bed.

She blinked, detaching herself from her fixed study of his throat. Maybe she was related to Black Liam Byrne, the evilest vampire in all Ireland. "We have a drink, joke around, talk about movies, then decide to play out a fantasy for fun. I'll fill in the beginning dialogue later."

He looked intrigued. "I've never created a fantasy with a woman. Except for the gypsy one I did with you."

"Have you ever fantasized on your own?" *Dumb question, O'Neill.* He's spent every working hour having sex. Men didn't fantasize when they had all the beautiful women they wanted.

His slow smile moved over her. "I fantasize a lot about the gypsy thing, especially the part where you dance naked." His smile widened. "In my private fantasy no one watches except me. In my private fantasy, I take you to my bed and perform incredible acts of—"

"Yes, well, we'll discuss the incredible acts later." For a moment she considered the wisdom of setting Brian's fantasies loose in her book. She straightened her spine. So long as she controlled the fantasizing while getting sensual details from

216

him, everything would be fine. "Now, about *this* fantasy. I belong to the harem of a powerful sheik. Hmm. I wonder if that's historically accurate. Did sheiks have harems?"

He shrugged. "Your readers won't be checking your historical accuracy. They'll be skipping pages to get to the sex part."

She sighed. "Right. The sex." No use putting if off any longer. "The sheik or whoever has sent me to get a massage so I'll be ready for him. You're the one who massages the women of the harem. But you can't control yourself with me and—"

"I'd be a eunuch." He frowned. "Your sheik wouldn't trust his women to a whole man. I don't think I like the direction this is taking."

"You can't be a eunuch." What an awful thought. What a *waste*.

His expression brightened, and Ally didn't like the gleam in his eyes.

"Why not reverse the fantasy? I could be the slave in a male harem, and you've been ordered to ready me for my mistress."

It was Ally's turn to frown. "Wouldn't it be the same thing? Wouldn't I lust after you? Your mistress wouldn't want that."

Brian's gaze turned calculating. "You hate me. I rejected you because you have . . . brown eyes. You've decided you'll make me suffer by driving me crazy with your massage, then turning your back on me."

Brown eyes? Didn't he like her eyes? What was

wrong with her eyes? "I don't know. After Dave, I swore I'd never do things just to please a man again. I said that during interviews, so my readers will have expectations. This scenario sounds like I'd be doing the giving." She narrowed her gaze. This was what Brian wanted. He'd said he'd like a woman who'd please him.

He glanced at her, and sensual promise heated his gaze. "It's about power, babe."

"Power?" What did power have to do with a stupid fantasy?

His stare grew thoughtful. "You held the power in the relationship. You did everything for him, so good old Dave depended on you."

Ally eyes widened. Ohmigod, it was true. Dave's troubles with Erica stemmed from his dependence on Ally. She'd never thought of herself as the power broker in their relationship. She'd need time to readjust her thinking.

"I'd say you have to make a decision, sweetheart."

Ally closed her eyes, but that didn't keep out the painful insight into her character. She wanted the power. And for the first time, she considered the idea that maybe Dave hadn't been the only one at fault in their marriage.

Now was not the time for soul-searching, though. She had a decision to make.

Never let it be said that Ally O'Neill didn't know how to twist self-discovery to suit herself. She could honestly state that she wouldn't be doing this to please Brian, but to feed her need for power. There was something wickedly sensual about a powerful woman. "I'll give you the massage."

He didn't try to hide his satisfaction. "No woman has ever given me a massage."

"Nebula's your trainer. Hasn't she given you one?"

Brian grinned at her. "Sure, but she's more than a woman, so she doesn't count. Besides, Nebula's massages are like getting body slammed by one of your sumo wrestlers. Pure pain."

His comment relieved some of Ally's tension. "I have one other suggestion." Her imagination was in hyper-drive now. "I still think your mistress would want to make sure nothing happened. So I think she'd have you tied so you can't touch me." Ally smiled. She liked that idea. A little kinkiness never hurt book sales.

Brian's expression told her all she needed to know about his opinion.

Ally leaped in with both feet before he could object. "You've never been the one who's powerless, have you? During the games, it's the woman who can't touch." She shrugged. "I'll understand if you can't handle it." She added the coup de grâce: "Hey, you've always wanted a woman who would do things for you. Well, here I am, prepared to do all the work in this massage fantasy."

She watched him wrestle with his male pride,

knew by his muttered oath and narrowed gaze the exact moment he gave in.

"Fine. Let's do it."

He didn't sound too happy with his role, but she thought it'd be . . . fun. Okay, so it excited the heck out of her. All that gleaming bare flesh and rippling muscle at her mercy. Just the thought gave her goose bumps . . . in strange and intriguing places.

Ally looked into his eyes, saw them change into the eyes of the man who'd had sex with someone-who-might-have-been-her that afternoon. This was his game face.

"My mistress wants me prepared for tonight. She's chosen you to administer to my body." He raked Ally with a contemptuous gaze. "I don't think she chose well."

Wow. He really got into the part.

"Your wishes mean nothing to me. Remove your clothing." Amazing how mere words affected her. She could feel pleasure seeping into the part of her most vulnerable to seepage when Brian was around.

With his gaze narrowed on her, he slipped off his jacket, then yanked his black T-shirt over his head. She sucked in her breath at the sudden exposure of so much wonderful bare chest. And held it as he pulled off his sneakers and socks.

The breath she'd sucked in was exhaled with a whoosh as he unsnapped his jeans, then slid them down over his lean hips and muscular legs.

Ohmigod! "You don't wear . . . ? Not boxers,

they wouldn't be called boxers in a harem. You don't wear undergarments?" She fixed her gaze on his groin. He was . . . excellent.

"My mistress wants access to her favorite part of my body without excess cloth in her way." He lifted his lips in a taunting smile that said he knew exactly how that part of his body affected Ally.

No kidding. She'd want access to that body part also. Especially if it kept gaining size and shape as it was now. "I have no interest in any of your body parts. You're less than nothing to me. Place yourself on the bed so I may bind you."

He bit his lip, and she knew he wanted to say no. Tough. He was a slave. He'd do what his mistress ordered or feel the lash. *Arrogant male animal.*

Was she getting into the fantasy, or what?

Reluctantly, he lay facedown on the bed.

Forget the foreplay. She'd have her climax right now. Brian facedown and naked was almost as great as Brian face up and naked.

She looked up at the ceiling mirror to get a better perspective. The contrast of golden skin tones against black satin sheets was a yummy décor triumph. And here she'd thought his choice of black sheets for his bordello-on-wheels was a bit . . . overdone. Silly her.

Now she had to tie him. Ally frowned. What to use? Finally, inspiration struck. Pulling open a drawer, she yanked out two of her black bras and two pairs of black panties. Coordinated in all things. Not exactly harem-quality bindings, but they'd do.

Brian's glower lightened a little when he saw the bras and panties. "Not too authentic, babe."

"I know." She pursed her lips as she thought. "But I left my chains and implements of torture back in Arizona so I could fit my stuffed ducky in the suitcase. Sorry." What could she tie his hands and feet to? Ah, there.

Ignoring his grumbles, she quickly bound his wrists and ankles to the mini-posts at each corner of the bed. She frowned. The bed didn't have king-size proportions, and the posts weren't too spectacular, but it was Brian who would fuel this fantasy. And he *definitely* had king-size proportions.

He turned his head to the side so he could watch her. "The other women who massage me wear no clothing."

Ally smiled. He was back in their fantasy.

"It matters not to me what other women do, because . . ." Her smile widened. "I am more than a woman."

He lowered his lids, hiding his expression. "The other women enjoy massaging me while they're naked."

She cocked her head to study him. "I suppose less clothing would give me more freedom of movement. I'll remove some of my clothes, but not all. You don't deserve to see all of me."

He turned his face into the bed. Was that muffled laughter? Ally narrowed her gaze on him. He'd pay for that.

Waiting until he turned his face to her again, Ally slid her red sweater over her head. She touched her red lace bra, tried to look thoughtful, then shook her head.

She ignored his groan of disappointment.

Next she unsnapped her jeans, then pulled them slowly down her hips. *Pause for sensuous shimmying.* When Brian looked suitably interested, she slid the jeans down the rest of her legs and kicked them off along with her shoes. She fingered the red panties, pulled one side down with her thumb, then glanced at Brian.

His gaze turned dark, heated. "Take them off."

Ally pulled the side back up. She gave him her best cruel-witch glance. "A slave doesn't give orders. I'll get my scented oil—" translation: vanilla almond body lotion—"so that I can relax your tight muscles." She tried for an innocent look, but from the glare he leveled at her, Ally figured it wasn't too effective. "Your muscles *are* tight, aren't they?"

"Your punishment will be long and excruciating," he ground out between clenched teeth.

"Promises, promises." She turned her back to him and wiggled her way over to the counter, where she retrieved the lotion. This was fun. How long had it been since she'd had fun with sex? *Try never.*

For just a moment she wondered at her lack of embarrassment. But after her Sex Super Bowl experience, she felt a familiarity with this man's body that didn't allow for false modesty. No matter who had been on that bed with him, she'd taken joy in her sexuality and wouldn't consider denying it. Ally had liked the sensation.

She drew a deep breath and took one last visual stroll down the length of his body. Ally paused for some mental still shots of his incredible buns. Wherever women gathered to discuss marvelous buns, Ally could say she'd seen the best.

Quickly straddling Brian's hips, she paused to study the situation, *to savor the feel of his body between her thighs.* Leaning forward, she brushed his long hair away from his neck, exposing a part of him that had probably never known a woman's lips. Hers would be the first. Softly, she kissed the base of his neck, touched the spot with her tongue, tasted his skin. "When I'm finished with you, slave, you'll never know another woman's touch without thinking of me." Okay, if you were going to fantasize, you might as well do it in a big way.

"If I were free . . ." His voice was husky, hinting that he'd finally realized the full scope of his folly.

Ally, the wicked-harem-massager, laughed at him. "But you are not free, and I can do whatever I want." To illustrate, she slid back to kneel between his spread thighs.

No matter how she fought to maintain discipline in her body systems, her breathing was breaking ranks with an embarrassing pant, pant. Could mutiny be far behind? Already her heart was out of step. She tried to ignore them. Pitter, pant, patter, pant. Ally concentrated on the job at hand.

Swallowing hard against an emotion that was part desire and part something she couldn't name, Ally reached between his thighs and cupped him, rubbed the base of her thumb back and forth, memorized his texture, his heat, then ran her fingernail lightly the length of his erection. "I have never seen a man more worthy of a woman." She meant it.

His large body shuddered. "Your words and touch make me hard, woman." Pause. "*Ally.*"

Thank you. "Enjoy what I do to you so that you may go to your mistress ready to give her pleasure." *Over my sensually deprived body.* Ally wanted all pleasure reserved for herself.

She ignored a small determined voice that was shouting, "Hello! Fantasy. Remember?" and got down to the nitty-gritty. Pouring some lotion into her hand, she rubbed her palms together to warm it, then straddled his thighs again. Ally rubbed the lotion into his shoulders and back with hard strokes.

Soft and gentle wouldn't do it. She felt a gnawing hunger, a craving that settled low in her stomach. No chance of a midnight snack tonight, though. Not with his contract hovering over them like a virtual Richard Simmons warning that sex would make them fat.

But she could touch him. Lord, how she could touch him. Bending down, she lingeringly kissed his back, following the line of his spine. For the rest of eternity, the scent of vanilla almond would evoke this moment, the memory of his flesh warm and smooth beneath her lips. "I could eat you, Brian Byrne."

"That's because I smell like a cookie." His words might be light, but his soft murmur echoed her own need.

He raised his hips, filling the space between her thighs, pressing his buttocks hard against her.

She couldn't stand it anymore. The panties and bra she wore had to go. Every possible inch of her body had to come in direct contact with him. Kneeling at the foot of the bed, she quickly stripped them off.

Finally free, she knelt between his thighs again and lowered herself until her nipples touched his back. Closing her eyes, she moved back and forth, felt her nipples scrape over his back, his buttocks. Her nipples were so sensitive she wanted to scream, to ease the pleasure that was almost pain. It was too much. *Too little*. She couldn't stand another second without his mouth on her breasts, surrounding her with moist heat, his tongue touching, teasing, drawing the need from her.

"If this is your idea of foreplay, I don't think I'll live through your book." His comment was an angry grunt. "Untie me so I can turn over."

She was tempted, so tempted.

"I want to taste you, Ally." His voice turned soft. "Your breasts, your belly, your—"

"No." She already wanted the whole thing. If he turned over, she wouldn't be able to stop herself. She'd probably ignore his contractual obligations and plant herself on his erection, ride him until everyone in Ireland could hear her cries, bringing the wrath of the Old One down on her and all future generations of O'Neills.

She straddled his buttocks, spread her legs, and pressed herself down hard until she touched him with the part of her that was hot and needy. And needy was the right word. She clenched around a want so intense she had to move, do something, or scream. Slowly, she slid back and forth, felt his buttocks tighten, press upward.

"Untie me. *Now.*" His voice was a hard command.

She'd as soon uncage a tiger. Besides, she couldn't think beyond the rhythmic motion that brought her most sensitive spot in contact with his body. A small spasm shook her, but she knew she'd have nothing more tonight because . . . something about a contract. She couldn't think.

Ally was startled out of her pleasure as he jerked against his bonds. *Get back into the fantasy.* What would be the expected response if a slave tried to break free? Sliding off his body, she tried to think. He pulled at his bonds again.

"Stop that." Ally didn't think; she reacted. She slapped his buttocks. Probably not an authentic punishment for a disobedient slave, but . . . Realization set it. She'd hit him. "I can't believe I just did that. I'm so sorry." Rubbing a circular pattern of regret on his firm buns, she mumbled more meaningless apologies.

With a muttered oath, he yanked one more time and freed himself. She edged to the side as he reached down to untie his ankles, then turned over and sat up. Ally wondered what her chances were of making it to the door. Not good. Besides, she was naked, and the Old One was probably camped outside.

Thoughts of escape disappeared as Brian pushed her onto the bed, then crouched over her. Uh-oh. This was not the same in-control man she'd seen during competition. His dark hair tumbled around his bare shoulders, his lips were a narrow line of anger, and his eyes were green heat.

"Don't *ever* take your fantasy and go off without me again."

She dragged in a deep gulp of air. "I was into the plotline. What can I say?"

He leaned back on his heels and stared at her. Unable to meet his gaze, she looked at the ceiling. Mistake. Something was finally happening in her bed, and the ceiling mirror was faithfully beaming it back: his dark fall of hair, tanned muscular body, and his enormous need for her. She narrowed her gaze. But who was that woman sprawled beneath him? Tangled blond hair, parted lips, and heaving breasts. Nope, Ally didn't know her.

She shifted her attention back to reality. "I guess you were into the plotline, too."

His smile was deadly promise. "You have no idea, babe."

He made her feel selfish. Okay, so she had been selfish. "I won't apologize again. You felt good. I was emotionally committed to the action. I was . . ." *I was completely out of control.*

"If I didn't hear Cap's car coming, I'd explore other directions this fantasy could've taken." He climbed from the bed and stepped into his jeans.

Cap's car? Katy! Quickly, Ally followed him off the bed and began dressing. "In my next fantasy I'll make sure—"

His slow smile touched her everywhere. Little Red Riding Hood would have recognized that smile in a heartbeat.

"The next fantasy is *mine*. And you'd better think long and hard before you take part in it because I'm going to make love to you, Ally O'Neill."

He'd said make love, not have sex. "You can't. Your contract. Remember?"

Brian walked to the door, then turned. "The Boss and I did some renegotiating." He nodded toward the bed. "Dream of me, babe." Opening the door, he was gone.

Ally stared at the closed door.

Oh boy.

Chapter Fourteen

"I can't wait any longer, Ally. Get up."

Ally groaned and pulled herself out of bed. Katy was like a snooze button on fast forward. Not even five minutes between naggings. "I'm up, I'm up."

"Good, because I can't wait to tell you about the other spirits that haunt this castle." Katy was holding a glass of orange juice. "Here. Drink. It'll wake you up."

Obediently, Ally drank the juice. It was good, but it didn't have the usual orange juice taste. "What brand is this?"

Katy shrugged. "Who knows? Cap brought us a pitcher of it this morning."

Ally closed her eyes. Oh, no. Another love potion. Yesterday's hadn't worked, so why should she worry about today's attempt? *Because you're not sure yesterday's didn't work.* Today she had a clear head, and Ally was almost certain that only a love potion could cause her to act the way she had yesterday. Heat rose to her face even thinking about it. She'd lost control. Twice. Okay, so maybe she hadn't been herself during her reality experience, but she should have felt *some* embarrassment. And last night? She'd used his body. It was that simple. She'd ridden him with only one goal in mind. Actually, her mind had little to do with the whole thing.

Now Cap had gotten to her again with his juice. Maybe today's concoction wouldn't work, but just in case, she'd keep away from Brian as much as possible. She'd be on guard against any lust attacks.

"I don't think you're awake yet." Katy peered at her. "That's what you get for staying up most of the night with that writing."

Her writing. Everything had flowed last night. She couldn't go to bed while the ideas were coming. She'd never remembered writing with so much emotion before. She picked up her legal pad and glanced back at what she'd written. So much of it was Brian. Ally frowned. What she'd written was good, but it didn't sound like a typical one nighter. And this *was* about one night. She had to remember that.

"You have that look." Katy grinned at her.

"What look?" How would she stay away from Brian when she didn't want to stay away?

"Never mind." Katy's expression was blandly

innocent. *A warning sign.* "I think I want to start taking a few day trips. See some of the sights. Thought maybe tomorrow we could go to the Cliffs of Moher. Bet they're spectacular. They drop seven hundred feet straight down to the ocean. I bet we'll hear all kinds of ghostly shrieks." She frowned. "I'm hoping for an overcast day. It adds to the atmosphere."

"Sea birds, Katy."

"What?"

"Your ghostly shrieks are the cries of seabirds. The travel guide said we'd see puffins, kittiwakes, choughs, and lots of other birds there."

Katy's expression turned mutinous. "I'm going there to hear ghostly shrieks, and I'd better darn well hear some."

Ally knew when to back down. "I don't know about ghosts, but you might see a merrow. She's supposed to be a beautiful woman who lives in the sea. She wears a long sealskin cloak, and some people say she'll marry a mortal man." She stopped to think. There was something else. "Oh, in some parts of Ireland she's regarded as a messenger of doom and death."

Katy looked appeased. "Well, I wouldn't mind seeing a merrow as long as she wasn't bringing her message to me." She smiled. "Now that tomorrow's settled, let me tell you what I heard about this castle. Yesterday, I—"

A loud knock interrupted Katy. Irritated, she flung open the door. "This better be important."

She looked up. "Oh, didn't expect it to be you, Nebula."

Ally walked over to stand beside Katy.

"I have decided to help Ally become worthy of Brian." Her expression said that everything should now be clear.

"Worthy?" Ally didn't dare consider what Nebula would demand she do to become "worthy."

Katy was not one to be closed out of any conversation. "You have it backwards, Nebula. Brian has to work a little to become worthy of Ally. First thing he has to do is get rid of his job. It's a great job, but I'd guess that Ally would think it was a conflict of interests."

Nebula looked insulted. "I have trained Brian for many years. He is as close to being more than a man as any male can be." Her glance grew conspiratorial. "Do not tell him I said so, but no male is capable of becoming more than a man. They are much too puny."

"He's *not* puny. He's strong, intelligent, and . . ." Uh-oh. Impulsive speech leads to much sorrow. Wasn't that an old proverb? If it wasn't, it should be. And why this sudden fierce need to protect Brian? She wasn't ready to examine that question yet.

Katy and Nebula exchanged looks that indicated females who were gifted with being more than women knew what they knew.

Katy smiled. "Would you like to come in for a bit?"

Nebula cast the wagon a dismissive glance.

"This puny vehicle would not hold a woman of my stature." She fixed Ally with a commanding stare. "You will be ready for your sensual exercises in two hours."

Ally and Katy watched her leave. Katy closed the door. "Think I'll tag along when you go for those exercises. Might want to get more sensually fit myself. It can't hurt."

Two hours later, Ally wasn't so sure of that.

She stepped out of the wagon with Katy right behind her. Nebula waited for them. Unfortunately, so did Brian.

Ally hadn't a clue why she was doing this. She looked up at Nebula. Actually, she did know. Ally wasn't stupid enough to make seven feet five inches of dedicated mass and muscle mad. The second reason? There was a chance that Nebula could really improve her sensual conditioning. Didn't every woman want to be sensually fit? Ally could open sensual fitness centers, make a fortune. And don't forget her book. This would be great stuff for her book.

The truth? She glanced at Brian, and he gave her an encouraging nod. She wanted to be the very best she could be for their next fantasy. Where had her original concept to use him merely as a research tool gone wrong?

Katy walked over to stand beside him. "I'll just stand over here out of the way." She looked up at Brian. "I think Nebula looks real feminine with that pink sweat suit and green hair. Green and pink are ladylike colors."

"It was not my wish to appear feminine." Nebula looked as though she might rip the sweat suit off right there. "Ally should be honored that I attempt the difficult task of making her worthy of Brian. My services are in great demand by every team."

Ally didn't like the feel of this, and she definitely didn't like the idea of Brian watching. "I don't know if this is a good idea, Nebula. I mean, where do you start? You're not going to have enough time to make me worthy. Making me worthy could take years. I'll understand if you change your mind."

Nebula was ignoring her, doing some strange breathing exercises and arm swings that were rather scary.

"Why does Brian have to be here? If he's at the almost-more-than-man stage, why does he have to watch a rookie train?" Ally was getting desperate.

Nebula segued into rhythmic hip and leg motions Ally had never seen in her fitness center. Of course, Ally didn't visit a fitness center too often. Fine, so she never visited a fitness center.

"Since I am doing this for Brian, I think it is fitting he be here to watch your progress." She continued with her routine.

Ally hoped Nebula didn't expect *her* to do those things.

Frantic, she turned to her last hope. "Brian, tell Nebula that you really don't care if I'm worthy."

He shrugged and slanted her a wicked grin. "Hey, got to be worthy, babe."

She leveled her deadliest glare at him. "No one would ever reverse the 'i' and 'a' in your name."

He didn't look insulted. "Katy and I can sit on the wagon while you're exercising and discuss your personal life. Maybe she has a few embarrassing baby pictures."

"Hmmph." When in doubt, make an intelligent noise. With a sinking feeling, Ally noted that Nebula had finished her warm-ups.

"We will begin with tongue and lip exercises."

Fascinated, Ally watched as Nebula stuck out her tongue and moved it in a circular motion, then made a puckering shape with her lips. When she'd finished, she glanced expectantly at Ally.

"These exercises will make your tongue flexible, able to reach . . ." She rolled her eyes up in her head, obviously searching for the right description. "As your commercials say, able to reach those hard-to-get-to spots."

Ally blinked. She wouldn't go there. "What about the lips?"

Nebula nodded. "Yes, the lips. You must pucker them so that they are full and soft, yet firm. The fullness and softness gives a man the mistaken impression that his woman is yielding. A woman must remember to inflate a man's ego."

Brian wasn't smiling anymore. Score one for Nebula.

"What about the firmness?" Ally didn't care

about the firmness, but the longer she kept Nebula talking, the less time there would be for puckering.

Nebula cast her an impatient glance. "Firmness is important. No man wants to kiss an overripe zeekee berry."

"Zeekee berry?" Ally cast a quick glance at Brian. He caught her glance, stroked it, held it.

"Lips and tongues are important, sweetheart. I love a woman with great lips. Soft, warm, welcoming. Practice hard so you can play hard." He leaned back against the wagon and offered her a slow smile that promised he could teach her things about lips and tongues she'd never imagined.

"What a man." Katy cast him a worshipful glance.

Ally sighed. "Okay, let's get started."

Nebula launched into drill-sergeant mode. "Tongue out. Circle to the right. Circle, circle, circle. Now to the left. Keep it up. Circle, circle, circle. Hold that extension. Lips next. Pucker, pucker, pucker. Tongue again. Curl, curl, curl. Work on that flexibility. Circle, curl, circle, curl. Now put it all together. Lips, tongue, lips, tongue. Rest."

Somewhere in the middle of that excruciating event, Katy left the wagon to join Ally. "The puckering part makes you look like a guppy. I think I'll try these exercises. Never hurts to be a kissing fool."

Nebula was just hitting her stride. "We will

now strengthen our pelvis muscles for those long nights, and in deviant individuals even days, of mindless pleasure. First we rotate our hips, then do our pelvis thrusts." She demonstrated.

At least Ally wouldn't feel stupid doing these. It looked like what the women did on some of the MTV videos, only they did it with a lot fewer clothes.

"Ready. Stomach in. Now rotate, rotate, rotate. The opposite direction. Rotate, rotate, rotate. Hold that stomach in. Now the pelvis. Thrust, thrust, thrust. Work it, work it."

Twenty minutes later, Ally had puckered her last pucker and thrust her last thrust. No way would she live long enough to be worthy of Brian. He might have to settle for someone unworthy but highly motivated.

Nebula frowned. "You will be my greatest challenge. We must firm your thighs next. When I finish with your thighs, you will be able to strangle a lennot with them. I will work with you again tomorrow at the same time."

Not if I can help it. Ally didn't know what a lennot was, but she had no intention of strangling one. And she fully intended to be on her way to the Cliffs of Moher at this time tomorrow. She walked over to the wagon, controlling the urge to wince with every step. Katy was still exercising away.

Finally gathering her courage, she glanced at Brian. If he laughed at her, she'd . . .

He wasn't laughing. His gaze was heat and desire. "I like the way you move, babe."

She was pitiful. All it took was a few words of praise from him to renew her energy, make her want to do more exercises. Okay, maybe that was stretching it, but Brian's approval sure made her feel great. This from a woman who'd sworn that men's opinions would never again matter to her.

"You owe me a fantasy, and I want you to move that way when you dance naked for me." His lips tipped up with a wordless promise that she would do exactly what he wanted.

She smiled at him, accepting his challenge. "Sounds sensual, if you're into dancing goose bumps. Because that's all you'd see if I danced naked here."

Goose bumps? Brian thought hard. No goose bumps. Another lapse in the Language Assimilation Program. But he could figure out what Ally meant.

"If the goose bumps are attached to you, then they're sexy. Dance with enough passion, sweetheart, and you'll keep both of us hot." He was having fun talking to her. Brian didn't joke with women, certainly not the ones he met during competition. There, he weighed every word for its arousal power. And off the field? Nope. For a moment he thought of Nebula, and smiled at the thought.

"Are you laughing at me?" Ally tilted her head, daring him to admit it.

"Laughing *with* you sweetheart. I'm thinking

we have a lot in common. Nebula has both of us under her thumb."

She laughed, a clear honest sound on the cool air. He couldn't remember the last time he'd heard a woman laugh like that.

"Nebula will never have you under her thumb, hotshot." She reached up, curled a strand of his hair around her finger, then pulled. Obediently, he lowered his head. She whispered in his ear. "If she gives you a hard time, I can strangle her in a thigh press. By the way, what's a lennot?"

He put back his head and laughed. Really laughed.

The smile she offered him had a touch of wonder in it. "You should laugh more often, Byrne. You could get anything you wanted with that laugh."

He drew his finger along her jaw, touched her lips with a fingertip. "I like being with you, Ally O'Neill. You make me happy." How could something be so simple and yet so profound? "And a lennot is a very large rodent. Think of an elephant with beady eyes and whiskers."

"Ugh. Someone else's thighs can strangle it."

Brian didn't get a chance to answer because Katy joined them.

"That was fun. Got the old juices flowing." Katy paused to consider her statement. "Problem is, at my age all those flowing juices don't have anywhere to go. Men my age are all a bunch of old farts."

Brian decided to let that pass without com-

ment. "Nebula will either kill you or cure you."
He noticed that Jupe had stuck his head from his
shelter. Brian still had a few things to discuss
with his agent. "I enjoyed watching—" he smiled
at Ally—"but I have to talk with Jupe before he
runs and hides."

Katy put a hand on his arm. "Wait up. I need
to tell Ally and you about the neat things I found
out about the castle when I went into town yesterday."

Ally looked suspicious. "Does this involve more
bloodthirsty spirits?"

Katy nodded. "Yep. Brian, you had some evil
ancestors." She looked like the thought gave her a
lot of pleasure. "All around here was O'Brien
country. If you were a Byrne and wanted to
build a castle, you'd better have had an in with
an O'Brien. To prove his friendship with the
O'Briens, your ancestor invited some of their en-
emies to a big feast. Lots of drinking and ca-
rousing. They didn't know your ancester was
tight with the O'Briens. Now comes the bad
part." She paused for dramatic effect.

Brian used the moment to glance toward
Jupe's shelter. Jupe looked his way, and Brian
glared at him. Jupe ducked back into the shelter.

"At the exact stroke of midnight, Byrne and his
men slaughtered every one of his guests."

Ally's horrified glance made Brian feel guilty
by association. "Didn't the people during that
time do anything but kill each other?" She looked

at Brian. "Don't *ever* take a vacation back to that time."

Brian studied the keep. For the first time, he considered the wisdom of repairing the old place. A lot of people had died here. Shouldn't he let them rest in peace?

Katy wasn't finished. "He had them dragged down to a storage area under the castle. Then he walled up the room so no one would ever find them. But servants talk, and after Byrne died, people went to have a look-see."

Ally joined the conversation again. "What is it about midnight? Have you noticed that everything bad or scary happens at midnight? Is this symbolic of the darkest, therefore the evilest, time of night? Maybe midnight just symbolizes the unknown."

Katy wasn't interested in symbolic implications. "Something awful started happening when people went down to where those poor souls were walled up. When anyone went down there, people waiting for them at the top of the steps could hear shrieking and sounds of rocks being thrown. And when the ones who'd gone down finally stumbled back up they were raving mad, screaming about bloody hands and stones flying at them. Had to be put in asylums for the rest of their lives."

Ally stared at her great-aunt. "No, we are *not* going down there."

Katy looked innocent. "I'm not stupid enough to go down there, but I'd like to see where it is.

The lady who owns the sweet shop said if you look along the north wall of the keep, you'll find a spot that's been boarded over. The police came out a few years ago and closed it up permanently because of all the things that had happened." Katy's smile turned wheedling. "I'm going to take a shower. Then maybe we can go see if it's still boarded up." She glanced at Brian. "Since this is your property, you'll probably want to make sure everything's safe."

Brian knew when he was beaten. Besides, if it gave him more time with Ally, it was time well spent. "I'll meet you after I talk to Jupe." He watched them return to the wagon, then headed for Jupe's shelter.

During his short walk, he symbolically washed his hands of the keep's horrifying history. He couldn't change the past, and he couldn't right the wrongs done.

Jupe surprised him by coming out to meet him, but that didn't blunt Brian's anger. "I don't have much of a personal life, Jupe, so it really steams me when someone interferes with it. You wanted Ally to back away from me, and you thought the reality experience would do it. It didn't work, but if it had, I'd be searching for a new agent as soon as I got home."

Jupe shook his head. "No, you wouldn't. We go back too far. I know you better than you know yourself."

Brian was usually pretty laid-back about Jupe's manipulating, but not today. "I like Ally. I like it here. I'm enjoying my vacation. Let it alone."

"Uh-uh. Can't do that." Jupe looked as serious as Brian had ever seen him. "We're the same inside. I came from the outer planets a lot of years before you, but I still remember what it was like. I'm at the top of my profession now, and I'm staying there."

Brian frowned. "What's that have to do with me?"

"You worked twelve years to get where you are now. You're the best. I don't want you to throw it all away. Ally O'Neill might enjoy having sex with you, but she wouldn't want the whole package. You don't belong with her. You don't belong here." Jupe's voice was rising by the second.

"I'm not thinking of staying." Brian shouldn't have been bothered by what Jupe said, but he was. Did Jupe have it right? Wouldn't Ally want him?

"Make sure you keep on thinking that way. You have too much to lose. If you stayed here, you'd blow it all: your career, your kids, everything you've ever worked for. No woman is worth that." Jupe looked a little more relaxed. "You think I manipulate you? That's nothing compared to what a woman would do." He grinned at Brian.

"Ally's not like that." If Brian was sure of anything, he was sure of that.

"No?" Jupe's expression turned sly. "I heard her talking with Cap. They were talking about how to get to you. Cap told her to make you open up about your childhood. Sounds like manipulating to me." He shrugged. "Doesn't matter. You're too much like me to fall for that. We both watch out for number one." He tapped Brian on the chest before heading back to his shelter. "Don't forget it."

Brian didn't even notice when Jupe left. He felt like someone had socked him in the gut. He couldn't remember the last time he'd felt this disappointed. *Sure you can.* But the first time he'd been a little kid. Now he was an adult. He accepted that people weren't always what you wanted them to be.

Why was she trying to "get to him"? What kind of deal had Cap offered her? And why did it hurt so much?

The scary part? Ally had crept up on his emotions when he wasn't looking. Brian squared his shoulders. He was okay, would always be okay, because all he really needed was himself.

He'd confront her, give her a chance to have her say, then he'd forget her. But before he forgot her, he wanted his fantasy night, wanted to bury everything he'd started to feel for her in one great night of sex. He'd walk away knowing it had *always* been about sex.

Jupe would be happy. Brian Byrne didn't belong in this time and place. He didn't belong with Ally O'Neill.

Chapter Fifteen

Brian was at about a nine on his personal mad-as-hell scale. And the fact that Ally could make him that angry ticked him off even more.

He strode toward her wagon, anger fueling every step. Another emotion simmered beneath the surface, one that bothered him. Hurt? No, he definitely didn't want to feel hurt. Anger was a strong emotion. It allowed him to vent on a major scale. Hurt burrowed inside and left a man bleeding.

He'd only known the woman for a few days. That wasn't enough time to feel hurt.

The Old One padded beside him. "You win, Boss. I don't like your methods, but this once you were right. I need to know my limits, stay inside the lines. From now on, I do what I do best and stay away from the emotional stuff. Happy now?"

He peered down at her. "Guess you won't be happy until we get back to 2502. You can't express too much as a cat." If he didn't know her so well, he'd swear she looked depressed.

Glancing up, he saw Ally and Katy waiting for him. Looked like he'd have to hold on to his anger for a while. Katy and the Boss would be way too interested in what he had to say.

"This is an excellent adventure." Katy looked at Ally and Brian for confirmation.

Brian wasn't convinced. It was getting less excellent by the minute. He glared at Ally. She returned his gaze, troubled. Good. If he weren't so angry, he'd laugh. His maturity level was dropping fast.

He walked silently beside Ally up the hill to the keep. She kept space between them, and perversely, that bothered him. Because no matter how mad he was, he still wanted her. His body didn't recognize emotional conflicts. It had its own agenda.

"Looks like someone got here before us." Katy sounded disappointed.

Brian glanced in the direction Katy was staring. A large wooden pallet lay on the ground beside a gaping hole. He frowned. If a person got hurt on his property, was he legally responsible? He drew a deep breath. Reality check. This was a tourist site and would stay a tourist site long after he was gone. At least until the place fell down, which according to history, wouldn't be too long into the future. He'd be pretty safe from lawsuits in 2502.

Thoughts of his departure should have made him feel better. They didn't.

He positioned himself beside Ally as they grouped themselves around the top of the ancient stone steps. She cast him worried glances.

"Is something the matter? You don't look too happy." She leaned closer so Katy couldn't hear. "Is it last night? Are you still upset about what I did?"

"I'm about sex, babe. That's all last night was." The absolute truth? Probably that was all it had been for Ally. He wasn't quite sure about himself. Everything he did with her seemed to be about something more, something just out of reach. He needed to pin down his feelings because mysteries bothered him.

She didn't like his answer. He could see it in her narrowed gaze, her tightened lips. "Well, then what?"

Katy was still occupied. Out of the corner of his eye, he could see her hesitating on the top step, trying to peer into the darkness.

"Every once in a while I feel like I want to talk about my childhood. Would that make you happy?" He wasn't doing a good job of keeping a lid on his anger. Why was he so angry anyway? According to Jupe, Ally was trying to "get to him." That wasn't bad. It meant she wanted him.

Maybe she was interested for her book, or maybe she just wanted his body. So what was the big deal?

"Why do I get the idea this isn't about your childhood?" She looked puzzled.

If she was faking, she was doing a good job.

Brian shrugged. "Forget it." He nodded toward Katy. "I think your great-aunt's getting ready to do some exploring."

Her attention diverted, Ally turned toward Katy.

Brian frowned. The big deal? She was trying to *manipulate* him. He hadn't a clue why he thought Ally shouldn't be a manipulator. Everyone he knew was one. Hell, *he* manipulated women during competition. So why shouldn't Ally do the same thing? He didn't have it all figured out yet, but he wanted Ally to be up front with him more than he'd wanted anything in a long time.

"I don't think we should go down there, Katy. You don't have your light with you, and you could hurt yourself in the dark." Ally joined Katy in staring into the dark opening.

"You wouldn't have to go. But you're right, it doesn't make much sense for me to go down without my equipment. Maybe tomorrow night . . ." She leaned closer to the opening. "I hear something."

Brian walked over to stand beside them. "Someone moved the cover, so the person who moved it might still be there."

"Yoo-hoo, anyone there?" Katy's shout echoed down the gaping hole.

The answer came almost immediately. "I'm on my way up."

"Well, poop." Katy backed away from the steps. "Someone beat me to it. Didn't sound insane either."

A short time later, a woman climbed from the hole. "That was so cool. I can't get enough of this place. Oh, hi, Ally."

Ally smiled. "You're a lot braver than me." She turned to her great-aunt. "This is Claudia. I met her in Liscannor. Old buildings are her thing."

"This keep is like—" Claudia seemed lost for words—"an obsession with me. I can't stay away from it."

Brian glanced up at the keep. Obsession? He should be the one with strong feelings for the old place. This was his family's heritage. He didn't. It was just an ancient building with a bloody history. He had better things to obsess about. Like Ally, and what he wanted to say to her. *What he wanted to do to her.*

Katy sidled close to Claudia and stared intently into her eyes. "How're you feeling? A little off-kilter? A little mentally unraveled?"

Claudia grinned at her. "Mentally unraveled is my natural state. Why?"

Katy sighed her disappointment. "It's supposed to be haunted down there. Are you sure you didn't see any bloody hands? Anyone throw rocks at you?"

Claudia shook her head. "Sorry. Maybe that only happens at night. Don't ghosts only come out at night?"

Katy brightened. "You're right. I'll come back tomorrow night. I'd come back tonight, but I need my sleep. We're going to the Cliffs of Moher tomorrow. I want to be wide awake so I don't miss the ghostly shrieks."

"Ghostly shrieks?" Claudia looked puzzled, but then her expression cleared. "I haven't seen the cliffs. Maybe I'll drive out tomorrow, too."

"How'd you get here today?" Katy glanced around. "Don't see your car anywhere."

Claudia laughed. "I stopped down the road to look at the scenery, then decided to walk up here instead of driving. I needed to stretch my legs anyway." She started walking away. "I might see you guys tomorrow."

Brian watched her stride down the hill, then turned to Ally. "What're you going to do with the rest of your day?"

She seemed distracted. "I think I'll ask Cap to run me into town. There're a few things I have to pick up."

Hah. She probably wanted to discuss her progress in "getting to him" with her partner in crime. He exhaled sharply. He was starting to sound as obsessed as Claudia. Let it go. Let *her* go. Whatever they cooked up wouldn't work.

Katy tapped his arm. "I want you to go with us tomorrow. You can help Ally drive the wagon.

After that crazy driver almost killed us, I'm a little nervous about handling the reins."

"And . . . ?" Brian didn't believe a word she said. Katy Gallagher would drive into hell and thumb her nose at the devil.

She grinned at him, then stood on tiptoe to reach his ear. "I want to give Ally and you some time alone without all the others around."

He'd go, but not for the reason Katy thought. The trip would give him time to say what he wanted to say to Ally. And when he was finished, he might end up walking home. But the satisfaction he'd get would make it worthwhile. "Sounds good, Katy."

Ally climbed into the passenger seat next to Cap. She was tagging along with him for only one reason: to get him to lay off his love potions, to convince him they weren't working.

The problem? They *were* working. The orange juice she'd had this morning was driving her crazy. While they were all standing around those steps, she'd done some heavy sensual imaging. If she'd been a snake, she would have slithered up Brian's leg and coiled around his . . .

"We're alone now. Are you making progress with the big guy? What about the potions?" Cap drove away from the castle at warp speed.

Brian suspected Cap had been their hit-and-run driver. If he drove this fast all the time, she could well believe he'd hit them by accident. But then why hadn't he stopped to offer help? How badly did he want Brian out of the way? Ally shook off the thought. She couldn't believe that Cap, with his phony red wig, picture of his daughter painted on his head, and book of love poems would try to kill anyone.

"They're not working, and I want you to stop making them."

Cap slanted her a sly grin. "Let's get this straight. You want me to stop making them because they're not working." He glanced back at the road in time to zip around a terrified flock of sheep.

Ally peeled herself from the door where his unexpected turn had thrown her. "Exactly."

He shook his head. "I don't think so. I think they're working just fine."

She shrugged. "Okay, do your thing, but I won't touch any more of them."

Once they reached town, Ally left Cap to his own devices while she tracked down a phone. After a brief call to her parents, she sat staring at the phone. Dave had been bugging them. She'd have to deal with him now. Forcing herself to do what had to be done, she called him.

"Am I glad to hear from you, Ally. You have no idea how much I want you back. I never realized how weird Erica was. She called yesterday, and I told her it was definitely all over, that you and I were an item again."

"You told her *what?*" Ally closed her eyes. How could she have ever believed she loved this man? She was so *over* him, and she wished he'd realize it.

"I really miss you, honey. I miss the little things you did for me, like turning down the covers and fluffing up my pillow each night. I gave Erica a list of all the things you did, but she threw it out."

Good for Erica. Ally wished she could relive her last five years. She sure wouldn't have spent them catering to Dave. Why hadn't she ever noticed what a whiny worm he was?

"Erica said she'd be home as soon as she took care of a little problem. She expects us to get together again. It won't happen. I won't take her back."

Lucky Erica. "We're finished, Dave. Accept it. And I want you to stop bothering my parents."

"It's another man, isn't it?" He sounded disbelieving.

Jerk. "Yes." Ally's eyes popped open. Had she said that? "Yes" was a dangerous word to think, let alone say. She couldn't say "yes" to Brian Byrne because he wouldn't be in her life long enough to give "yes" any meaning.

"He won't be able to compare with me." Whiny had given way to nasty.

"You're right, Dave. I would never compare him with you." Quietly, she hung up, then leaned back in her chair. There was no comparison.

Closing her eyes again, she saw Brian's forest-green eyes, his wicked grin, and his buns. Strong, firm, with a dimple on the right one. Buns a woman could get her fingers into. Buns that would always be there for her. Brian Byrne had dependable buns.

His voice tempted her memory: deep, warm, sexy. And she wanted him so badly her teeth hurt. Ally opened her eyes. This was not a good thing. He would leave in a few weeks, and she'd never see him again.

Now she was really depressed. Time to do something to get her mind off inevitable departures. She stared at the phone. Something Eamonn Clancy had said nagged at her. Brian's namesake was supposedly wandering the world somewhere, but Eamonn had said Brian's father, Kieran, had died twenty years ago. If Kieran had been a priest most of his life, a son seemed unlikely.

Just as Ally had felt compelled to research Irish fairies when she'd agreed to go to Ireland with Katy, she now knew she was going to call Boston. Fine, so she was a compulsive researcher. This time, though, she had an emotional stake in the results.

Two hours later, she sat in a restaurant staring at her lamb chop while across from her Cap chattered on about his team.

"I really like our chances if Brian doesn't come back to the Monarchs."

"Uh-huh." She'd discovered zip from her call to Boston, so she'd called the only person she knew who could squeeze information from a stone. Mavis. Her agent hadn't disappointed.

Ally now knew that Father Kieran Byrne couldn't have fathered a child because, according to everyone who'd known him, Father Byrne was the closest thing to a saint St. Joseph's parish had ever seen. He never would have broken his vow of celibacy. She believed Mavis.

Ally didn't want to think what the implications were for her Brian. *Her Brian.* She liked the sound of that.

"Within the next ten minutes, Earth will disintegrate and life as we know it will end."

"Uh-huh."

Cap laughed, and Ally blinked, wondering what she'd missed.

"I give up. It's no use trying to talk to someone in love." He winked at Ally. "Let's head home."

"I'm not in love with Brian. Your potions aren't that good." She was *not* in love. She was sensually attracted and personality-positive to him, but she didn't love him. Ally was glad she'd gotten that straight.

By the time they returned to the keep, night had fallen. Ally wasn't sure how she felt about that. She'd be better off not seeing Brian until morning, especially since he'd acted a little strange today. But she wanted to see him. Cap's potion must not have worn off yet.

Ally watched Cap walk to his shelter. She looked at the wagon and sighed. The lights were on, so Katy was still up. No doubt waiting to grill Ally on what she'd done, said, and thought. Putting off the inquisition, she strolled up the hill until she was sure no one from the wagon or shelters could see her, then gazed at the keep. Moonlight spilled over it, turning the scene into a silver fantasy. Through the opening in the wall, she could see the area that had once been the great hall bathed in pale light.

Ally sensed movement behind her, but relaxed almost immediately. She knew who it was, felt the recognition in a part of her that needed no sight. She turned to look at Brian. "It's a terrible kind of beauty. The moonlight makes it look pure, untouched, yet so many people have died violently inside its walls."

"Beauty doesn't have to be pure to be beauty." Brian moved to her side, but didn't touch her.

It didn't matter. He touched her in ways he didn't know. His scent: crisp Irish air mingled with the smell of the sea that clung to his hair, his jacket. And warm male, along with something that was essentially his alone. His voice, deep and as cool now as the light filtering through the ancient stone keep his family had built so long ago. But she knew his voice could touch her with heat, and she held the memory of that warmth close inside her.

"In my fantasy, the gypsy woman dances naked for me in my great hall, for me alone."

His breath fanned the side of her neck, and she shivered.

"Would you dance for me there, Ally O'Neill?" His voice was low, husky with his promise that all would not end with her dance.

Ally shook her head. Not even for him would she dance in that place of death. "How could I dance there after what we heard, felt? There's so much sadness there. Can't you feel it?"

"We'll give the old place a new memory, a

happy one. Perhaps years from now, people will stand where we stood and see us dancing in the moonlight." He took her hand then, pulled her into his arms, and danced.

She laughed as she allowed him to guide her across the silvered grass, felt his arm tighten across her back as she tripped on a stray rock.

If she listened carefully, she could almost hear the music, wild as the Celts who once wandered this land. Joyous music with penny whistles, fiddles, and bodhrans. No quiet harp for her.

He held her close as he swung her in the moonlight. She should have a gown on, one that swirled around her, lifted high in the sea breeze.

His body moved against hers, hard muscle and heated flesh. Her breath quickened, her heart beat faster.

"What would it take to get you to dance in the great hall?" He slowed, then stopped, but he continued to hold her against his body. Putting both arms around her, he ran his palms slowly up and down her back.

Ally relaxed into his rhythmic motion, thought about what he'd asked. It would take something extraordinary to make her dance in that place where so many people had been murdered. "I would dance as a gift of love, if I had nothing else to give, if I wanted to give something that would live forever in someone's memory." She grinned at him. "Memories are portable."

He nodded. "A gift of love, huh? Not much chance of that."

Beneath his low words, Ally sensed bitterness. Why?

"How about for lust? That's a good reason. You'd have something really exciting to put in your book." He abandoned her back and buried his fingers in her hair, lowered his mouth to hers. "What could I do to change your mind?"

Right now, with his mouth so close, she had no mind to change. "Why do I have to dance in that particular spot?"

"Because I want it, babe." His voice was soft, intense. "It's about family. Once in my life, I want to feel that connection, to know that this was where my ancestors danced . . ." His lips touched hers. "Loved."

Loved. The word touched her with warm breath. She opened her lips to it, and he covered her mouth with his.

His lips moved lingeringly over hers, and she savored the feel, the taste of him. His tongue slid across her lower lip, then explored her mouth, and she met him with an eagerness that would have been embarrassing if she were thinking more clearly. She slid her arms around his neck, felt the warmth of his nape beneath the heavy fall of dark hair. She cataloged every sense, so it would be there whenever she took out her memories of Ireland.

He abandoned her lips to place his mouth over the spot on her neck where her pulse beat hard and fast. Finally, Ally understood Katy's fascination with Black Liam.

Brian lifted his mouth from her neck. Gazing into her eyes, he reached down and pulled up her sweater. Without thinking, she raised her arms over her head to allow him to strip off the top. It seemed she had no shame where he was concerned. She needed his touch. Everywhere.

She waited for him to finish pulling off her sweater. He didn't. He merely lifted it until it covered her head, then stopped.

"What're you doing?" Her voice was muffled by the sweater.

"You need another fantasy to take the place of my gypsy one."

He captured her wrists above her head and held them there with one large hand while he deftly unsnapped her bra. She felt it slide off. She should stop this, but she couldn't, any more than she could stop the pounding of her heart, her rapid breathing. Ally moistened her suddenly dry lips with the tip of her tongue, savored her anticipation.

Thank heaven for loose-weave sweaters, or she would've used up her supply of oxygen in one frantic pant. But the cool night air still touched her parted lips, moved across the rest of her face.

"When this keep was new, slavery was a way of life in the world. We're back there now, and you're for sale to any man who can pay the price. You're head remains covered so that you won't see the many men who touch you, because it's only your body they're interested in." He unsnapped her jeans, yanked the zipper down, then slid them over her legs along with her panties.

Ally didn't step out of them, only stood there, feeling the chilly night air flowing across her exposed body, cooling her heated skin. There was pleasure in her total stillness, allowing his words to weave a sensual spell as real as the sweater's weave touching her face.

"Feel their hands on you, testing your firmness." His voice was a dark murmur of seduction as he clasped her breast, gently kneaded it, then rubbed the pad of his thumb across her nipple.

Without sight, all her other senses were heightened. Her nipple, hard beneath his stroke, grew so sensitive she thought she'd scream. He had to touch it with his mouth or she'd die right here in front of his precious keep. The ruling would come down: dead from sensory overload. They would add a footnote, though, that the deceased died with a smile on her face.

"They would test your softness." He slid his fingers over her stomach, up the inside of her thighs.

She sucked in her breath, wished he had ten hands so he could touch her everywhere at once. You'd think five hundred years of evolution would have taken care of that little problem.

"Your readiness." He pushed her legs apart and without warning slid his finger into her.

Ally moaned and pushed against his finger to drive him deeper. She wanted to tighten herself around him, hold him there forever. Kick her if she ever again whined about Nebula's clenching exercises.

But she couldn't focus on Nebula or anything else as Brian pulled her into the fantasy.

"Finally, a buyer chooses you, paying a price that draws gasps from those around him." He slowly drew his finger from her.

Gone. She felt deprived, as though he'd stolen something that belonged to her. But she wouldn't beg. Not right away, anyway. "How much did he pay?" No matter how strong she tried to make her voice, it came out wispy.

Ally sensed rather than heard the slide of his zipper. She had a great memory for detail. Last night. No boxers. Breathlessly she waited.

"The price of ten camels. You must work hard to please one who values you so highly."

"Ten camels?" She was insulted. "I'm worth a lot more than that."

Ally closed her eyes at the touch of his erection between her legs. Even though he still held her arms above her head, and the sweater still blocked her sight, she wanted a more intense blackness so she could concentrate every part of her being on the only sense that mattered now. Touch.

"Worth more?" He laughed softly. "You're a woman who doesn't want to please a man, who doesn't realize that in pleasing she'll gain pleasure. Your master must teach you this lesson. Are you worth more?"

She felt the slide of his erection between her legs. Back and forth. A rhythm she quickly picked up as she thrust against him, wanting closer contact where closer contact wasn't possible.

"Your master paid for you. He can do what he wants." His voice dropped to a soft murmur. "And he wants to do many things."

His lips closed over her nipple at the same time he released her hands. It didn't matter. She couldn't have moved if a whole army of spirits had marched past them.

He teased her nipple with his tongue, then nipped gently. She moaned into the sweater even as his mouth tormented. Everything blurred as his mouth closed over her other nipple. Pleasure built as he kissed a path over her stomach, kneaded her buttocks with hands that shook.

Air. She had to have air. Ally pulled the sweater off her head in time to see him drop to his knees. No thought was involved, only instinct, as she spread her legs wider and tangled her fingers in his long hair.

He clasped her bottom, then pulled her to him. He put his mouth on her, warm, wet, searching. His tongue found the spot that was the center of her personal universe at this never-to-be-repeated moment.

No scream of pleasure could do justice to the sensation, so she gripped his hair more tightly, anchoring herself to earth, as the spasms shook her.

And even as the waves of sensation washed over her, slowly receded, leaving her so weak that she sank to her knees, she knew that this wasn't *it*.

He'd given pleasure, but taken none. There'd be another time, the *right* time for it, when he'd join her. Almost fearful, she lifted her gaze to his eyes, then relaxed. These weren't the eyes of the man in her reality experience. This man's eyes were heated with emotion, hot desire. He didn't have his game face on tonight.

But it wasn't right that she'd done all the enjoying. "I want to—"

Reading her intent, he shook his head. "There'll be another time." His gaze drifted to the great hall. "My time." He glanced back at her and smiled.

"You're really fixated on your gypsy fantasy. You're a stubborn man, Brian Byrne. Do you always get what you want?" Surprised, she paused. *Stubborn.* A character flaw. If she were really searching for the perfect mate, he wouldn't qualify.

"I *never* get what I want."

She followed his gaze down to where his arousal rose hard, strong. It triggered a twinge that indicated her body would be eager again as soon as it caught its breath. Meanwhile, she'd allow herself one touch. One touch to hold her over. Reaching down, she slid her fingers along the length of him, felt his deep shudder, his iron control. She wanted to test his control. Soon.

"But I will, babe. Count on it." His words were a harsh whisper.

Overconfidence. Another flaw. The scary part was that she didn't care. She wanted every inch of his imperfect self. Her body wasn't discriminating, and her mind was growing less so by the minute. Maybe perfection was overrated.

Besides, why should she worry about his lack of perfection, when she was clearly far from perfect herself. She was greedy, self-indulgent, impulsive, shameless—

Brian interrupted Ally's cataloging of her questionable character traits by standing, then helping her to her feet. She stood docilely as he handed her bra to her, pulled up her panties and jeans, then pulled her sweater over her head.

She fastened her jeans and shoved her bra into a pocket as she watched him try to fasten his own jeans. He winced. She felt a totally inappropriate twinge of pride that he was still hard for her. Was that pathetic, or what? Other people took pride in things like curing disease and building better rockets. She took pride in making a man hard. No, not *a* man. *This* man. There was an important truth in that distinction. She'd think about it later.

"I think we have a visitor." Brian's voice was low, alert.

"What?" She turned, expecting to see Katy or the Old One.

A dark horse stood watching them. Sleek-muscled and the color of the night, the horse turned its head to stare at the field where their horse rested hip shot. The horse's long wild mane blew in the wind that had gradually picked up.

Ally took a fearful step closer to Brian, and he wrapped his arm around her waist as the horse turned its gaze back to them. It watched them with glowing yellow eyes for what must have been only moments, but seemed forever.

Finally, it turned away and galloped toward Ally's horse on silent hooves.

"Ohmigod! The pooka. Katy has to see it." Ally raced toward the wagon. Standing outside, she shouted. "Katy. The pooka!"

Katy pulled open the wagon door and peeked outside. "Where?"

"There . . ." Ally turned to the field. She saw nothing but their horse . . . and an open gate. The pooka had done his mischief and was gone.

Katy frowned at her. "I don't like to be fooled. I haven't seen one darn fairy or ghost on this trip. I'd better see one soon." She took a closer look at Ally, then smiled. "Seems like your bra slipped off when you weren't looking." She went back inside.

Ally exhaled sharply. Damn. She looked up toward the castle. Brian had gone to his shelter. He was the cause of all her emotional turmoil, and now she was seeing pookas.

Alone she stared into the night, and somehow wasn't surprised when she saw the pooka standing on the other side of the wagon. Its yellow eyes mocked her.

"Oh, shut up." She climbed onto the wagon and went inside.

Chapter Sixteen

Ally rubbed her eyes while figuratively scratching her head. What the heck had happened last night? She glanced out at the pale morning light, then took a sip of her coffee. Neither action inspired her.

Last night she'd stood naked in front of fairies and any wandering ghosts who cared to stand around and watch. Oh, and pookas. She couldn't forget her pooka.

Ally enjoyed sex. Even sex with Dave had been okay. Not great, but okay. *Ordinary.* She was an ordinary woman. She usually had sex in darkened bedrooms, not because her body embarrassed her, but because ordinary people did it in ordinary places.

Last night? How would she describe herself? How about totally out of control? Not a hint of pink anywhere on her bare body. Blushing hadn't been an option.

She'd explained away her reaction during the reality experience. *That* woman wasn't anyone she knew. The sensual massage gone wrong? No excuse, but at least she'd done it in an enclosed space.

Last night had simply been . . . Wow! Why this reaction to Brian? She didn't have a clue. Hmm. Cap's potions? Ally smiled. She'd forgotten about those potions. Good. Someone else to blame. Her conscience was clear.

"If you didn't stay up so late writing that book, you wouldn't be half asleep in the morning." Katy was putting things away, getting the wagon ready for their trek to the Cliffs of Moher. "Too bad this wagon doesn't have headlights. We could've gone at night, seen tons of spirits."

"Right." Thank heavens for no lights.

"When're you going to let me see your book?"

"Soon." Never. This couldn't be the book she'd send to her editor. It was too personal, too much about emotions, not enough about the sex Mavis wanted. It was too much about Brian, not the faceless one-night stand her editor would expect. She couldn't seem to stop writing about what she felt inside when she was supposed to be writing about surface sensations.

"I'll get the horse ready." Ally put her empty cup in the sink, grabbed her clothes, and left the wagon. Luckily, no one was around as she headed for the bathroom.

When she came out, she found Brian already busy with the horse. He turned to gaze at her. How did he do that? Just a glance, and poof, she was standing in her emotional birthday suit.

"You look tired." She fiddled with the harness.

His smile was rueful. "Couldn't sleep last night. Troubling thoughts." His gaze turned intense. "It's your fault, babe."

Ally felt a lot better. Misery really needed company to be fulfilling.

An irritated hiss warned Ally they weren't alone. The Old One sat on a nearby wall, and she wasn't a happy cat.

Brian smiled. "The Boss doesn't feel she should be shut out of this trip. She thinks it's her right to go wherever she wants." His smiled widened. "I tried to sneak past her, but she'd sprawled herself across my doorway." He offered an aside. "The Boss likes to protect her investments against marauding night visitors."

Katy had left the wagon and wandered over to listen.

"Anyway, I stepped on her tail. I don't know what she called me, but I'm pretty sure it had two syllables." He shrugged. "She's here, and she wants to go with us."

"I'll talk to her." Katy's militant expression didn't bode well for a calm discussion as she walked over to the wall.

Ally focused on Brian. "I'll drive." She'd definitely try to convince him to ride inside the wagon with Katy. If cell-phone use while driving impaired concentration, she didn't even want to think what Brian Byrne beside her might do. The police would arrest her for driving while under the influence of the most intoxicating male in the universe. How dangerous would *that* be? "Keep me company?" So much for definite tries.

"Interfering old biddy!"

Ally frowned. Every interfering old biddy within ten miles would hear Katy.

"Wouldn't ride anywhere else, sweetheart." He gave the expected response as he stroked the horse's neck.

Ally followed the motion and recalled the slide of his fingers across her skin, felt the prickle of goose bumps along the remembered path.

But just as she had yesterday, Ally sensed an underlying emotion, a tension that had nothing to do with his words. She didn't have time to analyze that hunch, though. They had to get moving before all the noise woke Cap and Jupe.

She paused to listen to the assorted feline screams, growls, and mad-as-hell spitting noises. She sighed. "This will *not* help us sneak away unnoticed."

Unexpectedly, the *calm* discussion ended and Katy rejoined them. "Let's get moving fast. I think she's going to wake the others."

Uh-oh. The Old One was headed for Jupe's shelter in bounding leaps.

As one, Ally, Brian, and Katy clambered onto the wagon.

Brian settled himself close to Ally as she guided the horse down the path to the main road.

Katy hovered in the doorway. "I'll go inside and read that book of yours on Irish fairies, Ally. If there's one of those merrows around, I want to know all about her." She started to close the door behind her, then paused. "Oh, remind me to thank Cap for bringing that thermos of coffee over real early this morning. With everything going on, I wouldn't have had time to fix any before we left." She glanced at Brian. "There's some left. Would you like a cup?"

"No. He doesn't want any." Ally hoped she didn't look as frantic as she felt. "It was awful coffee. Bitter. Yuck." *Calm down.* Logic said that all her reactions to Brian couldn't be potion induced. But logic wasn't on her menu this morning. Ally *wanted* to believe Cap's potions were the culprits because the alternative would plunk responsibility for her actions, her feelings, directly on her own slumping shoulders. And she *wouldn't* fall for someone like Brian, a man she'd have to share every Monday night while the universe watched.

Katy cast her a curious stare. "Tasted great to me. Made me feel all tingly and perky. Bet Brian would like to feel that way."

"Thanks, but I'll pass."

Katy nodded and closed the door behind her. Ally's relief was short-lived.

Brian moved even closer. Now *she* felt all tingly and perky. Wow! If this was potion-induced, it was good. She'd have to tell Cap to go commercial with the recipe. There wouldn't be a droopy sex drive anywhere on Earth.

Ally was as far over as she could go without leaping from the wagon. She considered that option for a moment, then dismissed it. He'd only stop the wagon and scrape her off the road.

"Look at all the empty seat you have. Maybe you should use it. I'm feeling a little scrunched here." She cast him a glance she hoped said, *I am not responding to your body, nana nana.*

His wolfish grin didn't reach his eyes. "I want to get as close to you as I can—" his smile disappeared—"while I tell you about my childhood." He didn't move away.

"Okay, let's get this out in the open. What's with this sudden need to tell me about your childhood?" She would have crossed her arms over her chest if she hadn't been holding the reins.

He narrowed his gaze. "Don't you remember? Cap was giving you some helpful hints. I think it went like, get Brian to open up about his childhood and you'll have him. Lucky for me, Jupe heard you." Anger and something more gleamed in his eyes. "So I'm making it easy for you, babe."

"Jupe heard *Cap.* He didn't hear me say anything. And we all know what a disinterested party Cap is." Now she remembered. The rustling sounds.

Brian's anger horrified her, but it also intrigued her. Women must want to get to him on an hourly basis, so why all the anger over what he thought *she* had done? A thought worth exploring.

"But hey, I can see that telling me about your childhood will start your day right, so I'm all ears." She tried to grin, but it didn't quite work.

He looked startled. "You really want to hear about it?"

She didn't try for casual this time. "I want to hear about *all* of your life, so your childhood is a good place to begin." Ally's intensity surprised even her.

This could be a huge mistake. The more she learned about him, the more she'd have to remember once he'd gone. And sometimes more wasn't better.

"Why?" His tone suggested he couldn't care less about her answer.

Ally gazed at the horse's ears, searching for the perfect lie. "It's part of the 2002 dating ritual. Telling a partner about your life gives a sense of intimacy, a feeling that you know each other, care about each other. It's part of the foreplay." What a bunch of garbage.

Brian shrugged away her comment, as he probably shrugged away so much in his life that he didn't want to hear.

"I don't remember much before I was six years old. When I was six, my mother left me in a spaceport. She told me she'd be back and to be a good boy. She never came back, and I was never a good boy. Guess we were both batting zero."

His voice sounded neutral, as though he were telling someone else's story.

Ally didn't believe that voice. She glanced at his face, but he'd turned away to watch some sheep grazing by the side of the road.

"How did you survive?" Ally leaned against him, as if bodily contact could ease the pain of the boy he'd once been.

He didn't move away from her. "There're lots of things a six-year-old can do to live on the outer planets. Social programs are pretty much nonexistent, so it's every kid for himself. I learned to steal and carry messages that an adult couldn't carry safely."

He paused, and for a moment she thought he wouldn't continue.

Six years old. Ally couldn't imagine a six-year-old on his own. At six, she'd felt safe, cherished. Her most traumatic moment had been her first public appearance. She'd been a celery stalk in her class play.

"There were other . . . services I could perform."

She had no words to describe her emotions. Her churning stomach, her *rage*, were enough.

He scowled, and she had the feeling he hadn't meant to tell her this much. She wasn't sure she could *take* this much. But if he thought he'd drive her away with the horror of his childhood, he didn't know Ally O'Neill.

Brian glanced away from her. "I did what I needed to do to survive."

Ally didn't care whether he wanted her touch

or not; she put her hand on his thigh and squeezed. "If this is supposed to send me screaming into the night, it isn't working. I just wish I could reach through time and strangle the bastards who'd prey on a small child."

She felt the tension leave him as he placed his hand over hers. His soft laughter washed over her, leaving her feeling warm inside.

"I guess I never thought it would scare you away." He rubbed a circular pattern with the pad of his thumb on the back of her hand. "I was *hoping* it wouldn't because Cap was right about something. You get to me, babe."

His admission hung between them, a connection Brian didn't need, but wanted more than anything he'd wanted in a long time.

He sensed her sigh, felt her fingers pushing into his thigh, massaging the tight muscles. Amazing. No matter what part of his body she touched, she always touched *him*. Brian had always thought he knew who he was, but the part of him Ally touched was a stranger.

"Then you don't believe I'm plotting with Cap?" She slanted a small smile his way.

Brian shook his head. "When Jupe first told me what he'd heard, I lost my temper and jumped to conclusions." He gazed at the passing rock walls, and green checkerboard fields relieved by yellow-flowered gorse stretching into the distance. "I don't know why it made me so mad."

She didn't follow up on his comment. "How did you get started in your career?"

He grinned. "I picked Jupe's pocket while he was waiting at the spaceport. He caught me, but didn't press charges after I agreed to listen to his proposal. He'd been scouting the outer planets looking for men he thought had the right look, attitude, and sex drive to make it big in the games. Jupe's always been a great judge of talent." His grin faded. "I owe him a lot. I was sixteen when he caught me, and I trained for two years, then went pro. I never looked back. I've been in the league for twelve years."

"So how do you spend all your wealth?" She tightened her fingers on the reins and stared fixedly between the horse's ears. "I asked you once before, but you didn't give me a straight answer. Guess you didn't trust me. Do you trust me enough now?"

She wanted his trust. Her body language shouted how important it was to her.

Suddenly, he relaxed. He'd tell her the truth. No one else besides Jupe knew what he did with his earnings, but he wanted Ally to know. "I support homeless kids all over the outer planets. Make sure they have places to live, enough to eat, education, and career choices."

"Like *you* never did."

She didn't sound teary, and he didn't hear any pity in her voice. Good thing. If he had, he would have joined Katy inside. He couldn't believe he'd told her about his kids, but the telling felt good. "Don't make me into a martyr. I'm at the highest level of my career. I'm a hero to *Monday Night*

Sex fans everywhere." He hoped she'd smile because all this emotion was making him uncomfortable.

"You're a hero to me, too, Brian Byrne." Her soft answer made his day. No, it made his lifetime.

Brian decided that no matter how spectacular space was, there were still places on Earth that could make you suck in your breath. The Cliffs of Moher had that effect. The caution sign they'd passed on the way in, warning of "very dangerous cliffs ahead," was a classic understatement. And not one guardrail. He wondered how many people had taken a header off these cliffs.

He stood with Ally and Katy on the sandstone ledge where dozens of other tourists milled, staring down almost seven hundred feet to where the Atlantic dashed itself against the cliffs, sending jets of spray into the air. Wow was about the only comment that came to mind. He stepped back.

"I think we have company."

Ally's comment shifted his gaze to where a small group of people and one calico cat were carefully making their way down to the path. It didn't take Nebula's green hair to identify them.

Great. Just great. He turned back to Ally. "They won't come over. They're just keeping track of me." Brian had expected them to follow, but their presence still made him angry.

Katy peered over the edge of the cliff. "I don't hear any spirits, just a bunch of birds." She

277

glared at Ally. "I know, I know. You told me there'd be birds. I don't see any of those merrows either. Can't write a book about nothing. I think I'll try another spot." She started walking farther up the path.

Ally took a step closer to the edge even as Brian took a step back. Extreme heights made him . . . uneasy. Okay, so he was afraid of high places.

"Brian, maybe I'm seeing things, but it looks like there's a woman down there. Come and look." Ally's voice was edged with excitement.

Brian knew his would be edged with fear. "I'll take your word for it." He stared straight ahead, so he wouldn't be tempted to look down. For the first time since he'd arrived in Ireland, he was relieved to see the gray mist rolling in off the ocean. Within minutes, visibility would be gone and they'd return to the wagon.

"It's hard to see, but she doesn't look like she's in trouble. How did she get down there? It's too rough for a boat. She looks like . . ." Ally turned to Brian with widened eyes. "A merrow? I have to get Katy. If she misses this . . ." She turned back to scanning the cliff's base. "Darn. The mist is moving in, and I can't see now. Maybe I just imagined it. What should I do?"

Leaving came to mind. Brian knew his fear was irrational, but knowing didn't end it. The mist cloaked everything in shades of gray. It was like some mythic monster moving in from the sea, touching him with a cold, damp tongue. He shivered, afraid to move for fear he'd step off the now invisible cliff and plunge into the abyss. *Get a grip.* He closed his eyes, blocking out the mist, gathering the shreds of his courage so he could drag Ally and Katy back to the wagon without their knowing he was scared witless.

He opened his eyes to the sound of Ally's surprised gasp.

And stared, horrified, as she teetered on the edge of the cliff. Ally flailed her arms wildly in an attempt to regain her balance. Useless. She would fall to her death.

He reacted. No time to think. Stepping to the cliff's edge, he grabbed the back of her jacket. But her forward motion caught him off guard. He hadn't had a chance to set his feet, and her weight yanked him off balance.

In a moment of clarity, he knew if he didn't let her go, he'd go over the edge with her.

He held on.

Suddenly, someone grasped him from behind and pulled. The backward yank was just enough to give him a chance to get his feet under him. With a last effort he didn't think he had in him, he jerked Ally back from the edge.

She fell into his arms, her legs barely supporting her, and just shook. His own legs felt like he'd returned to Earth after a month of space's weightlessness. Weak and shaky. He wrapped his arms around her and forced himself not to crush her with his need to keep her safe. He took several long, calming breaths.

Then he turned to thank the person who'd

grabbed him. He stared into the eyes of the woman he'd seen at the keep. Claudia? She looked as shaken as he felt.

"Thanks. We'd be lying at the bottom of the cliff by now if you hadn't grabbed me." He smoothed his hand over Ally's hair, felt her shaking ease.

"I'm glad I was standing close enough. Another few feet in this mist and I wouldn't have seen what was happening." Claudia focused her attention on him, never once glancing at Ally. "I couldn't let you go over."

Brian frowned. Why did he feel Claudia's message was for him alone? He abandoned that thought as Ally drew a deep breath and stepped away from him.

"What can I say? Thanks, Claudia." Ally didn't glance toward the cliff's edge. "I think I've seen all I ever want to see of the Cliffs of Moher."

Katy materialized out of the mist. "Didn't see a darn thing. Maybe Ireland doesn't have any fairies or ghosts. I sure wish something exciting would happen. Did you guys see anything?"

My life flash in front of me? No, Brian now knew that in the moment before death there were no thoughts, just the frantic effort to stay alive. He glanced at Ally, saw her shake her head. He took his cue from her. "Nothing to see, Katy."

"Hmmph. I'll meet you in the wagon. May as well take a nap so I'll be fresh for tonight. Maybe those tortured spirits buried under the keep will make up for this." She disappeared into the mist.

Brian glanced around. Claudia had left, and the others were nowhere in sight. In the distance, he could hear the faint echo of voices, but within their gray cocoon he and Ally could well be the only people on Earth.

"Thanks for not telling Katy what happened." Her voice seemed disembodied, as though she were speaking outside herself. "How could I explain that the cliffs almost gained two more spirits, that the next time she visited this spot she'd definitely hear ghostly shrieks? Mine."

Brian knew she expected him to laugh. He didn't.

Ally leveled a stare at him, searching, emotionless. Brian sensed the emotionless part was simply an attempt to hold reaction at bay.

"Why didn't you let go, Brian? If Claudia hadn't grabbed you, you would've gone over with me." Her gaze never wavered from his face.

Because in that instant where thought ended and inner truth began, I knew I couldn't lose you. What did that mean? He couldn't explain something to her that he didn't understand himself.

So he gave her another reason, one he'd just realized. "Redemption comes at unexpected moments. I told you that I broke a promise once, but I never told you the promise." He could close his eyes and pull up the scene with Landis as though it were yesterday. Funny how the really ugly moments in life stuck with you. "I was sixteen. It was right before Jupe found me. Landis was one of the guys I ran with. We were just a gang of petty thugs, but we'd vowed to take care of each other. He'd climbed a bilectron power pole to try to reach the window of a gem distribution center, a place where precious stones from across the galaxy are kept in controlled conditions until dealers order them."

"You don't have to tell me this, Brian." Her voice had softened, grown warmer.

"I want to." It was that simple. He wanted her to understand. "I didn't go up with him because . . . I'm afraid of heights." He glanced at her to make sure she wasn't laughing.

She studied him, unsmiling, not judging, just letting him speak.

"He'd almost reached the top when something snagged him, and he couldn't get loose." The telling got harder now. "He called down for me to climb up and help him." Brian gazed into the mist, seeing the pole, feeling his fear. "I yelled for him to relax because I'd be up to get him. I stood at the bottom of that pole, tried to step up, and froze. I was so afraid I thought I'd throw up. Maybe I would've eventually gone up to him, but in the end I didn't have to."

He knew his voice had turned bitter, rank with all his old self-loathing. "In some faraway power station, someone pressed a button." His breathing caught with the remembered horror. "The force of the energy bolt threw Landis from the pole. He was dead before he hit the ground." Brian exhaled on a long breath of old pain. "I broke my promise to Landis, but I never broke another one."

She closed her eyes, and within her silence he touched peace. Her understanding wrapped him in warm, caring arms.

Opening her eyes, she slid her palm along his clenched jaw, then gently massaged the tense muscles along the back of his neck. "You need to let it go."

He felt everything go at once: his tension, his bitterness, his belief that he would never face his fear. The relief left him weak. "I did." He fixed his gaze on her, wanting her to understand what the last few minutes had done for all his yesterdays. "Today."

She nodded, her gaze warm with something he'd never seen in any woman's eyes. Something more than desire. "I'm glad." But before he could do any analyzing, the wind picked up, and the swirling mist dissipated enough for them to see the path that led back to the wagon.

Brian could make out the shapes of other people who'd been standing near them when the mist drifted in. He was no longer alone with Ally, had never really been alone. "What made you lose your balance? Did all that open space make you dizzy?" He shook his head. "Makes sense to me. I was dizzy, and I wasn't even at the edge."

Ally didn't answer him as she peered into the mist at the people surrounding them. There wasn't much to see beyond darker shades of gray.

Finally, she turned to look at him. "I didn't lose

my balance." She started walking up the path that would lead them away from the cliffs.

Now he was puzzled. He caught up with her. "What happened, Ally?"

This time she didn't look at him, didn't pause as she walked toward the wagon.

"Someone pushed me."

Chapter Seventeen

"Someone *pushed* you?" He clasped her shoulder and swung her to face him. "Are you sure?" His voice was low, deadly, suggesting that if she was sure, he'd hunt down the person responsible and do some serious bone breaking.

Was she sure? Her eyes filled as the reaction she'd kept at bay set in. She'd been sure a few minutes ago. She could still feel the press of a palm against her back, the hard shove . . .

Had the shove come before or after she lost her balance, before or after Brian reached for her? Had it really been a shove, or the accidental brush of an arm against her back? Details faded when compared to her recollection of the moment she knew she would die. *That* memory had a sharp clarity that would fuel nightmares for years.

Ally took a deep breath and swiped at the corners of her eyes. She would *not* cry. "I'm not sure." Only one person had been close enough to know for sure. "Did you see anyone?"

He cursed. She didn't understand what the words meant, but she understood their intent. "I didn't see a thing. I had my eyes closed." He glanced around. "We need to go back, ask some questions."

Ally shook her head. "It was probably an accident. Why would anyone want to push me off a cliff? Wait, I forgot. My favorite reviewer, Mrs. Scowly, thinks the world needs to be saved from more of my books." Her attempt at a joke sounded lame even to her.

Brian frowned. He didn't look convinced.

Ally pressed on. "Whoever bumped into me is probably long gone. Besides, no one could've seen anything in this mist. Claudia was close to us, and she didn't see anyone." A shiver slid up her spine. "I want to get out of here."

Reluctantly, he nodded. He clasped her hand, and they walked the rest of the way to the wagon in silence.

Katy stood in the doorway waiting for them. "It's about time. Jupe and the rest drove past a few minutes ago. Didn't look too happy." She grinned. "I couldn't resist pulling someone's puffed-up calico tail. When Jupe rolled down his window to ask if you were in the wagon, I said you hadn't gotten back yet. Made a big show of being mad because I had to wait for you to finish making hot love down on the cliff. Said you'd wanted to do it dangerously. Jupe got real pale and the Old One did some whisker twitching. Guess they pictured you rolling right off that cliff in a fit of ecstasy."

Katy chuckled, Brian looked thunderous, and Ally was beyond confused. Not about her near-death experience. She'd convinced herself that was an accident. Nothing else made sense. Murder needed a motive, and no one would profit by her death.

Ally was confused about Brian. Distracted, she allo.ved him to help her onto the wagon, said nothing as he picked up the reins and guided the horse back to the main road. She barely noticed when Katy disappeared into the wagon.

It seemed natural for her to sit close to him. When he shifted both reins to one hand, wrapped his free arm around her shoulders, and pulled her against him, it felt right. Ally knew nothing could happen to her now.

Okay, she could explain away the safety feeling. If you couldn't feel safe with a man who'd saved your life, who could you feel safe with? But what about her other feelings? The feelings of desire mixed with yearning?

Desire she could understand. It was lips, nipples, and lower-body specific. A clenching need that kicked in automatically when Brian was around.

The yearning? Troubling. It wasn't specific. It was a need, but a need for what? It was sadness, but not for today. It was sadness for her tomorrows when Brian Byrne would be only a memory. It was a wanting for something *more*, something just out of reach.

"When we get back to the keep, you need to lie down and rest. I'll take care of Katy and the others. You'd better eat something, too. All you had was Cap's coffee this morning." He tightened his grip on her shoulders.

She turned her head to study his profile. A strong jaw, clenched now as he worried about her. Eyes and lips narrowed in concentration, no doubt ready to do battle if she dared argue with him.

"I'll tell everyone the coffee made you sick. Do you need anything from town? I could borrow Cap's car and get it."

"You don't know how to drive." She couldn't help it; she smiled.

A scowl line formed between those incredible eyes. "If Cap can drive, I can drive. No one's going to stop me, babe."

Stubborn, hardheaded, bossy. He would never be anyone's perfect husband. So why did her yearning for him fill her until she felt she would explode with it? One of life's great mysteries. "I have all I need here, Brian."

She was quiet for the rest of the trip home. Home? When had she started thinking of the keep as home?

As soon as Brian stopped the wagon, he went back to talk to Katy while Ally sat staring at the keep and the cliff beyond. She couldn't seem to keep away from cliffs. One misstep and she'd fall a long way. Brian? Maybe she'd already stepped off her own personal cliff where he was concerned.

Brian came out of the wagon a few minutes later with Katy in tow.

Katy hopped off the wagon, then peered up at Ally. "You look a little pale. Brian's right, you need to rest. He's going to unhitch the horse. Then we'll take a stroll up to the keep. See if there're any tortured spirits around." She glared up at the afternoon sky. "Guess I won't see anything while it's still light, but Brian said he'd tell me some great stories about his sex games. Maybe I can work those into my book. Need to fill some pages since the fairies are a bust."

Ally smiled. *Thank you, Brian.* She went into the wagon and grabbed some chocolate chip cookies. Hey, a diet rich in chocolate led to emotional balance. Then she lay down on the bed Katy had fixed for her. She didn't bother undressing.

Ally didn't know how long she'd been staring up at the ceiling mirror, thinking deep thoughts of maybes and what-ifs, when a calico reflection leaped onto the foot of her bed. Glancing down, Ally narrowed her gaze on the Old One, who stared fixedly back at her. "How'd you sneak past Brian?"

The Old One's yellow-eyed gaze suggested it

Nina Bangs

wouldn't be hard for a female with a talent for sneaking.

Ally linked her hands behind her head. "I don't know why you're here, but since you are, maybe I can run some ideas past you. You look like a woman who can keep a secret." Maybe it was her imagination, but the Old One's whiskery expression seemed to soften into almost friendly lines.

"I did some checking up on the man who's supposed to be the father of the Brian Byrne in this time. Our Brian is impersonating his son."

The Old One's eyes narrowed on the word "our."

"Understand that this present-day Brian Byrne was mentioned in our Brian's family history. He really existed. Or should I say exists? Funny thing, though. When I did some investigating, I found that Kieran Byrne, father of the 2002 version of Brian Byrne, was a priest totally devoted to his calling. So there could never have been a Brian Byrne. What do you make of that?"

The Old One's eyes gleamed, and the ancient intelligence Ally saw there was scary. Ally had no doubt the cat was turning the information over in her mind and coming to a conclusion. Unfortunately, the Old One wouldn't be able to tell her what she concluded.

Suddenly, the Old One's eyes grew rounder, if that was possible. A cat might not express much emotion, but Ally had no trouble reading horror on every fuzzy inch of the Old One's face. She leaped from the bed, ran to the door, and slipped outside. Probably running to Jupe to try and pass on her information. Ally smiled at the mental picture.

Her smile faded as she tried to think of what might be serious enough to scare the Old One. Okay, for the Old One, disaster would be Brian not returning to win another championship for her. Ally thought back over the conversation. What had she said that would make the Old One think Brian wasn't going home?

Kieran Byrne had no son, but history recorded that a Brian Byrne, the son of Kieran Byrne, lived during this time. How . . . ?

Her revelation didn't come as a clap of thunder. Ally just knew. Kieran Byrne never had a son. *Her* Brian was the one history had recorded. He'd never returned to 2502. He'd stayed in this time to live out his life. *To become his own ancestor.*

Her first explosion of joy was quickly followed by a mental "Huh?" and some symbolic head scratching.

This level of weirdness was beyond Ally's grasp. If she had been standing, she would have fallen down. How could something like this happen? But what did she know about cosmic truths and time travel, the possible and impossible?

Okay, don't get too excited. Think this out. Maybe Brian wouldn't stay. The people in Liscannor knew he was here, knew he was a Byrne, so they'd record him as such even if he left tomorrow. But if he went back to 2502 without siring a child, *he* wouldn't exist, would he? She drew a deep, steadying breath. That was what had scared the Old One. Because worse than losing her star player would be if he had never existed, had never won her a championship.

Ally had to tell him. She'd explain what she'd found out, then let him come to his own conclusion. The scary part? What if he didn't believe her? He would never *want* to stay in this time. With his attitude toward promises, he'd never walk away from his contract with the Old One. And what about the children he supported, the famous life he lived in the future?

She tried to relax. Maybe she'd overreacted. If he already existed in 2502, surely his existence couldn't be canceled. *Could a person change history?* Ally closed her eyes on that frightening thought.

She opened her eyes and put a lid on her out-of-control imagination. Okay, maybe this was all a big fat mistake. Maybe Brian's mother lied about his history. Maybe he was some other Brian Byrne. It was a common Irish name. If she looked, she'd find a perfectly logical explanation for all this.

She thought about everything that had happened since she'd met Brian. Fine. So logical was out.

She felt relieved when Katy entered the wagon. Ally needed a distraction from the dark paths of speculation her mind was wandering.

"Hmmph. I won't be bothering with those tor-

tured souls for a few days. Nebula said it'll be a
full moon tonight, and there's not a cloud in the
sky. I want to give it my best shot, so I'm going
to go down those steps on the darkest night I can
find." She reached into a cabinet and pulled out
a pack of crackers. "Think I'll turn in early tonight."

*No need to go rooting under castles for tortured
souls, Katy, when you're sharing a wagon with
one.* Ally sighed. Guess Katy wouldn't think she
was exotic enough to qualify as a genuine tortured soul.

"Nothing is happening here. If things don't li-
ven up soon, we may as well move on." Katy
quickly converted the bench seat into a double
bed, then plopped down on it. "I might even turn
cynical in my old age. Really thought I'd see
some paranormal action in a place like this."

Ally frowned. She, on the other hand, could do
with a little less action.

"You did *what?*" Brian glared at Jupe.

Jupe paced nervously in front of his shelter
while Nebula completed what seemed like her
thousandth deep knee bend. Inside the shelter,
Cap was probably taking a nap. The Old One
sprawled across a nearby rock wall taking in the
last dying minutes of Ireland's long summer daylight.

Jupe paused in his pacing. "I thought I was doing you a favor. I figured you'd be bored stiff after
a few days, so I changed your schedule a little."

"*How* little?"

Jupe wouldn't meet his gaze. "I told the travel agent to have a stag pick us up this Sunday."

Two days. "I won't go." A little more than a week wasn't nearly enough time to explore his new feelings for Ally. A year, a century, wouldn't be enough.

Jupe rubbed the back of his neck in a weary gesture. "The longer you stay, the harder it'll be. You signed a five-year contract. That's a promise to the Old One, to your fans."

"When does *my* life begin?" He'd felt the stirrings of discontent this past season, but nothing like this.

"You have one of the best lives in the universe. You're famous, wealthy, in the prime of your life." Jupe sounded a little desperate.

Jupe had left one thing out. Brian had no one to love. And the concept of love as a need rocked Brian's world. He'd never thought beyond his job, his obligations. He enjoyed the senses, especially touch. A good meal, a soft bed, a hard workout. Love was an abstract, an *emotion*. Abstracts made him uneasy. How did you touch an emotion? *You touch an emotion every time you slide your fingers across Ally's body.*

"You and the others can go home in two days. I'm staying. Oh, and tell the travel agency I'll stick with my original time of departure." He needed to be alone to sort out his feelings, to figure out where the love-and-Ally connection was going.

He turned and walked away from Jupe. Stopping at his shelter just long enough to grab something to eat, Brian wandered into the keep. The mystery of the great hall beckoned. Seating himself on a large stone, he stared across the open space that had once been the center of the castle's life. Now overgrown and shadowed by growing darkness, he could still imagine how it had once been.

Ally found him there. She'd wrestled with the problem of the very real Brian and the Brian who might never be until her stress headache had driven her to Advil. When the pain had finally eased, Katy's snoring had driven her from the wagon. With the light of a full moon to guide her, she'd gravitated to the keep's great hall, a place of mystery and violence that might take her mind off her own unanswered questions.

She stood studying him. His leather jacket emphasized broad shoulders she knew instinctively would always be able to bear life's problems, *or the ones of anyone he loved.* Even seated and relaxed, his back was straight. He'd never bend under pressure or abandon obligations he saw as his. She frowned. This might not be a good thing, especially if honoring his contractual obligations by going home led to his ceasing to exist. He'd stretched his legs out in front of him, and she couldn't help wondering if they'd ever again carry him into a packed stadium, if frenzied fans would ever again scream his name.

And as much as she didn't want to think about his returning to the Monarchs, she'd choose that scenario a million times if it meant he would still exist.

He glanced up and caught her stare. Patting a spot beside him, he returned his gaze to the moonlight-bathed center of the great hall.

Wordlessly, she sat beside him.

"Feeling better?" He cast a searching look.

"Yes." No.

"I've been sitting here wondering about them." He rubbed a spot on his thigh that must ache in the damp Irish weather. "They must've had their own problems, things they thought were really important. Then they died." He shrugged. "And nothing mattered anymore. *Nothing.*"

"How does that translate to our lives? Does it mean we should just relax and let fate decide what happens to us, that in the end nothing matters?" No, she could never think that way. As long as she had a breath in her body, things would matter. *He would matter.* Despairing, she knew that particular truth would follow her to the last minute of her life.

He shook his head. "Never, babe. It means take joy where it's given, because tomorrow doesn't come with a guarantee."

Tell him now. He'd offered her a lead-in. Ally took a deep breath for courage. "When I was in town with Cap the other day, I started thinking about what Eamonn Clancy said. He thought

Kieran Byrne never had a son. I was curious, so—"

"Why were you curious?" He turned a strangely intent gaze on her.

Because, God help me, I've fallen in love with a man from the future who makes women happy by the thousands. "I read mysteries. I *love* mysteries." Did her lie carry the right degree of indifference?

"Sure. Makes sense." He glanced back at the great hall. "What did you find out?"

Ally had the feeling her answer had disappointed him.

"Kieran Byrne was a priest, a man who never would have broken his vow of celibacy. He couldn't have sired a child." There it was. She'd wait for him to think it through, to come to his own conclusion.

He grew still. She sensed the moment he realized the implication.

"What you're thinking is that if Kieran Byrne was the last of his line, then I couldn't possibly exist." He didn't sound upset, only thoughtful.

She nodded. "Someone had to carry on the line."

"You're thinking that I stayed, that *I* was the Brian Byrne history recorded as Kieran Byrne's son." He didn't pause to let her answer. "But I wouldn't stay even if I wanted to."

The last pitiful spark of hope she'd tried to keep alive flickered and died. "Of course not."

"I have a five-year contract with the Monarchs."

"You could come back." She knew it wouldn't happen. He probably knew it wouldn't happen either. People changed. Life got in the way. Memory faded. In five years his life wouldn't include a trip back to a barely remembered interlude. "But what if—"

"What if I don't exist anymore? I'm not worried." His voice was grim with his determination to exist. "History can't be changed. Besides, after so many years, records aren't always too accurate. Most of the Byrnes came from County Wicklow. Maybe my history chip is wrong. Maybe I'm a County Wicklow Byrne."

History can't be changed. The statement hung between them. And she wondered whether he was as sure as he sounded. She wouldn't think about it any more right now, or she'd need another Advil.

"Why are you sitting here?" It was warm for an Irish night, but still chilly.

He grinned. "Getting over my anger at Jupe. Before he left 2502, he decided that since I'd probably be bored after a few days here, he'd move my departure date up a little."

Ally's stomach clenched. "When?"

"In two days. But I told him to forget it. When the stag comes, it can take Jupe and the others home. I'm staying my full three weeks."

Ally mentally pried loose the stomach muscles that had shifted north and clamped around her heart. As her heart picked up its former rhythm, her stomach plopped back into place. Her internal organs didn't handle shock well.

"You never explained much about the stags. How do they travel through time?" Ally glanced at the moonlit center of the great hall. She let the peace of the place seep into her. For the first time, she considered the joy rather than the tragedy that had taken place here. Weddings celebrated, children born. Long-dead Byrnes had probably loved this place. Warts and all, home was still home.

Brian stood, then stretched. Ally followed the motion, and hoped her hunger for him didn't show.

"No one knows. They've always been here. Legends of white stags have existed during most periods of history." He sat down again. "We keep them safe because if they feel threatened, they won't return to that particular time period." His gaze shifted back to the great hall.

Okay, what to talk about now? Should she leave? Had she overstayed her welcome? Infringed on his privacy? She sighed. The heck with his privacy. She wanted to be with him as long as possible. Ally O'Neill had no pride where he was concerned.

"We need to get back to your book soon." He slanted her a grin. "Better think up some good fantasies before my consultation time expires."

She glanced around her, at the ancient stone walls, the open space filled only with moonlight that both drew and repelled her. And remembered. *Why do I have to dance in that particular spot?*

It's about family. Once in my life, I want to feel that connection, to know that this was the spot where my ancestors danced . . . loved.

There weren't many things she could give him. He already had fame, wealth, and millions of fans. She couldn't give him back his lost childhood. But there was one thing no one but Ally O'Neill *could* give him.

She would dance for him.

Chapter Eighteen

Brian watched as Ally stood, then walked to the center of the grassy space. The sensual sway of her hips drew him. She couldn't disguise the erotic message of those hips even under her oversized tunic sweater. He'd noticed that sexy walk the first night they'd met. Coming or going, Ally O'Neill was a treat.

He smiled. He'd never thought of a woman's walk as arousing, but then he'd never watched women move. Not enough time. No, that wasn't the truth. It was Ally. Only Ally's walk could affect his body.

Brian frowned as she stopped and twirled to face him. What was she doing?

"If the great hall were still here, where would I be?"

"A long table would be there. Why?" He

301

watched, puzzled, as she moved away from him to stand close to the far wall.

"Here?"

"The fireplace."

She grinned. "The one big enough to roast a whole ox? It's a yucky thought, but at least I'll be virtually warm."

He returned her grin. "You don't need to be virtually warm when you're wearing the wool from a thousand Aran sheep in that one sweater."

"Not for long." She turned her back to him, grasped the bottom of her sweater and started to pull it over her head.

"Have you lost your mind? What's this all about?" Any minute now he'd have to cough because his heart had leaped to his throat, and he couldn't breathe.

"Nope. My mind's not the part I lost. Guess again." Her voice was muffled by the sweater that briefly covered her face.

He rose and strode to the center of the great hall, then stopped as though he'd walked into a stone wall. She'd finally managed to remove her sweater and drop it to the ground.

No bra. He stared at the long slim line of her bare back, the slight indentation of her spine, and the smooth expanse of skin shaded golden by the sun, and heard the roar of his inner beast, alive after thirty years of silence. "Okay, what's this about?" Mild words that gave her no hint of what churned inside him.

Ally didn't turn to him, but kicked off her shoes

and worked at her jeans until she could slide them down over her hips. He narrowed his gaze as she made a big production of wiggling her bottom to make the jeans slide more easily. His inner beast had added breathing fire to its repertoire.

No panties. Her narrow waist flowed into a rounded bottom that made him weak. He wanted to go down on his knees, slide his fingers up her long legs and touch each soft cheek with his lips, his tongue.

"It's about a fantasy, Byrne." Slowly, she turned to face him. "Tonight, a gypsy will dance for you." Her voice died on a whisper as she began to move.

He stood riveted by her motion. She raised her arms above her head and her breasts lifted, swayed gently to the rhythm of the music only she could hear.

If he went to her now, he could fill his palms with her breasts, rub his thumbs across her nipples until they grew hard, as hard as the erection pressing against his jeans. He was in pain, pain he wanted to end by burying himself inside her. Pain he wanted to savor and enjoy until he couldn't stand it anymore. His body was undecided about which he wanted more.

But his mind knew. He'd been trained to finish fast, but tonight he'd make it slow. An endless feast of looking, touching, and tasting. And if the doing killed him, the on-site spirits could drag his satiated body from the great hall.

"Why'd you change your mind?" *Idiot. Don't question, just enjoy.*

Her smile mocked. "I had a change of heart." She looked past him and her gaze grew distant. "Do you hear the harp?"

"No." How could he hear anything with the roaring in his ears?

Her smile turned teasing. "If you could, you'd probably recognize it as the famous Irish harper Turlough O'Carolan's 'Carolan's Welcome.'"

"Sure." Brian edged closer, the better to see what she was doing with her hips. "You know a lot about everything, don't you, sweetheart?" Her hip motion looked like one of Nebula's clench and thrust exercises but with a rhythm guaranteed to bring a strong man to his knees.

"I'm a thorough researcher."

He figured she was thorough in all things as she turned her back to him. Spreading her legs, she lifted her long blond hair from her neck in a display of blatant temptation. She finished him off by slowly rotating her hips.

"Like to see a man suffer?" He moved closer.

Ally turned to face him, then lifted her breasts in her palms, an offering no man could resist. "Are you suffering?" She looked hopeful.

"Payback is sweet, babe." Every body part he owned seemed swollen with need; his throat was no exception. He didn't even try to get rid of its huskiness. "Is that an authentic gypsy dance?"

She rolled her eyes up in her head as proof she was giving his question great thought. "Umm, I don't think so. I think an authentic dance has more kicks and twirls. But when I twirl too much I get dizzy and fall down."

He was close enough now to see the thin sheen of sweat that made her body glisten in the moonlight, her wide-eyed uncertainty that belied the boldness of her dance.

Tentatively, she reached out and touched a strand of his hair that lay on his shoulder. He clasped her hand, holding it to him. "I want you, babe. Here, where generations of my family made love." Love? He'd never thought of having sex as making love.

She shivered, and he didn't know if it was from the chilly air or fear. *Excitement?* He could hope.

In a part of him that recognized cosmic truths, he knew this would be one of the determining moments of his life. Why? He didn't know, didn't care. All he understood was his need, and his need went beyond anything he'd ever felt, beyond the hard demand of his body, beyond his drive for release. "I'm safe, Ally. An inhalant that won't wear off for another couple of weeks." His smile was grim. "I've traded away my incentive clause for this." The incentive clause would have been useless anyway. Right now, he couldn't imagine feeling any incentive for anything that didn't involve Ally.

She shook her head, and her hair moved in a golden tangle across her shoulders. "You'll never be a safe man. That's part of your charm." She cast him a teasing glance, her brown eyes luminous in the moonlight. "*You* might be safe, but *I* don't feel very safe right now."

The topic had shifted. "Smart lady. The Byrnes were lords of this keep, and they were a dangerous lot." He shrugged out of his jacket and flung it to the ground. "But a dangerous man is nothing in the hands of a beautiful gypsy woman." With one motion, he drew his T-shirt over his head and let it drop beside his jacket.

He'd reached to unsnap his jeans when she laid her palm flat against his chest. He froze.

Slowly, she ran her palm down the center of his chest, let the weight of her hand rest right above where his fingers still touched his jeans. He sucked in his breath as his erection reacted to her anticipated touch.

"Do you know how much joy touching you gives me?" Her voice was a low murmur of seduction.

Did she understand the power of what she'd said, how much it aroused him? During a game, *he* did the touching, but no one drew pleasure from touching him.

Holding her gaze, he unsnapped his jeans. Stepping back, she watched him discard them along with his shoes. He was glad he wore nothing beneath his jeans, wanted her to see the full extent of his need for her.

She stepped close to him again. "I want to explore your body first, before you touch me and I lose all rational thought." Her voice was a soft purr of anticipation. "I've figured something out.

Touch is all about perspective. I touched Dave because I thought I had a duty to our marriage." Her words were barely a whisper. "I touch you because I know I'll die from want if I don't."

Brian couldn't have said anything if his life depended on it.

Ally feathered her fingers along his jaw and throat. He clenched his jaw in response to the heat she left behind. Her fingers rested at the base of his throat where his pulse beat hard and fast, his blood pounding with a level of need he'd never thought to feel.

When she allowed her fingers to linger at his throat, he spoke in a guttural voice he didn't recognize. "During the games I've waited hours to take my pleasure. But with you . . . ? Don't press your luck, babe."

Her laughter echoed off the ancient walls, the ripple of it filling dark corners where laughter had fled hundreds of years ago. Brian could almost feel the keep expand with the long-absent sound.

She slid her hand behind his neck, lifted his hair, let the strands glide through her fingers. "I've always wondered what men found so erotic about a woman's hair. I understand now."

Continuing her path of discovery, she trailed a line of sensation over his chest, pausing to touch each of his nipples, to squeeze gently, then roll them between her fingers.

He sucked in his breath, calling on all his vaunted discipline to keep from reaching out to her, to keep from begging her to touch him with her mouth. But his discipline wouldn't save him. He knew this with every despairing particle of his soul.

He looked into his heart, and found the truth. The control that had made him the best in the universe was a sham. He'd only exercised rock-hard control because he'd never wanted a woman, never *really* wanted her. His *body* had wanted other women. Everything that made him a man wanted Ally.

Once again, she placed her palm flat against his stomach, pressed firmly as she moved her hand down to his groin and paused, as though she wanted to make sure he felt her.

He felt. And would feel her again and again through the long years, every time he closed his eyes, every time he *remembered*. "Not a good time to rest, babe."

She smiled a shaky smile. "Give me my moment of enjoyment, Byrne."

He moved his legs apart: wanting, anticipating.

Ally didn't disappoint. She slid shaking hands roughly up the inside of his thighs. He understood the roughness, the shaking. This much hunger wasn't gentle. The friction of her hands on his flesh seared him, and the heat spread in a flash of desire that almost buckled his knees.

"This is what I want." She cupped him, rubbing her thumbs in a circular pattern over his skin. Then she clasped his erection in both hands, squeezed gently. "I want you inside me, filling all my emptiness, filling me with memories to get me through the long, cold nights of winter." She touched the tip of his arousal with a forefinger.

He looked down, watched her finger touch him, then stared at the drop of moisture that appeared in response. He could stand no more.

Stepping back, he bent and quickly spread her thick sweater on the ground. Then he lifted her in his arms and laid her on the makeshift bed. He straddled her legs as he knelt over her. "I need your lips on my body. I need to slide my fingers over you, into you. I need to taste you."

With a moan, she wrapped her arms around his neck and pulled him down to her.

He took her mouth with barely controlled savagery, his hunger clenching his stomach, tightening his groin. She opened her lips to him, her tongue exploring his mouth as his did hers, her taste forever a part of his present, his future.

Abandoning her mouth, he kissed a path from the sensitive skin behind her ear down to her breasts. Sliding his tongue over each nipple, he felt her tremble, her soft pleading as she arched her back.

Discipline disappeared. The determination to make this long and sweet died a quick death. He felt himself sliding down the slippery slope of raw desire, gaining momentum with each touch.

He closed his lips over her nipple, savored the sensation of her flesh against his tongue. Gently, he nipped her, felt her buck beneath him.

"If you don't go faster, Byrne, I guarantee your family tree will lose its last limb." Her threat was born of heat and desperation, whispered between panted breaths.

Her desperation was catching. He slid his tongue down the middle of her stomach, watched the muscles contract, breathed in the scent of lavender soap and aroused woman.

Straightening, he gulped a deep breath of chilly Irish air, let the cool breeze play across his heated flesh. Then he deliberately tortured himself by rubbing his erection the length of her inner thigh, purposely paused as she spread her legs in encouragement, and then denied himself the almost overpowering need to plunge into her.

Ignoring her muffled curses on his family ten generations removed, he placed his hands beneath her buttocks and lifted her to his mouth. Touched her with his lips, his tongue. Slid his tongue along her hot slickness, teased the one nub of female flesh that had no resistance to this particular type of teasing, then probed her with his tongue. He plunged deeply, in a sensual mimicry of what he'd soon do with another body part that was fast losing patience.

She cried his name and shuddered within his grasp. He memorized the sound, the feel, the taste. Forever.

His own shudder ripped through him. And he knew if he went on he wouldn't be able to control himself. He, who'd spent his whole adult life dedicated to control. He lowered her to the sweater and sat back on his heels. Drew breaths in deep gasps, tried to think of icy pools and ugly women.

"I want to touch you with *my* mouth. Now. You're not the only mouth in town, you know." Her demand was raw hunger. "Hah! No one takes away an O'Neill's right to use her mouth."

"So you're saying O'Neills are mouthy?" He tried to grin, but he was afraid it came out more like a grimace. "Isn't this the way you wanted it, babe? You, zip effort?" He thought about her initial touching. Okay, so maybe not zip effort. "Me doing all the pleasing?"

She stuck out her bottom lip and glared at him. He didn't know how long he could resist that bottom lip.

"I changed my mind. Mind changing is a woman's prerogative."

She wiggled down farther between his spread thighs until her mouth was so close to his erection, he could feel the warmth of her breath. He beat back the urge to once again lift her, to push into her, bury all his flesh in her, then slide out only to plunge deeply again and again.

Brian was a master of control. He had to keep reminding himself. He'd make it last for Ally.

But she put a major hole in his resolve when she slid her fingers around his length and pulled him down to her. Before he could do more than suck in his breath, she slipped her lips over him, took him deeply while her tongue sealed her doom.

Nina Bangs

All thoughts of slow and sweet disappeared. Hot and dangerous took their place.

"I tried, babe." What had happened to all the gentle words he'd intended to say? Gone.

Her mouth held him in molten bondage while her tongue slid along his length, finding every sensitive nerve guaranteed to drive him toward the inevitable explosion of the senses. When she gently nipped him, he could stand no more.

Once again he slid his hands beneath her bottom and lifted her to him. He'd always prided himself on the controlled power of his thrust. Now his hands shook, and his body wasn't answering to him anymore.

His erection was strong between her spread thighs, and as he glanced down in his last moment of lucidity, he recognized that this was the final moment of his old life, his last chance to back off and leave the future untouched. If he entered her now, nothing would ever be the same again.

He thrust deeply, burying himself smoothly in her heat. Her body welcomed him, clenching tightly to hold him inside her. She wrapped her long legs around him, urging him on with small cries of frantic pleasure.

His body automatically picked up the familiar rhythm, each plunge pushing him closer to his release. *Too fast.* He could feel the mounting wave pushing at him, carrying him along as he flailed frantically to slow things down. He

312

couldn't finish before her, never had left a woman behind.

"No!" His cry was one of denial. Denial that his body had failed him in his most important moment. And pleasure. A pleasure so intense his breath stilled for a moment as he tried to prolong the sensation.

It was the thunder of the wave as it crashed against the rocks, the instant when sea spray shot high into the air, the moment when the wave was at its most powerful. *The second before the wave died.*

He heard Ally's cry join him from a distance. And as he emerged from his shuddering release, he felt her legs still clamped around him. Gently, he lowered her to the sweater and leaned over her, drawing in deep, gasping breaths.

"I'm sorry, babe." He'd made it last for so many women, but he'd failed with the most important woman in his life. And even though he wasn't yet capable of much coherent thought, he knew she *was* the most important woman in his life.

Ally stirred beneath him, and he reached down to smooth her hair away from her face.

She stared at him with wide-eyed awe. "Sorry? You mean it can get better than that?"

He shook his head, focused only on his own failure. "I've always been able to control my release. Nothing like this has ever happened before. I wanted to make it long, make the pleasure last, but I couldn't stop. . . ." His explanation died into shame.

She put her palm against his jaw, forced him to look at her. "Do you know how good that makes me feel? That *I* made you lose control? You've given me a wonderful gift, Brian." She smiled, her lids still heavy with her own climax. "Besides, if you'd made me wait one more second, the spirits would have a whole new vocabulary by now."

He smiled down at her. "That's what I love about you, sweetheart. You take all my negatives and make them into positives."

The word "love" hung between them, then drifted into the quiet night.

Ally gazed up at him, memorized every line of his face, every strand of hair that lay tangled across his gleaming shoulders . . . and wondered if he knew.

I would dance as a gift of love, if I had nothing else to give, if I wanted to give something that would live forever in someone's memory.

Did he know how much she loved him? She hoped not. He'd be going home soon. His sense of honor demanded he fulfill his contract. She wouldn't interfere. But God, it hurt. She glanced away, hoping he didn't see the glisten of tears in her eyes.

"Ally?" He didn't try to hide his concern as he touched her face, forcing her to meet his gaze.

She smiled through her tears. "It's nothing. I'm emotional. Great sex always makes me emotional. It's a weakness."

He frowned. "How much great sex have you had?"

She tried on her thinking-hard expression. "Umm . . . I think this is the first time. Initial experiences are the ones we remember most."

He studied her for a moment, then let it go. "Sleep with me tonight, Ally."

I'd sleep with you forever. "Only if you guarantee the sleeping-to-great-sex ratio will be balanced."

His smile pushed back the sorrow building in her heart. "Can't do. Wouldn't guarantee any sleeping at all."

She made a pretense of thinking deep thoughts. "Sounds fair to me."

Brian lifted her to her feet, helped her dress, then pulled on his jeans. He slanted her a wicked grin. "My thigh's aching again. Guess I overworked it. Think you can do anything for it?"

"Oh, yes." She let the words out in an anticipatory sigh.

Laughing, he wrapped his arm around her waist, and they walked from the great hall toward his shelter.

Just before entering the shelter, she looked up. At the foot of the hill, a dark horse with yellow eyes watched them by the gate he'd just opened.

Ally wasn't surprised. This place, this man, would always remain the magical home of her heart. She raised her hand and waved.

An answering whinny faded into the night.

Chapter Nineteen

How did you measure the length of a day? As Ally sat on the rock wall watching night creep up the sides of the old keep, she decided today had been the longest day of her life.

She'd left Brian sleeping in the early hours of dawn and crept back to her wagon. She didn't wake him because she hadn't a clue what to say that wouldn't involve "I love you." When he left, she didn't want his final impression of 2002 to be her clinging frantically to his ankle, begging him to stay. And the more time she spent with him, the likelier that scenario would be.

He hadn't approached her today, but she'd caught him watching her, his expression brooding. Good. She hated suffering alone.

Ally watched Claudia poking around the keep in the fading light. The old building sure obsessed Claudia. But Ally couldn't criticize when the keep's owner obsessed her.

She forgot about Claudia as Katy wandered over. Katy had given Ally her space today, and Ally was grateful.

"I'm getting all my gear together and going down to that walled-up room as soon as it's dark enough." Katy's expression said the only way Ally could keep her from the room was by tying her hand and foot. "That room is my best chance of seeing some spirits in this blasted place. I'll tell you I'm a disappointed woman right now. If this doesn't pan out, we may as well leave." She cast Ally a searching look. "Whenever you're ready."

She'd never be ready to leave. Not until the moment Brian faded into the future. Then she'd leave Ireland and never return because seeing this place again with Brian not here would destroy her. Okay, maybe when she was eighty years old and living in her memories, she'd make one last visit.

Ally forced her attention back to Katy. "I'll go down with you." She met Katy's gaze and knew her great-aunt recognized the O'Neill stubbornness in her grandniece.

Katy only nodded, then headed back to the wagon. Ally hoped a kind spirit or fairy would appear for Katy. All the technology Katy had stored in her fisherman's vest shouldn't go to waste. And the truth was that Ally wanted Katy to go home happy.

Katy had barely disappeared into the wagon

when Cap sat down on the wall beside Ally.

Ally smiled at him. "What's the matter, Cap? I haven't seen a potion in a couple of days. Running out of recipes?"

He cast her a sly glance. "I only tried one recipe."

"But you said . . ."

"I lied."

"Then the other things you sent, the coffee and juice . . . ?"

He grinned. "Nothing in them. Placebos. I was counting on the power of suggestion."

Ally felt no surprise, only relief. Every bit of emotion she'd experienced, every bit of the love she'd felt, had been hers alone. "Why'd you give up so easily?"

His smile faded. "I didn't need any potions. Love didn't need any prodding with you and Brian. I only hope he makes the right decision."

She couldn't miss the sympathy in his gaze as he stood and headed toward his shelter.

Ally sighed as Nebula headed her way. It seemed if you sat on a rock wall in Ireland long enough, the whole world came to you.

Nebula didn't sit. She probably considered sitting a weakness. "Did the exercises I showed you help last night?"

"What?"

Nebula's expression suggested she was speaking to a slightly dense child. "Did you have enhanced lower-body control in your sexual encounter with Brian?"

"How did you know?" Suspicion flared.

Nebula's glance was dismissive. "Brian has achieved great control of his body, but his face hides nothing." She shrugged. "His feelings are plain to see for someone with heightened sensitivity."

Heightened sensitivity? Ally didn't think so. Emotions would bounce right off Nebula's "more than a woman" superiority like pingpong balls off a steel wall.

"What *are* his feelings?" She shouldn't play into Nebula's need to expound on her many talents, but she needed to know.

Nebula smiled. A real smile.

For the first time, Ally looked beyond Nebula's overbearing exterior and saw the woman within.

"He loves you."

Did he? Ally wanted to believe it, but she had doubts about Nebula's qualifications in the recognizing-undying-love department. "Were you ever in love?"

Nebula's smile faded. "Yes." She looked uncertain.

Ally checked to make sure her jaw hadn't dropped. Nebula with doubts? Amazing.

Nebula's gaze shifted away from Ally. "He was very . . . short. He had superior intelligence, but his body lacked overall tone. He was . . . flabby."

Flabby. It amazed Ally that Nebula even managed to get the word past her lips. Nebula's shallowness in the understanding-love area boggled

Ally's mind. "Too bad. Guess he'd never make more-than-a-man status."

Nebula's expression turned defensive. "I asked him to strengthen himself for me, but he said I must accept him as he was."

Ally got the picture. "I bet you didn't ask. I bet you demanded."

"Perhaps." Nebula still avoided her gaze.

"Has being more than a woman made you happy, Nebula? Has being *alone* made you happy?"

Nebula finally met her gaze. "No."

Ally smiled. "I'm going to share a hard-learned truth with you. It doesn't matter whether he's perfect, if he's perfect for *you*. So I'd suggest you find your short flabby lover and give him a big hug." She glanced at Nebula's massive arms. "Well, maybe not so big."

Nebula nodded. "I accept the advice of one who is also—" she smiled at Ally—"more than a woman." She turned and strode away.

More than a woman? Ally could grow into that title.

Darkness now enveloped the keep, making it no more than a black silhouette. The waves were muted thunder, and Ally shivered. No moon or stars tonight. A cold wind hinted at rain.

Tonight in the great hall, the keep's ancient tragedy would live again. And Ally knew it would bear no resemblance to the moonlit memory of last night.

Tonight she and Katy would visit a different

part of the keep, with a no less bloody inheritance. With Ally's luck, she'd be left fighting off hundreds of tortured spirits, while Katy fiddled with her latest technical equipment and saw zip.

Ally sighed. May as well get it over with.

She'd just pushed herself off the wall when she heard the unmistakable sounds of Eamonn Clancy's donkey cart drawing near. The creaky wheels and plodding hooves of the donkey grew louder until the cart materialized out of the darkness. Eamonn reined the donkey to a halt and waited for Ally to reach him.

Ally stopped beside the cart. "There's no moon, and it feels like rain. They'll drag Bridget's body from the great hall again tonight, won't they?"

Eamonn nodded, but didn't speak.

"Why did you come tonight, Eamonn?" Ally decided the old man was as obsessed with the keep as Claudia.

"Something will happen this night." He turned a confused gaze on her. "I was called."

Called? Like on the phone? Ally had no chance to question Eamonn before he spoke.

"Stay away from the keep." He turned his gaze back to the old building.

"Why?" Great. He was creeping her out.

Eamonn shook his head. "I do not know."

"Hey, that's a good enough reason for me."

He didn't smile and his gaze grew distant. Ally sensed he was alone with his memories.

"Fillean meal ar an meallaire." He stared at her, *through* her.

321

"If you say so." Eamonn made her want to run back to the wagon, jump into bed, and pull the covers over her head. She straightened her shoulders. The old man's cryptic words wouldn't intimidate her.

Eamonn smiled, his gaze once again recognizing her presence. "It be an old Gaelic saying. 'Evil returns to the evildoer.' Much that be evil still dwells here. The evil will leave this night."

"How do you know?"

He shrugged.

"Fine." Okay, this wasn't so bad. If the evil left, it would be a good thing, wouldn't it? But logic didn't work with her brain still on scary alert. "Guess I'll be going. I have to get Katy so we can explore that room beneath the keep. Katy's determined to see a fairy or ghost." She sighed. "I appreciate your warning, but when Katy sets her mind on something, there's no stopping her."

He'd turned his gaze back to the keep, and Ally sensed his attention had drifted again.

"Ye'll do what ye must."

How encouraging was *that?* He could have at least offered her a hearty "Good luck" in parting.

Busy thinking about Eamonn's strange behavior, Ally didn't realize Katy was sitting on the wagon seat waiting for her until her great-aunt spoke.

"I'm loaded for bear tonight. Pulled out all the stops." Katy handed Ally her fisherman's vest. "Here, you check as I go through my equipment list."

Ally almost dropped the vest. Talk about heavy. Katy would need help getting back up the keep steps. Ally set the vest on the stone wall beside the wagon. "Sure you didn't forget something?"

"Cut the sarcasm." Katy glared at her. "Start checking."

Ally smiled down at the bulging vest. Black. Everything Katy had on tonight was black. Katy used to tell Ally about a program she listened to on radio years ago. *The Shadow.* Tonight Katy would be The Shadow.

"Electromagnetic meter. Raytek Mini Temp to measure temperature changes. Still camera. Camcorder." Katy paused for breath. "Digital voice recorder and . . ." She touched her head. "Spelunkers headlight."

"All here." Ally didn't for a minute think Katy would use any of this stuff. If she did see a ghost or fairy, she'd be so excited she'd forget what was in each pocket.

Katy shrugged into the vest, turned on her Spelunkers Headlight, and trudged toward the keep. "Think Brian might want to come along? I wouldn't invite anyone else. Spirits don't like too many people." She cast Ally a critical glance. "Wish you'd wear more black."

No. Ally wasn't ready to face Brian yet. "He's been in his shelter most of the day. I don't want to bother him."

Katy nodded. Thank heavens she was too fixed on her coming adventure to question Brian's nonappearance.

As they reached the stone steps, Ally stopped to stare. "Someone moved the pallet."

"I did. I moved it aside this afternoon so I wouldn't have to mess with it tonight." Katy started down the steps.

"Wait. A little caution is in order here." Ally stopped on the second step.

"Why?" Katy turned her head, catching Ally in the glare of her headlight. "We know it's just an old room down there. I want to see those spirits." Determined, she continued down the steps.

"Wait. I just talked to Eamonn Clancy. He said to stay away from the keep."

Katy paused. "Did he give a reason?"

"Not exactly. But he seemed pretty sure something would happen tonight."

"Good. I've waited too long already for something to happen." Once again, she started down the steps. "Let's do it."

Not willing to allow Katy to go it alone, Ally reluctantly followed her.

They stopped at the foot of the steps, and Ally shivered. The room smelled of damp stone and earth. The smell of . . . No. She wouldn't go there. But her writer's imagination was already there and enthusiastically drawing its own conclusion: the smell of death.

"Smells a little musty down here."

Katy Gallagher, queen of understatement.

"Musty. Right." Ally rubbed her arms in an unsuccessful attempt to soothe her goose bumps.

But her goose bumps were no fools. They knew what they knew.

Katy turned in a slow circle, exposing the ancient stone walls to the glare of her headlight. Damp wall, damp wall, Claudia aiming a gun at them, damp wall . . .

Whoa! Katy backtracked and spotlighted the gun in her headlight's shaky circle of light.

"Claudia? What . . . ?" Ally fought to swallow the boulder lodged in her throat.

"Uh-uh." Claudia shook her head. "I'm Erica today."

Erica. Ally allowed a cold, ugly possibility to take shape, become solid. "Dave said you had long dark hair. You cut and colored it. Why?"

Erica shrugged. "I have a different color for every occasion." She smiled. "Red's my killing color."

"I don't understand. What's she talking about, Ally?" Katy's voice was scared and uncertain.

Katy's fear fueled Ally's anger, her protective instinct. Erica wouldn't get Katy. She started to push her great-aunt toward the steps.

Erica laughed. "Wouldn't do that, Ally. I can shoot both of you before you take three steps." She gestured with the gun. "Move over by that wall."

Ally tried to remain calm, to assess the situation, but the frantic pounding of her heart canceled logical reasoning. She needed to keep Erica talking until she could decide what to do.

Ally moved to where Erica had indicated, pulling a strangely quiet Katy with her. Erica then shifted her position to a spot that not only gave her a clear view of the steps, but cut off Ally's escape.

"What's this all about, Erica?" Ally clasped Katy's cold hand in her own.

"It's about Dave. I got sick of hearing what a perfect wife you'd been, so I decided to remove all that perfection. After you're gone, he'll forget about you."

"If he doesn't?" Ally wasn't sure she wanted to know, but she needed to say something.

"I'll *make* him forget." Erica's smile no longer looked young and perky. "Out of sight, out of mind. Isn't that how it goes?"

Ally felt Katy stir beside her. *Don't say anything, Katy.* But getting Katy to keep quiet was like holding back the sea.

"A trashy woman's like one of those black widow spiders. Looks intriguing sitting in a dark corner of the barn, but when a fly flits up to take a closer look at her, he finds out he messed up big time." Katy glanced around hopefully. "Where's an exterminator when you need one?"

Ally jumped into speech before Erica could decide she didn't like what Katy had said. "Why didn't you let me fall off the cliff?"

She could hear Katy suck in her breath. "You didn't tell me about falling off any cliff."

Erica ignored her. "When Brian grabbed you, I figured he'd pull you back from the edge. Then he'd turn around, see me, and know I was the only one close enough to have pushed you. And with so many people milling around, I couldn't take a chance on trying to push both of you over. So the only way to avoid suspicion was to play the hero." She frowned. "You sure are hard to kill. I mean, I was sure that dumb horse would get so scared he'd run off the road, but no such luck."

Erica shrugged. "Mercury must be in retrograde or something because my luck's been nothing but bad. I had you dead in my sights when I pushed that hunk of stone off the top of the keep."

Erica glanced at Katy, and Ally saw cold resolve in her gaze. "Aunty has to go, too. She's seen too much."

Ally felt the icy slide of horror at Erica's casual dismissal of Katy's life. "Someone will find us."

"Not for a while. I'm a demolitions expert. It's what I do. I've planted enough explosives in this old keep to make sure nothing's left but a pile of rock. I gave myself plenty of time." She took a quick glance at her watch. "I have exactly fifteen minutes. I'll leave your bodies here, replace the pallet, and walk away. I'll be on my way by the time the place implodes."

You're crazy. A phrase Ally had thrown around her whole life, but for the first time, it was true. And she didn't dare say it.

Ally drew a deep breath and tensed her muscles. Talk wouldn't change Erica's mind. She'd have to try to rush her. If Erica used her gun, the sound of a shot might bring someone. But even as Ally thought it, she could hear the wind whistling and the rumble of thunder echoing from the top of the steps. The ancient drama in the great hall would be unfolding about now, masking the modern one happening so close by.

Ally drew on all her courage and focused on two goals. She wanted Katy to live, and she wanted to see Brian one more time to tell him how much she loved him. To hell with being unselfish. Life was too short, too precious to not take a shot at happiness.

She edged a little closer to Erica and felt Katy do the same.

Brian left his shelter and glanced toward the wagon. Dark. They wouldn't be asleep this early. Wind whipped around him and lightning flashed, followed by the hollow rumble of thunder. He shifted his attention toward the keep. They wouldn't be there, would they?

For the first time, he noticed the donkey cart in the shadow of the keep's wall. Brian frowned. What was Eamonn doing here? Then he remembered. The great hall would live again tonight, and Eamonn seemed drawn to the haunting.

Brian was about to wander over to speak with the old man when the sound of a car stopped him. In a sudden flash of lightning, he saw Mr. Fitzpatrick from the bed-and-breakfast in Liscannor push open his car door, hunch his shoulders against the rising wind, and hurry toward him.

"I'm glad I found ye here, Byrne. This isn't a place I'd choose to search on a night like this." He glanced at the darkened wagon. "I have a message for Miss O'Neill. Ye might pass it on to her. A man named Dave called. He didn't seem to know if Miss O'Neill would still be in the area, but he sounded upset, so I decided to deliver it as soon as I could. He said to tell her Erica booked a flight for Ireland. He seemed to think that was important. I don't know . . ."

Brian followed Fitzpatrick's gaze up to the keep where Eamonn still waited. He shifted his attention back to Mr. Fitzpatrick's face at the man's sharp gasp. Puzzled, Brian watched Mr. Fitzpatrick cross himself.

"It's himself." Mr. Fitzpatrick started to back away from Brian.

"Eamonn?" It didn't take a genius to see the terror on the older man's face.

Mr. Fitzpatrick nodded. "Over three hundred years he's waited for his wife at this cursed place." Turning, he bolted for his car.

Stunned, Brian watched the car bump and skid down the path to the main road. He looked back at Eamonn. Three hundred years? Impossible. But considering what he'd seen at the keep so far, probably not impossible at all. Determined to get to the bottom of Mr. Fitzpatrick's story, Brian headed toward the donkey cart.

He didn't get far before he saw the Old One

padding toward him. Brian waited for her to catch up.

"Something's going on, Boss. I don't know where Ally is, someone named Erica's in Ireland, and Eamonn's a little older than I first thought." Erica. Where had he heard that name? Then he remembered. She was the new woman in Ally's ex-husband's life. Why would she be in Ireland, and why was it important?

He didn't have time to ponder his question, because he'd reached Eamonn. "Mr. Fitzpatrick says—"

"Ye must go to her." Eamonn turned a fierce gaze toward him. "Ye must not fail her as I failed my Bridget." He looked back at the keep. "Ye'll find her below."

"Below? Where . . . ?" *The room beneath the keep.* The one Katy had been so set on exploring.

Eamonn's sense of urgency propelled Brian toward the keep. He didn't know what was happening, but he understood he had to find Ally.

Brian had taken only a few steps when a sound froze him in place.

A high, keening wail swept over him, surrounded him, carried on the rising wind. It went on and on, the cry of a woman, filled with sorrow and loss. It wrapped around his heart and squeezed.

And when he looked toward the place where the pallet and steps would be, he knew what he'd see.

A woman stood by the steps. Clothed in a gray

hooded cloak, she was as insubstantial as the night, as ageless as the stories told about her. Brian didn't need her mournful cries to identify her. *The banshee.*

She'd come to claim an O'Neill.

Not if he could help it. He ran. He'd defy a dozen banshees, rip Ally from the arms of death itself if he had to.

Brian should have slowed down and formed a plan, but his fear for Ally drove him. He raced down the stone steps . . . and pulled up short as Claudia swung her gun to cover this new threat.

She frowned. "You know, this is the pits. Now I have to kill you, too."

Brian's gaze searched for Ally and found her in the darkness. He moved to her, then wrapped his arms around both Ally and Katy. He faced Claudia, no *Erica*. "This won't work. You can't get away with killing three people. Dave knows you're here, and he'll go to the police."

Erica's smile was eerily undisturbed. "Dave will believe anything I tell him. He loves me. And once Miss Perfect Wife is out of the way, he'll love me even more."

Brian recognized evil and knew it was too late for a plan. He'd have to rely on reaction speed honed by hours of Nebula's exercises and hope for the best.

Erica sighed deeply. "Well, better get this over with before someone else wanders . . ."

Someone else wandered. The Old One padded down the stone steps and trotted, unconcerned, behind Erica. Erica narrowed her gaze. "A person can't eliminate one ex-wife without the whole damned world showing up."

"Something a lot scarier than the whole world is about to show up."

Brian's whispered comment caught Ally's attention.

"What . . . ?" She turned frightened eyes up to him.

He bent down to Ally's ear. "I'll try to keep Erica talking for a few more minutes. The Boss is going to change."

Brian straightened and stared at Erica. "What'll you do after you shoot us?"

Erica glanced at her watch. "I'll leave. I've placed explosives so that in a few minutes this place will implode. The keep will come straight down and bury this room forever."

Hurry, Boss. Brian cast a nervous glance behind Erica, then relaxed a little. The Old One had huffed and puffed herself up to the final moment of change.

Brian knew what to expect, but it was still a scary experience. The Old One demanded that all members of her team know her true form, so each new player went through the experience of watching her change. She probably figured it gave her an intimidation advantage at contract renewal time. Seemed to work.

"Oh my God!" Ally pressed her body against him.

His reaction exactly. Brian tightened his grip

on her. A dozen Ericas couldn't have torn his gaze from the shimmering cat form growing and flowing into something huge, *alien*. And even though Brian lived in a time when "alien" was normal, the Old One still remained *really* alien.

"That's not going to work." Erica waved the gun at them. "I'd be crazy to look behind me."

Katy was actually quivering beside Brian, but he didn't think it was from fear. She was finally experiencing something strange and wonderful in Ireland. Brian took an unbiased look at the Old One. Well, maybe not so wonderful.

"She sort of looks like the alien in that movie with Sigourney Weaver, only better. Saw that movie five times back in seventy-nine." Katy ignored Erica and her threat as she cocked her head to gain a different perspective. "Maybe it's all those jaws with all those big shiny teeth. Can she talk out of all of them? Bet she has more tentacles than an octopus." Katy paused for thought. "Good thing she isn't any bigger, or we'd need to grease her up to get her out of here."

"Oh my God!" Ally was stuck in one-phrase mode.

"Shut up!" Erica shouted. "I'm not turning around, and all of you are going down now." She aimed her gun.

Uh-oh. No one told the Old One to shut up. This wouldn't be pretty. Brian wished he could stick his fingers in his ears, but he was afraid a sudden move might startle Erica into a wild shot.

The Old One roared.

She sounded like one of those old dinosaur movies.

Everybody screamed. The Old One in full voice was an eardrum-shattering experience.

Erica spun around, looked up at the Old One, and fainted.

Convenient. Brian ran over and scooped up her gun. "Thanks, Boss. Great show."

Katy raced past Brian and craned her neck to look up at the Old One. "Well, look at you. Aren't you the sneaky one? Never thought you'd look like this. Let me get my camera out and take a few shots. Then we can go with the camcorder." Katy's gaze was worshipful. "Don't worry, no one will know you're from the future. I'll tell everyone I took these pictures next to Loch Ness."

"Loch Ness is in Scotland." Ally's voice was weak, but recovering fast.

Katy shrugged off that small detail.

"Let's get the hell out of here before this place blows." Brian pushed Katy and Ally toward the steps just as Nebula raced down them.

"I am here to save you. The old man said you would need me." She ran her gaze around the room, searching for victims in need of saving.

"She's planted explosives." Brian nodded toward Erica. "Get her, and let's get out of here."

In one stride, Nebula reached Erica, scooped her off the floor, and slung her across one massive shoulder. Then they all ran. Except the Old One. She slithered and scuttled.

They reached the top of the steps and kept running.

Brian yelled as they passed Jupe's shelter. Cap and Jupe joined their mad scramble down the hill and away from the keep.

They'd just reached the wagon when the keep imploded in a series of muffled explosions. For a moment the ancient building looked as though it was trying to withstand this attack, as it had so many others for hundreds of years.

It didn't.

The keep collapsed in on itself with a muted thunder that blended with the storm sweeping in from the sea. Lightning flashed and thunder boomed, a light and sound show to celebrate what the castle had once been, would be no more.

Everyone stood riveted as out of the gloom a small donkey emerged pulling a cart. A woman sat on the seat, a shawl wrapped around her shoulders, her long red hair blowing in the wind. She laughed up at the man beside her, a young man with an easy smile. His black hair whipped across his forehead as he turned to meet Brian's stare. And in the man's eyes, Brian saw the Eamonn Clancy he'd known for such a brief time.

"Brigh gach cluiche gu dheireadh. The essence of a game is at its end. May your game end well, Brian Byrne." He raised his hand in farewell as the cart shimmered and disappeared.

And with Eamonn's leaving came the rain, sweeping in from the sea. Jupe, Cap, and Nebula—with Erica still slung across her shoulder—scrambled into the wagon. The Old One wouldn't fit, so she scuttled into the bathroom.

Katy paused, staring at the spot where the cart had disappeared. She turned an awe-filled gaze toward Brian. "Was that . . . ?"

Brian nodded. "Ghosts."

Katy's eyes shone. "That was an excellent adventure. I didn't get a picture, but it doesn't matter. I'll remember Eamonn here." She tapped her chest.

Without another word, she hurried into the wagon to join the mob already there.

Brian stood staring at the dark pile of stone that had been his family's legacy. His hair lay heavy on his shoulders, and water ran down his face. Tears or rain? Probably rain. It was hard to cry over something he'd known so briefly.

A movement beside him signaled not everyone had run for shelter. He looked down into Ally's face. Her hair hung in wet tangles, and she'd hunched her shoulders against the torrent. Her eyes were warm with emotion, and he'd never seen a more beautiful woman. *His woman.* And in the thinking, everything became so simple.

When it was time to leave her, he'd have to make a choice. Either he'd return to 2502 and honor his contract, *his promise,* or he'd stay with the woman he loved.

"Will you use the Constructor to rebuild the keep?" Her voice was soft beside him. Calm, accepting of what he'd decide.

Will it ever stop, Eamonn?

Aye. When the keep topples, never to rise again, then he'll take her home forever.

Brian shook his head. "Eamonn waited too long for his Bridget. I wouldn't take her away from him." His memories of this time would never be about the keep, but about the woman standing beside him.

Ally wrapped her arms around his waist and settled her head against his chest. "You're a wonderful man, Brian Byrne, and I love you."

Chapter Twenty

Ally had told Brian she loved him, and he'd just hugged her. Guess that pretty much defined their relationship. She loved, he liked.

She stood beside the wagon with Katy and watched him walk toward her. This would be one of her enduring memories of him. He strode down the hill in the morning light with his long hair lifting in the breeze, the rubble of his ruined keep behind him.

The essence of the man lay in that jumbled pile of stone. He could have easily rebuilt the keep, but his generosity extended to an old man he'd met only a few times and who'd died more than three hundred years ago.

He stopped in front of her and smiled. Brian's smile lit the morning and dispelled her poor-pitiful-me feelings. She'd live in the moment, enjoy the little time she had with him, and let the future take care of itself.

"The others are leaving today. The stag should be here any minute now. I thought you might want to see it." He included Katy in his invitation.

Ally's heart caught, then started beating again, but twice as fast to make up for the skipped beats. "And you?"

His smile faded. "I'm staying the full three weeks. You don't think I'd leave now, do you?"

She didn't know what his question meant. The important thing was he wouldn't be leaving today. "What do you say, Katy? Want to see time travel in action?"

Katy nodded enthusiastically. "I'll go get my camcorder."

Ally watched Katy disappear into the wagon. Anything rather than look at Brian. She'd better say something. Silence that lasted more than thirty seconds made her nervous. "At least the rest of your vacation should be uneventful. Erica admitted everything to the authorities. They'll probably schedule a psychological consultation for her. She kept babbling about a monster under the keep."

For a moment, Ally thought he wouldn't comment.

"I guess that frees up Dave. Ever thought of going back to him?" Brian's voice gave no clue to his thoughts.

Shocked, Ally finally met his gaze. "Why would

I do that?" It would be like . . . She couldn't think of a comparison that would do justice to the difference between Brian and Dave. Wait, she had it. She hated raw oysters. It would be like eating raw oysters after a box of Godiva chocolates. She shuddered.

Brian shrugged. "Just checking."

Katy hurried from the wagon, freeing Ally of the need to fill the silence with speech. Speech that might stray into the personal range and lead to her blurting out the "L" word again.

"With everything happening, we haven't done much with your book. Do you think you have enough material?" He turned to look toward Cap and the others gathered near the small grove of trees.

"Sure." She'd *never* write that book. How could she when every word would remind her of Brian?

He slanted her a wicked grin, one that turned his gaze to smoke and fire. "Still need a night of endless foreplay. Thought you said women in 2002 wanted lots of foreplay."

She widened her eyes. "Did I say that? If I did, then I was wrong. Too much foreplay can kill you."

Katy reached them. "What's that you said about foreplay?"

Brian started walking toward the others. "Ally doesn't want it."

"I'm a main event kind of woman." She made sure Katy walked between Brian and her. It gave her the illusion of safety.

Thank heavens they reached the others before Katy could comment.

Jupe turned a worried glance toward Brian. "Sure you won't come back with us?"

Brian shook his head. "I'm staying the full three weeks."

Conversation ceased as the air shimmered and shifted around them. Suddenly, the white stag was there. It stood, large and majestic, its antlered head turned expectantly in their direction.

Cap cast Brian a searching look. "Think real hard about what you want out of your life."

The Old One looked as though one of her mouths was about to comment on Cap's advice.

She never got the chance. A shot rang out from the small grove. With an expression of shock in its wide eyes, the stag went to its knees.

"What the hell!" Brian moved toward the trees just as a man emerged with gun in hand.

Ally knew him. It was the heavy-set man who'd eaten breakfast at the Fitzgeralds'.

He blinked as he took in the outraged circle of people. "I was after doing a little hunting." He fixed his gaze on Katy. "Ye mentioned that ye'd seen a white deer here. I . . ." Realizing that Katy didn't look encouraging, his glance shifted away.

Suddenly, the Old One reared up from the back of the group. At her full height, the Old One was a scary proposition. She roared her fury.

The man opened and closed his mouth a few times before he was able to get out a screech.

Dropping his gun, he turned and raced back into the trees. No one followed him.

Brian ran to the stag, which had managed to push itself back to its feet. It stood there trembling while Brian ran his fingers over its side. He turned to the anxious group of travelers. "There's a bad gouge here, but it's not life-threatening. I'll get my first-aid supplies." He ran for his shelter before anyone could speak.

Silence moved in uneasy waves around the huddled group of travelers. For once Katy had nothing to say.

Ally's heart had left its normal position and was quickly sliding into despair. Ally knew what they all knew, but weren't saying. The stag had found danger in 2002. It would never return to this time.

Brian would have to go home with the others, or not go home at all.

No! She wasn't ready for this. She hadn't worked herself up to final good-byes.

Brian returned and pushed his way through the silent group. He worked quickly and efficiently, then backed away from the stag. "That should do it."

Jupe stepped forward and said what they all knew. "You'll have to come back with us, Brian."

Ally heard his words as though from a distance. She stood amidst the rubble of her own belief in what she'd wanted for her life, her plans for her future, and knew her personal pile of despair was a mountain compared to the keep behind her.

Strangely calm, she did a final checklist. In a choice between Brian and everything she knew and cherished—her family, her home, her career—which would she choose? She mentally put a check beside Brian's name. It was that simple.

And if he didn't want her? She'd watch him leave. But she wouldn't let him go without giving love a chance. "I want to go with you."

"Be sure, Ally." Katy's voice was quiet, her usual spunk gone.

Brian turned toward her, and for a moment something warm and welcoming darkened his gaze. Then he looked past her, at the remains of the Byrne legacy. "You don't want to do that, babe. You'd be giving up everything you've ever known to go with a man who makes his living by—"

"I don't care." Ally didn't try to hide her feelings, but she sure wished she could do something about the tears filling her eyes. She blinked madly. Pretty soon she'd be sniffling and hunting for a tissue. A runny nose would *not* add to her sensual mystique.

But I do care. Brian looked back at the avid audience hanging on every word Ally and he exchanged. They all cared because each owned a piece of his past. His gaze returned to Ally.

But Ally owned his future. He'd fought the good fight through the long night. His code of honor demanded he return to play out his contract.

After hours of wrestling with his soul, he'd reached the only possible conclusion. The hell with his contract. He'd break a thousand contracts for Ally.

And in choosing the one person he wanted for all time, he'd discovered something important. Maybe he'd been wrong about his mother. What did he know about the choices she'd had to make? Life-altering decisions touched a lot of people, just as his decision would affect many people in 2502. He could never judge his mother without first looking into her heart, knowing *why* she'd left him. He felt free for the first time in his life.

Taking a deep, steadying breath, he prepared to break a promise for the second time in his life. "I'm not going back to 2502. Ever. I'm staying here."

Ally's eyes widened, her face paled. "Your contract . . . I know how you feel about promises."

Brian heard Jupe's oath and Cap's triumphant shout. Strangely, he heard nothing from the Old One. But then, she'd always been a pragmatist. The Boss would cut her losses and go on to win with someone else.

Right now, Ally was the only person who mattered.

Brian touched her face with the tip of his finger, felt the dampness of tears on her cheek. *"Ta' gra' agam duit.* I love you, Ally O'Neill."

She gazed up at him and smiled through her

tears. "Where'd you learn Gaelic, Byrne?"

He returned her smile. "I had the Language Assimilation Program tuck in a few common Gaelic phrases."

She swiped at her tears. "And how common is *that* phrase?"

"More common than you think." He finally gave in to temptation and pulled her into his embrace. "An Irishman is always prepared, babe."

Ally planted her palms against his chest and pushed. Puzzled, he backed up.

"What about your contract? We have to get the Old One to release you. I don't want you to feel bad about going back on your word."

He shook his head. "You know, I always thought breaking a promise was the worst thing I could do. Wrong. The worst thing I could've done was to walk away from you." He took her hand and started toward his space-age bathroom. "Fate has a way of evening things out. Years from now I'll tell my grandchildren how broken promises brought me my greatest sadness and my greatest joy."

"Wait. Where're we going?" She yanked on his hand, forcing him to stop.

"You're right about one thing. I owe the Old One an explanation. She probably scuttled off to the bathroom. It makes her feel secure. Reminds her of home."

Ally dug in her feet. "We have a bit of unfinished business before *we* face the Old One."

Before he could voice his question, she stood

on tiptoe, wrapped her arms around his neck, and kissed him. She covered his mouth with soft lips, while the tip of her tongue traced a path of fiery exploration. He opened his mouth to her, and her tongue tangled with his. Her sweet seductive taste, the slide of her tongue over his, and her breathed words of love were a promise for all his tomorrows.

When she finally moved away, he just stared at her. "Hate to tell you, sweetheart, but that didn't finish anything."

Never breaking eye contact, she slid her fingers over his erection. "Oh, yes." Her murmur was warm anticipation. "I'm going to enjoy pleasing you, Brian Byrne."

He raised an eyebrow. "I thought you were through pleasing men."

Ally smiled a wicked, feline smile. "Your pleasure will be my pleasure. Of course, if you expect me to fluff your pillow, you're out of luck." Her gaze slid over his body and stopped at his groin. "I'm not totally against fluffing, though."

His groin was into fluffing possibilities. He exhaled sharply and yanked his attention from sexual imaging. Tonight he'd explore growth, expansion, and fluffing issues with Ally. "We'd better find the Old One before I drag you into the wagon and lock the door." He continued walking with Ally at his side.

He knew she was thinking of that wagon. Locked doors, erotic paintings, and steamy ceiling mirrors. So was he.

Brian flung open the bathroom door without knocking and strode in with Ally close behind.

The Old One squatted in the center of the pristine white bathroom. She radiated outraged majesty.

Brian controlled his urge to shift from foot to foot. She might have an overwhelming presence, but he had love behind him. Ally moved to his side. Okay, now he had love on his side.

He drew a deep breath and faced his angry employer. "Okay, Boss, here's the deal. I'm staying here and nothing can change that."

The Old One's bulging eyes narrowed. All twenty of them.

"You're a survivor, and you'll figure out a way to win another championship without me." He turned thoughtful. "The fans will probably expect you to retire my number sixty-nine."

The Old One's narrowed gaze suggested what she'd like to do with his number 69.

"Look, you'll save all kinds of money. You can steal a great young player from some other team. There's Reylan from the Raunchy Raiders or Kestor from the Carnal Cowboys. Both will be all-stars some day. And both are free agents."

The Old One's gaze had turned assessing.

"Why isn't she talking?" Ally edged closer to his side.

"She's sulking. She never talks when she sulks."

Ally stared at the Old One. "That's a pretty im-

347

mature reaction, Boss. Reasonable adults should be able to discuss things—"

The Old One opened her jaws and roared.

"Reasonably," Ally finished on a mutter. "Boy, she's touchy."

"Comes from too many years of getting her own way." Brian had one more thing to say to his former boss. "I'm sorry about the contract, but you're smart and I guarantee you'll find someone to replace me for a lot less money. You're a winner, and you'll always come out on top." A little flattery never hurt anything.

The Old One was almost preening. Now was the time to get out, while the getting was good. Pulling a reluctant Ally behind him, Brian left the bathroom.

The rest of the group still clustered around the stag. Cap was giving an unresponsive Jupe a few hearty backslaps, while Nebula was no doubt commenting on the puny qualities of stags who let a little gunshot wound stay them from their appointed rounds.

Ally and he rejoined the group.

Jupe fixed Brian with a somber gaze. "We have to talk."

Brian nodded. "Ally, I—"

She touched his lips with her finger. "I understand. Go."

Jupe followed him to the wagon. Once inside, they sat side by side on the bench seat. Their silence spoke of all the memories of so many years together, all the sadness of knowing they'd never see each other again.

Jupe coughed, then spoke. His voice was unfamiliarly husky. "As soon as I get home, I'll make arrangements for someone to travel back to 1980 and put half your wealth into a Swiss account. It'll last you for the rest of your life."

Brian nodded. He didn't seem able to get words past the lump in his throat.

"I'll invest the rest of your wealth for your kids."

"Thanks." He watched Jupe rise.

"I just wanted to say . . ." Jupe hunched his shoulders and finally met Brian's gaze. Jupe's eyes had a suspicious shine. "It's been a great fourteen years. There'll never be another one like you, kid."

Brian rose and clasped him in a silent goodbye. Then Jupe walked to the door.

Brian knew there was one thing left to say. "Jupe."

Jupe paused, but didn't turn around.

"I've done a lot of griping, but you have to know one thing."

Jupe waited.

"You're the only father I ever had. Ally and I will name one of our children after you."

"Hey, being named after a big ball of gas isn't so bad." His reply was choked. He left and closed the door quietly behind him.

Brian sat and, unashamed, let the tears slide down his face. He cried for the first time since he was six years old. He cried for the last time over a world he would never see again.

"Someone has to get her out of that bathroom. We have to go home now before someone from Liscannor comes looking for the monster." Cap's good humor had given way to worry. No matter how much he might want to leave the Old One behind, league rules frowned on abandoning team owners in the past.

Brian stood with Ally in the darkness. They'd given the stag all day to recover its strength, and now it was ready to lead its clients home.

Ally tightened her grip on Brian's waist, as though she feared he might disappear into the growing mist with the others.

He chuckled. "Don't worry, babe. It's not going to happen. You're stuck with me."

She looked up at him and smiled. "This reminds me of the night we met. Misty with a chance of rain."

"Those are the best kinds of nights." He slid his fingers through her hair. "Want to live here?"

"Yes." Ally didn't waste words. "We can build a house right where the wagon is parked, with a great view of the ruins and the sea." She stared into the darkness as though she were searching for something. "Maybe I'll get a horse. A dark horse with yellow eyes."

He nodded. "*We'll* build our house. No Constructor. It's going back with Jupe to 2502 where it belongs."

"In a short time, I'll have you all to myself. For the rest of our lives." Her voice was soft, disbelieving.

Cap interrupted thoughts of lifelong love. "Okay, who's going in there?"

Nebula heaved an exaggerated sigh and cast Cap a contemptuous glance. "I will go."

She hadn't taken a step before the bathroom door slowly opened. Everyone stared at the door.

Brian shook his head and grinned. Each was hoping the Old One had gotten over her fury. An angry Old One didn't make for a great traveling con. panion.

The Old One appeared in the open doorway.

Brian stopped smiling.

And watched dumbstruck as his mirror image strode toward him.

"She . . . looks exactly like *you*." Ally was having trouble getting her words past her disbelief.

"Yeah." Talk about stating the obvious.

As the new Brian Byrne stopped in front of them, Cap was the first to find his voice. "What the hell is this?"

"This is me recouping my losses, stupid. What do you think it is?" The Old One grinned. "The greatest talent in the universe still plays for the Sex Monarchs, and I pay myself his salary. Can't get better than that."

Cap was left sputtering as the Old One turned to Jupe. "You can represent me." The reborn Brian's grin was sly. "Just like you always have."

Jupe could only nod.

The Old One's attention shifted to Brian and Ally. "This is great. I haven't been a male for over four hundred years. It'll take getting used to." He shrugged. "But hey, I can do anything. Always have, always will."

Brian frowned. "I liked you better as a cat."

"Have you thought about hooking up with Nebula? You and she have similar life views." Ally sounded intrigued.

Cap had finished sputtering and now was in full attack mode. "You won't get away with this. When we get back I'll tell—"

"You won't tell anyone." The Old One's tone was scary in any form. "You can't prove anything. Every test will show I'm Brian Byrne. And when the tests are finished, the forty law firms I own will each sue your skinny butt for defamation of character."

Cap huffed, puffed, then subsided. "I don't care who you look like, you'll be a bust. How many years has it been since you had sex?"

The Old One looked thoughtful. "Three hundred or so. But no problem. I pay people to get my players in shape." The new Brian Byrne turned his gaze on Nebula. "*You* can get me in shape."

Nebula looked somber, dedicated to duty. "My greatest challenge."

The Old One didn't look sure if Nebula's statement should offend him. He evidently decided it wasn't worth getting bent out of shape over.

"Let's go home. Oh, and Brian, *Sexual Survivor* will start airing in about ten years. Keep in shape and you could blow away the competition."

"I don't think so, Boss." He smiled. The Old One wouldn't offer him advice if he wasn't forgiven.

Brian pulled Ally close to him as the small group of time travelers moved away, following the white stag into the mist.

Cap brought up the rear. Just before he disappeared, he turned one last time to fix Ally with his gaze. He smiled and winked. "I'm not as upset as I sounded. The Old One will never win the Monarchs a championship. Know why?" He switched his gaze to Brian.

"Because Brian Byrne was simply the best."

THE PLEASURE MASTER

¾NINA BANGS¾

Stranded by the side of a New York highway on Christmas Eve, hairdresser Kathy Bartlett wishes herself somewhere warm and peaceful with a subservient male at her side. She finds herself transported all right, but to Scotland in 1542 with the last man she would have chosen.

With the face of a dark god or a fallen angel, and the reputation of being able to seduce any woman, Ian Ross is the kind of sexual expert Kathy avoids like the plague. So when she learns that the men in his family are competing to prove their prowess, she sprays hair mousse on his brothers' "love guns" and swears she will never succumb to the explosive attraction she feels for Ian. But as the competition heats up, neither Kathy nor Ian reckon the most powerful aphrodisiac of all: love.

___52445-7 $5.50 US/$6.50 CAN

HIGH ENERGY DARA JOY

Zanita Masterson knows nothing about physics, until a reporting job leads her to Tyberius Evans. The rogue scientist is six feet of piercing blue eyes, rock-hard muscles and maverick ideas—with his own masterful equation for sizzling ecstasy and high energy.

___4438-2 $4.99 US/$5.99 CAN

Dorchester Publishing Co., Inc.
P.O. Box 6640
Wayne, PA 19087-8640

DARA JOY
HIGH
INTENSITY

WHAT IS HIGH INTENSITY?

Silken Caresses. Steak bomb sandwiches. A hot press of lips. A haunted chef. Seductive touches in the dark. Spirits who gobble the haute cuisine. A master strategist. A miscreant ghost. And a very, very fat cat.

Join the most sizzling, provocative physicist to ever solve a case or heat up a bedroom and his equally passionate partner as they investigate the perfect equation for love! Tyber and Zantia invite you to come along for their madcap, sensual journey into high intensity. . . .

___4747-0 $5.99 US/$6.99 CAN

Dorchester Publishing Co., Inc.
P.O. Box 6640
Wayne, PA 19087-8640

Please add $1.75 for shipping and handling for the first book and $.50 for each book thereafter. NY, NYC, and PA residents, please add appropriate sales tax. No cash, stamps, or C.O.D.s. All orders shipped within 6 weeks via postal service book rate. Canadian orders require $2.00 extra postage and must be paid in U.S. dollars through a U.S. banking facility.

Name_____
Address_____
City_____ State_____ Zip_____
I have enclosed $ _____ in payment for the checked book(s).
Payment <u>must</u> accompany all orders. ❏ Please send a free catalog.
CHECK OUT OUR WEBSITE! www.dorchesterpub.com